PORTISVILLE

PORTISVILLE

a novel by STEVE CUSHMAN

[signature]

NOVELLO Festival PRESS

CHARLOTTE 2004

Library of Congress Cataloging-in-Publication Data

Cushman, Steve, 1969-
  Portisville : a novel / by Steve Cushman.
    p. cm.
  ISBN 0-9708972-9-4 (hardcover)
  1. Terminally ill—Fiction. 2. Fathers and sons—Fiction. 3. Parent
and adult child—Fiction. 4. Conflict of generations—Fiction. 5.
Murder victims' families—Fiction. 6. Secrecy—Fiction. I. Title.
  PS3603.U84P67 2004
  813'.6—dc22
                          2004013159

Printed in the United States of America
FIRST EDITION
Book design by Bonnie Campbell

For Juliet and Trevor
And in Loving Memory of my Father

JIMMY WILLS pulled hard on the cigarette between his lips as the Ford F-150 rocked beneath him in the first moments after dark. To his right, on the faded red vinyl bench seat, a duffel bag filled with a couple days' worth of clean clothes moved slightly side-to-side. The night blackened as Jimmy headed south through North Carolina, and the blinking lights of mountain cabins shone before him. He'd always thought they looked like runway lights guiding planes in for a safe landing, but he was not thinking about that on this night. His mind was filled with the ragged voice on the other end of the phone line and the words it had spat at him: *Come Home Boy, I Got Cancer, Kill Me.* It was his father's voice, a thing he hadn't heard in twenty years.

Vehicles passed Jimmy going the other way every five minutes or so as if on timers. He stared straight ahead, the persistent angry cries of cicadas buzzing in his ears, as he gripped the steering wheel at two and ten. A tractor-trailer's lights grew brighter and then blinding as it approached. Jimmy closed his eyes and held onto the steering wheel and a second or two later felt his half-ton truck shake under him.

The back of the truck was filled with his painting supplies—ladders, cans of white, green, red and yellow latex along with the compressor and spray gun—all under a blue tarpaulin. Across Jimmy's fingers and T-shirt were specks of paint, like some kind of abstract art, that he hadn't bothered to wash off before leaving. He coughed and looked out the window at the blanket of darkness all around him, let out a solemn *motherfucker* and then dragged hard on the cigarette again.

The sign up ahead read GILL'S HUNTING CAMP. Jimmy squinted at it and thought of the one time he'd gone hunting. He had stood scared, next to his father, cheeks wet from tears, looking down at the deer lying in the high grass before them, watching the quick, clipped rise and fall of the animal's chest. Its eyes moved across Jimmy and his father, searching for something. A squirrel clung to a nearby pine tree, as if waiting to see what would happen. Jimmy wanted to reach down and hug the deer, pet it, tell it everything was going to be all right. In his nine-year-old mind it was nothing more than an over-sized dog, one they had wounded. His father tried to hand Jimmy the rifle, but when he shook his head no, the old man aimed and shot the deer between the eyes.

A mile past the Georgia state line, Jimmy stopped at a Wilco's Gas Emporium. He pulled up to the pumps and checked his wallet. There was a twenty, a ten and three one-dollar bills tight up against the uncashed check from the job he'd finished earlier. After working the nozzle into his gas tank, Jimmy turned to the darkness that surrounded the bright station. A large raccoon and her two kits scavenged through an overflowing garbage can. The mother pulled with her teeth on a variety of paper and plastic bags before finding a box of old chicken. The box fell to the ground—the softness of it preventing any noise, only a slight puff of dust. Swarms of flies and gnats swam away through the air. The two kits jumped down and each pulled a piece of the old chicken from the box and ran off toward the woods.

The girl behind the counter had a mole just below her right eye, like a brown ever-present tear, or a scar that would never go away. She smiled cute, playful, at Jimmy and he nodded back at her. He figured she was eighteen at the most, about sixteen years too young for him.

At the back wall of the store, he surveyed the varieties of beer and grabbed a six-pack of Miller Lite in cans. He turned toward the counter and that little thing—Sally, the nametag read—smiled at him again, blinking twice. Jimmy figured she wouldn't be worth the trouble, her boyfriend probably sitting out there in the parking lot just waiting for some reason to fight and her wanting somebody to prove, in some way, that he loved her and that she was worthy of that love.

Back on the interstate, Jimmy popped the first of the beers. He finished it in three mouthfuls, considered tossing it on the floorboard, which was already littered with a half-dozen paper cups and a week's worth of cellophane cigarette wrappers, but instead he threw it into the bed of the truck where it bounced around on the tarpaulin for a few seconds before settling in the back corner. He opened a second beer and took a mouthful of that one. Almost instantly, he felt some of the tension and anger slide away from him. Tension and anger that, in some ways, he had liked and that had propelled him forward in a blur of highway. But as it left him, Jimmy thought again of the raccoons and of his day thus far. The last side of the house painted. Then standing on the shore of the mountain stream. The sun starting its own descent as every bird on the mountain let out one final call. Cigarette ash falling on the soft ground. The splash and quick, silver brilliance of trout and Jimmy smiling as he brought the fish to his face, looking into its already close-to-death eyes. Then the fish, unmoving, in his kitchen sink and the telephone ringing, something telling him not to answer, but he had anyway.

Truman Wills was slumped over in the yellow La-Z-Boy on the porch of his off-white, Florida cracker house. A few dozen stray gray hairs littered his head and his chin rested on his bare chest. The flesh of his chest and arms hung forward like the old nipples of a many-times-bred dog. A tabby kitten sat curled in Truman's lap, nestled in the faded, blue overalls while a pair of mosquitoes took turns landing on his right shoulder, biting down hard and pulling the blood away. But he did not feel this. Under his bare feet, the porch swayed in his dreams, dreams that were full of guns and woods and cars. Of him driving a green Cadillac through an open pasture with his left hand sticking out the window catching the thick North Florida air, moving southbound with the unmarked police car behind him, then the two cars side-by-side on the bridge. Truman making a quick left, clipping the car, sending it over the rail into the mouth of the river thirty yards below.

With sunrise still an hour away, Truman opened his eyes. He sat up slowly and stared out into the blackness. He knew that the house was surrounded by pine trees and that the ground around the house was all dirt and a slick carpet of pine needles. He knew where his old unwashed Cadillac sat under the lone oak tree in the middle of the front yard and where her car was, to his right, over by the pine trees that hid the house from the highway. He also knew of the gravel road that led one in a zig-zag pattern the thirty yards from the road to the house and about the small orange wading pool on the side of the house, under the kitchen window. But he could see none of it; it was dark out there and the only light was a shadow cast from one 75-watt light bulb in the kitchen behind him. Truman looked down at his crotch and petted the kitten, who rose up upon his touch, stretched its legs and then jumped off onto the wooden porch floor, scurrying away past the bottle of Wild Turkey by Truman's right foot and the pearl-handled .38 by his left.

He bent forward in the chair, almost lost his balance and then regained it. Then he reached down again, this time slower, this time with a grace and patience no one would've believed he was capable of. When he sat up again, he held the gun and bottle. He set the gun on his right thigh and loosened the bottle's cap. Its smell traversed the air—hot and musky, full of spirits—and then he turned it to his lips, feeling the fullness in his mouth and throat, happy with the burn that filled his stomach. He lifted the gun up toward a pine tree he had shot at hundreds of times. He'd drawn a bull's-eye on it eleven months ago, after getting out of jail, with a piece of white chalk he'd found in Jimmy's old room, but an afternoon storm had washed it away. He couldn't see the tree, or the quarter he'd nailed to it last week, as he squeezed the trigger and laughed a moment later after hearing the soft thud of copper slicing into pine.

Behind Jimmy, in the back of the truck, the six empty beer cans rocked against each other. It was still in those few sweet moments between darkness and first light; those moments when one's fate did not yet seem sealed. Jimmy turned off the interstate onto Highway 144 and drove past a sign that read PORTISVILLE, FLORIDA—POP. 9,078. Traveling along the two-lane road, he began to see little streams of light, like ultraviolet rays, which shot across the blacktop through the multitude of palmetto bushes and tall pine trees lining the highway.

His heart quickened for a moment when he spotted the red and blue lights of the police cruisers up ahead. Passing the caravan of police cars and news trucks parked on the soft shoulder of the road, he saw the gray Honda Civic, which sat in the center of it all like a wash of silver against the wall of pine trees. Jimmy wondered if Davis was still the sheriff but didn't see him among the police officers looking in the windows and the cameraman scanning the trees behind the car.

A few of the pines were burned short from the latest brush fires, but for the most part they stood towering over whatever passed them on the nearby highway. Billboards lined the road, advertising phone companies and places to eat thirty miles east in Tallahassee. Jimmy kept his right hand on the steering wheel and watched the side of the road for any signs of life.

The thick pine brush opened up every half-mile or so to reveal patches of grazing land and cows chewing on high grass, the cows not even lifting their heads to the white truck speeding by, as if they were thinking of nothing but the dew-softened grass in front of them.

As quick as Jimmy would hit these patches of open land, he would be thrown back into another wall of pine trees. Jimmy knew that behind these trees dirt roads led to huge, arcing, curved cypresses and patches of water and ponds and untouched lakes. He saw blueberry farms and sod farms a hundred yards off the road and stands where old men would soon start setting up their little harvest for sale: watermelons and tomatoes and all varieties of peppers.

Jimmy felt tired now. He wasn't sure why he'd made the trip. Anger and then this tiredness. He had to piss and considered pulling off the side of the road. There was an intersection he didn't recognize up ahead and he stopped at the flashing red light, looked both ways, and then proceeded. Just past the light, a cut in the road led down to a new Walgreen's, which looked out of place in the sparse landscape, shrouded by leaning pine trees. The parking lot was empty, and he figured the store wasn't open yet.

He followed the road another quarter mile and up on the left was a small convenience store and gas station, a square block building with a tin garbage can on each side of the door. Jimmy smiled when he saw the familiar sign above the door: DAN'S GROCERY. The front windows were covered with poster-sized Marlboro and Coors ads. Behind the store, yet another wall of pine trees. Jimmy pulled into the gravel lot and idled past the two gas pumps and parked the truck by the side of the building and walked into the men's room.

At the urinal, he read a message written in black magic marker. On the white-tiled wall, somebody had originally scribbled *Ruth loves Ryan*, but this had been revised by scratching out the word *loves* and inserting *fucks* above it.

When he walked back outside to his truck, a few minutes later, Jimmy was shocked, dazed by the presence of sunlight as if it hadn't been there at all when he'd gone in. He squinted past the truck, toward the front of the store and saw a man with graying, short, curly hair, wearing jeans and a white button-up shirt, staring at him. It was his father's old friend, Dan Fausey.

Dan walked toward Jimmy, his face a little contorted, as if he was unable to believe what or who was before him, and then he smiled and said, "Jimmy, Jimmy Wills?"

Jimmy stuck his hand out to shake, but Dan reached past his hand and grabbed his arms and shoulders and hugged him, startling him for a moment before Jimmy hugged back.

"Goddamn, Jimmy Wills. I thought I'd never."

Jimmy smiled and said, "Good to see you." He reached into the cab of the truck and pulled the pack of cigarettes off the dash, tapped the box and then took one from the front. "Still here?"

"Shit, where am I gonna go?"

A buzzard circled overhead in the woods behind the store. Jimmy offered Dan a cigarette. Dan touched his chest and said, "No, I quit a few years back." But Jimmy still held the pack out as if he hadn't heard him at all. Dan reached in and pulled a cigarette out. "You've grown up. You look good."

Jimmy said, "Thanks, so do you."

Dan said, "Bullshit." They both laughed and Jimmy lit Dan's cigarette and then his own. As a boy, Jimmy had spent many afternoons at this store while his father and Davis and Dan sat inside making plans and deals for things that Jimmy wouldn't understand until later, after he'd moved away and his father went to prison. But back then, when he was a boy, he would pop in and out of the store after running down to the stream, digging for worms, and putting them—still wiggling, as if unable to believe that they'd been pulled from the safe softness of their dark homes—onto a hook and catching bream and suncrackers.

Dan said, "I haven't seen you since you was what, twelve, thirteen?"

Jimmy said, "Fourteen. I went and lived with my aunt."

"I know. Last I heard you was in the Carolinas."

"Still am."

"I'd venture to guess that you are in the housepainting business."

Jimmy looked down at his clothes and truck and smiled at Dan. Dan returned the smile and then looked away, into the woods, across the street. Neither one was really sure of where to go next with the conversation, both knowing where it would eventually lead. A truck passed on the road in front of the store with a half-dozen Mexican men in the back, leaning against the weathered planks of wood that made up the truck's bed. Dan waved to the man who drove the truck and the man waved back. Jimmy didn't recognize the driver or any of the migrant workers, but Dan's eyes followed the truck a couple of hundred yards down the road.

Jimmy said, "He called me."

Dan turned back toward him. "He's sick. They say he doesn't have much time. Got him some kind of round-the-clock nurse living in the house."

"Nurse? Is he that bad?"

"He was. I hear he's doing a little better now."

"You seen him?"

"I went to see him after he got out, but we didn't have much to say to each other. Just stood on the porch for a few minutes looking out into the woods. He was away a long time. I could've gone away too. We were friends, but that was a long time ago."

Jimmy squinted, his face hardening now by the turn in the conversation. "A lot of stuff happened a long time ago."

Dan pulled the cigarette out of his mouth and looked at the tip of it, as if it were something he'd never seen before, the quick folding embers of orange and white to black. He said, "Life is too short to go around hating people for what they done, or didn't do, so many years ago."

"You don't understand."

"Maybe I don't."

"He said that he wanted me to kill him, put him out of his fucking misery. Haven't heard from him in twenty years and that's what he calls to say."

Dan looked Jimmy in the eyes. "Kill him?"

"That's what he said."

"Naw, that's just crazy Truman talk."

Jimmy didn't know if it was crazy talk or not, but his father had sounded serious on the phone. "Still, you just don't do that."

"You're right." Dan looked back out toward the road, as if hoping another truckload of Mexicans would move by so that he could wave again. Without looking at Jimmy, he said, "You may not believe it, but he loved you and your mother. When we'd go on runs up to Kentucky, he'd talk about the two of you. Like when you got stung by that wasp and were running around screaming and she thought it was maybe a snake or a scorpion that bit you. How she started sucking on the tip of your finger until her mouth went numb."

Jimmy hadn't thought about his mother in a long time, hadn't wanted to, but now he could see her clearly in one of her red or white print shirts. Her long black hair falling down her neck, her thin fingers with the unpainted nails. Jimmy threw his cigarette down and stepped on it. Dan did the same and Jimmy handed him another one and lit it, then opened the door of his truck and climbed in. "Good to see you, Dan."

"Good to see you. You need anything at all, come up here and don't you dare leave without saying goodbye."

"Thanks."

Jimmy pointed the truck toward the road again. In the rearview mirror, he could see Dan standing there by the front door, taking his time smoking that cigarette, as if it were the last one he would have for a while.

Jimmy held the steering wheel with his right hand and let the left hang out of the window, catching the hot, dense air. He felt better after seeing Dan and knew if he were smart, he would turn the truck around and drive home. He told himself that his father didn't deserve to see him. This life, his father and this town, were all things Jimmy had spent twenty years trying to forget about. If perhaps he hadn't seen Dan it would be different, but he felt like he'd come too far not to look and see what those years had done to Truman.

A rust-covered Pinto pulled out of a driveway onto Highway 144 going the opposite way as Jimmy. It reminded him of how there were twenty or thirty houses along this road, behind the wall of pine trees, just like the one he had grown up in. Most of the houses were hidden pretty good, so that you wouldn't even know they were there if it weren't for the driveways and mailboxes marking them.

Highway 144 ran north and south, splitting the town evenly east and west. It started a few miles south of town and forked at the northern edge of Portisville, allowing you to either take a left and head downtown or take a right and go up through Tallahassee and into Georgia. There was no way around 144 if you wanted to travel through Portisville—all roads led to or from it. The elementary and middle school and cemetery were all off the road, as were the small pockets of neighborhoods, which were nothing more than three or four streets lined with houses and surrounded by pine trees. Jimmy figured that he had probably been on the road, for one reason or another, every day he lived here.

He remembered the last time he had been on this road, the day Davis had driven him away from Portisville to go and live in North Carolina with Aunt Carly, his mother's sister. Aunt Carly was a schoolteacher and single and Jimmy recalled how she would hug him at night, as if she believed that hugging and loving him could make up for every wrong in the world. She didn't look like his mother: his mother had been beautiful, tall and thin and wore jeans and tank tops without a bra and Aunt Carly was not beautiful and wore nothing but long yellow or blue dresses over her stocky body. The one thing the two women shared was a smallish, pug nose.

The words Aunt Carly used to describe his father rang in Jimmy's ear: *evil, the devil, better off dead.* She said she knew the first day she'd seen Truman that her sister was making a grave mistake. He'd come to pick her up in a beat-up Mustang and he wore dirty jeans and pulled her to him, kissing her with his hands all over her body, in the driveway before speeding away, slicing a strip of tire tracks into their front yard. Aunt Carly told Jimmy he was not going to end up like him. That he was going to be a good man and she was going to see to it.

Every Saturday, they would go fishing together at a stream a few miles from her house. She showed Jimmy how to clean and stuff a trout with spices and vegetables, to wrap it in aluminum foil and let it broil for six minutes. She taught him how to identify birds by sight and sound. He didn't think she was trying to be his mother, but was just trying to help him. But because she wasn't his mother and because of the anger Jimmy felt at having his mother taken away, he did things to Aunt Carly which he later regretted.

One afternoon, as they sat by the fire—the middle of January and school cancelled—snow climbed along the border of the house and spotted the naked dogwoods. The only sound was the wind whistling, a wind that if one climbed on and was small enough and strong enough would carry him all the way down south to a town named Portisville where it didn't snow and where boys played shirts-and-skins football in January. Where people swam in hollow lakes ten months out of the year. But Jimmy was not small or strong enough and on that cold day he and Aunt Carly sat by the fire as she sipped green tea and graded papers. Jimmy had a copy of *The Red Pony* in his lap that she'd given him for Christmas, but he didn't care about people in a book. After finishing a stack of papers and placing them on the coffee table between them, she turned to him, smiled and said, "Jimmy, what are you thinking about?"

And to this Jimmy replied by dropping the book on the floor, raising his right hand, squeezing every finger inward except for the middle one, then standing and walking away to his room. He could hear her start to cry behind him. He was not proud of what he'd done and hadn't known he was going to do it until that exact moment she asked the question. Even now, years later, he couldn't say why he'd done it. It didn't make sense, except that youth makes people do things even they don't understand. He hoped that she forgave him and felt sure that she did. They lived fifty miles apart now and spoke three or four times a year. On his birthday, Jimmy and Carly still met at the stream they had fished at years ago. After slaying trout, they'd drive to a nearby restaurant where, for a special fee, the chef prepared the fish.

Jimmy saw the figure on the side of the road from a great distance. At first, he couldn't make out what it was, but as he got closer he could see that it was a dark-haired woman in her early thirties, wearing a bright white T-shirt and blue shorts, jogging on the side of the road. As he passed her he thought how strange it was that someone would be out jogging on this country road. But he knew it was no accident; she was dressed as if she'd been running her whole life and knew exactly where she was going.

Jimmy pulled the bag he had brought closer to him. On the side of the road an armadillo lay dead with stiff, yellow claws pointing straight to the sky. Jimmy knew the house was close when he saw the old billboard on the side of the road. The billboard had been owned by a local grocery store and used to advertise whatever their weekly specials were, but after the store went out of business the sign stayed up like a reminder of how quickly it could all go away.

The pine trees had grown considerably since Jimmy had last seen them, overtaking the half-dozen slabs of plywood that made up the billboard. A tourist passing through, or someone who didn't know it was there, would not have noticed it at all. Jimmy tried to read the billboard but couldn't. All he could see was the red-brownness of the boards and his distant memories of huge loaves of bread and jugs of milk as big as a car, floating above his head.

Jimmy spotted the aluminum box with his family name in black electrical tape and turned into the gravel drive. He immediately faced another wall of pine trees and had to make a quick left. As he followed the narrow zig-zag trail, his heart rate increased. One time his mother, driving home a little drunk, had hit a couple of the pine trees that lined the driveway, not bad enough to knock them down but enough to splinter the bark. She had looked over at Jimmy after hitting them, put a finger to her lips and said, "Shh."

Jimmy turned the final corner and there was the house where

he had spent the first fourteen years of his life. It needed a fresh coat of paint and the front porch listed slightly to one side and the windows on each side of the door could stand to be replaced. The roof was covered with so many pine needles that Jimmy could see no shingles.

Truman sat in the chair on the deep side of the leaning porch. He seemed to be looking past Jimmy, out at the woods around the house. Jimmy parked next to the old green Cadillac and left the engine running as he waited for his father to acknowledge him. To his left was a blue Toyota Corolla and Jimmy figured it must belong to the nurse Dan had mentioned.

When Truman shifted in the seat and looked in his direction, Jimmy turned the truck off. Climbing out, he heard two angry blue jays yell at each other, then the leaves rustling behind him. Jimmy had no idea what he would say. His father didn't look as bad as he was expecting. He was expecting emaciation and close-to-death weakness, his father propped up in a bed, or a wheelchair, with oxygen tubing spread across his body, a table full of medicine next to him, bedpans and tissues. But really, Jimmy thought, he looked in so many ways just as he'd remembered him: a compact, thickly-muscled man, the remnants of his hair cut in a flat-top, and forearms that seemed capable of many things. A bit balder, older and softer, but he still looked like a man you didn't want to fuck with.

As he walked toward the house, Jimmy noticed a frayed, yellowed rope hanging from the oak tree a few feet above his head. The rope had been used as part of a swing, but now only a foot or two of it hung down from a withered branch. He had played on the swing as a child with his mother standing behind him, pushing him forward. Some days, Truman would sit on the porch drinking a tall glass of iced tea, watching the boy, laughing, yelling, "Jump, jump." After soaring so high that he could see the black shingles across the roof and the trees behind the house, Jimmy would jump off the swing into the soft, thick pine needles.

Occasionally he'd stay on the ground for a few extra seconds, faking an injury, waiting for his parents to help him up.

As Jimmy took the first step of the porch, Truman began to stand, his face showing no emotion that Jimmy could read, his lips a thin horizontal line of flesh. Jimmy stopped, and the two men exchanged a look in which they both searched for something, a thing for each so different from what the other wanted. Taking another step, Jimmy advanced slowly as if he half-expected the stairs to give under his weight.

Then the two men stood a foot away from each other. Behind Truman, the chair settled. The last time they had been together, Jimmy was the same height as his father, but now he had a good six inches on him. He considered, for a second, sticking his hand out, perhaps reaching for his father and pulling him forward as Dan had done to him. He remembered his mother and father sitting at the dinner table on either side of him and how his father would say the sweetest prayers, thanking God for blessing him with a beautiful wife and son, asking God to watch over his family and to allow him to have enough love for both of them.

As Jimmy shuffled another step closer, his father reached into the chest pocket of his overalls. Jimmy stared down at Truman's hand and wondered what the old man was fishing for, maybe a key, maybe something of his mother's. Truman pulled the .38 out of his pocket and said, "You ready?"

Jimmy stepped back and felt a rush of blood flood his face and neck. Truman held the gun out toward him, handle first. Jimmy descended backwards another step, staring at the old man, whose face had changed from blankness to an unkind smile. There was spittle-like pus at the edge of his lips. Pain shot through both of Jimmy's arms. *Oh Christ*, he thought. He felt stuck in time, weighed down like he was out in a pond somewhere and his shoes had filled with water, making each step more difficult than the one before. Were the gun, his father, and a leaning porch all part of his imagination? He closed his eyes and opened them, hoping that might be enough to change the scene in front of him, but the old man still stood there, holding the gun a couple of inches away from him. Truman said, "We don't have a lot of time. The girl will be back from jogging soon."

Jimmy turned back to his truck and stepped down onto the bottom step. The trees and truck blurred before him. He reached out for a handrail on the steps that wasn't there. Truman said, "Come on boy, it ain't like you never killed anybody before. Do your old man a favor."

Jimmy stopped as if about to turn around and say something, then continued walking to the truck, bracing himself, waiting for the sound of the gun and what he imagined would be a quick, piercing feeling in his back.

Bobby Webster pedaled the spray-painted black BMX bike fast and hard, his heart thumping with excitement, his mind filled with the smell and sliminess of fish. Across the handlebars, he held onto the cane pole with both hands.

Riding along the edge of the pavement, his goal was to stay in the six inches between the white line and the grass. To avoid running over a worm as it swam its way along the not-yet-hot asphalt, Bobby swerved his bike onto the grass, swung it around and stopped, standing directly over the fat brown worm. He grabbed the worm, and it folded around his right index finger like a ring. After pulling it away from his finger, Bobby placed it on the small hook on the end of the line, which was wrapped around the pole. He took the worm as a good sign, because he wouldn't have to go digging for bait before he started fishing.

Bobby turned his bike onto the dirt road, just past the square, brown MILLER's POND sign and rode down to the water. The pond was perfectly round and no more than fifty yards across at its widest points. After resting his bike against the picnic table by the water's edge, Bobby sat down on the top part of the table so that his feet fell forward, barely touching the seat in front of him. He held the pole straight out from his body and flicked his hand in a counter-clockwise motion, letting the fishing line unwrap from the pole. The worm hung down in front of him, wiggling, making tiny brown letters, a question mark. Bobby said, "What's your name? Alfred, huh? Kind of silly name for a worm, but that don't matter much I suppose. I need you to catch me a fish."

He climbed down, took the three steps to the water, and tossed his line out into the pond. The tiny pool from his cast settled a moment later. Sitting back on the edge of the table, with the pole in his hands, he looked across the water at the cypress trees that bordered the far side in a big *U* until they met the pine trees and brush that hid the pond from the road. A white bird with black legs walked on one of the beanbag-sized boulders over there.

Something hit in the middle of the pond. Bobby thought he saw a huge bass, with a mouth the size of a prizewinning muskmelon, come out of the water and pull a dragonfly under. As the water settled, he felt a light pull in his hands and the end of the pole bobbed. He pulled straight back, and after a moment of tension, the line popped. Bobby yelled, "Shit, shit, damn."

He jerked the line in but the hook and worm were gone. Bobby said, "Thanks, Alfred." From the front pocket of his cut-off jean shorts he pulled out a sandwich bag full of coins — mostly pennies — and held it up to the new sunlight for a better look. It took a few seconds before he spotted a hook at the bottom.

As he tied it to the line, Bobby wondered what kind of fish had taken his other hook and imagined it was the bass he'd seen — huge and hungry, and Alfred wiggling down there, sticking his tongue out for everyone to see, taunting them. Or maybe it was one of those blue-black catfish that rest on the bottom of the water, waiting for something to fall into their fat faces.

After tying the knot and tugging on it a couple of times to test it, Bobby bit off the excess line and spit it onto the ground. He crawled underneath the table and sat in the cool dirt. An assortment of hardened balls of gum clung to the underside of the table. He wished he had some gum and considered, for a second, pulling one of the old pieces down. As he dug in the dirt, he re-membered going to Panama Beach with his parents a couple years ago. He was eight then and his mother had helped him make a sandcastle with different sized buckets. After the castle, they made a small three-member family out of debris, using sticks for their bodies and multicolored — purple and red and blue — shells for their heads. As Bobby ate lunch, the water washed the castle and family away. He hadn't been back to a beach since, and it wasn't long after that trip that his mother left.

Under the table, he pulled away a fistful of the dark dirt, felt his middle finger touch something solid, perhaps the root of a tree, so he turned his hand in the other direction. In a couple of minutes, with three worms in hand, he climbed out from under the table. The fattest of the worms Bobby placed on the edge of the hook, white traces of insides dripping out as the fine tip pierced through the opposite side of the worm. He dropped the other two on top of the table where they moved in slow spas-modic bursts, forth and back, as if lost and confused. Bobby lifted the end of the pole above his head and then stopped. He looked at the worm again, considered naming this one, but no names came to him, so he tossed it out into the water nameless.

As Bobby stood on the edge of the pond, staring at the water, waiting for the next strike, two purple and black grackles flew down on the table behind him. When he turned around and lunged at the birds, they flew away with the worms hanging in their mouths.

Bobby told himself that when he got older he'd get a regular fishing pole and use lures or maybe even get one of those fly rods. With them you could stand on one end of a pond and cast all the way over to the other side. He was convinced that all the good fish swam over there on the other side, just beyond his reach.

Davis sat in a corner booth at the Portisville Diner with Bird, his deputy. The deputy was in his mid-twenties and broad-shoul-dered and had a tanned face and kind, blue eyes. Davis felt tired already. He'd been up for three hours, walking around the woods where they had found the car. Bird fingered one corner of his menu and said, "Think we'll find her, Sheriff?"

"I don't know, son."

"You never know."

"I hope we don't."

Bird burrowed his eyebrows in a questioning gesture and Davis felt certain his comment had disappointed the deputy.

"Why's that?"

"She'll probably be dead."

"What?"

"Missing girls usually end up dead."

"I don't know. Seems possible she might be okay."

Davis appreciated the kid's optimism, even if it was built on ignorance. He wished he could feel more optimistic about this, but he didn't. It had all the signs of bad news.

Bird said, "Find anything else about her?"

"Nothing really. The sheriff in Tallahassee said she was a college student and she's been gone for five days now."

"Into drugs or anything?"

"Bird, I don't know any more than what I just told you. Her roommate told them that she left the dorm with plans to go to the library Saturday morning and that was the last anybody has seen her." Davis turned away to the front window of the diner where two old men were sitting on a park bench and pointing out cars that passed by on the road. "They're supposed to fax us a folder on her today. State police are going to come by."

"This is a pretty big deal then."

"Somebody is missing and they find her car abandoned next to woods thirty miles away from where she was last seen with no signs of forced entrance, then it becomes a big deal. Don't suppose we're going to get much rest until we find her." Davis liked his deputy, but sometimes his constant questions got to be too much.

"This the biggest case you ever had?"

"Well, it's not exactly our case yet."

"You know what I mean."

Davis wondered if he knew about the Dot Wills case, twenty-two years ago. It was his first real case. Made the newspapers as far south as Orlando. He'd only been the sheriff for a little over a year when he'd had to arrest Truman Wills, a man as close as a brother to him, for the crime of killing his wife. The only evidence they had was some of Truman's hair and skin under her fingernails, which Truman said was from sex the previous afternoon. When he was found not guilty, there had been other trouble for Davis: people didn't think he tried hard enough, two of his deputies quit, and he almost lost the next election. But hell, at the trial the doctors couldn't prove exactly when the hair and skin had gotten under her nails, whether it had been that night or afternoon. His alibi also checked out: Dan swore that they'd gone to Kentucky and had gotten back early that morning when Truman discovered her missing. Davis had never been convinced of his friend's guilt in the case, but the prosecutor was young and wanted a conviction even if he had no concrete evidence.

Davis figured the deputy was probably a baby at the time, but it was still possible, and very likely, that Bird knew about the case. That and the murder five years ago of a middle-school girl named Vikki Dobson were the two biggest cases during Davis' time as sheriff. Every couple of months, all these years later, he would still occasionally stumble in on a conversation where Truman's guilt was being discussed.

Davis said, "Yeah, I guess it is."

"Damn."

Davis stood and pulled his pants up a bit. He hadn't eaten. He was still hungry, but needed some fresh air. The man seated behind them kept coughing and Davis could feel himself getting agitated. He thought it best if he was alone for a while, went for a drive to clear his head. The coffee in front of him wasn't doing much good either, probably making him jittery; he'd already had four cups since he'd been up this morning.

Bird said, "Where you going?"

"I'm gonna go check out the car; they're supposed to tow it to the station. Then I'm gonna head back out to the crime scene. Walter is running his dogs. Maybe he found something."

Bird began to stand. "I'll go, too."

"Don't be silly; eat."

"What about your food?"

"You eat it. You're a growing young man." Davis turned to walk away, felt relieved somewhat that he'd left the deputy with a smile on his face.

Bird called, "See you in a bit then."

Davis walked to the front of the diner, and stepped outside into the hot air and sound of slow-moving traffic without turning back.

Jimmy's mind flashed hot and fast and red as he moved through the winding driveway, kicking up gravel behind him. Around the final corner, his back fender hit a thin new-growth pine, knocking it down and tumbling into the other trees around it.

Turning onto the blacktop, he wondered why he had come so far. What exactly had he been expecting? Was he expecting the son of a bitch to be standing there with his arms open, out in an I've-missed-you hug? *Shit*, Jimmy thought, *I should've just fucking killed him, done us all a favor.*

Jimmy felt the muscles tense in his leg from the pressure he held on the pedal. His head ached, his eyes felt heavy, and his hands squeezed the steering wheel. He spotted the MILLER'S POND sign and slammed on his brakes. The truck jerked to the right and settled so that he was straddling the edge of the asphalt. He stared at the sign and the road that led down to the pond, hardly able to breathe from the anger. Jimmy had fished here five, six days a week as a boy. And something about the new sign, the way it was so different from what he remembered—back then, it was a simple piece of plywood with the words MILLER'S POND in white spray paint—and his tiredness, and his anger, and the way he felt like he'd already, in a matter of hours, started to slide back to a life he didn't want, made Jimmy start to cry. He leaned forward and his head touched the steering wheel. He didn't want to cry, pulled against it like a motherfucker, but a few tears came nonetheless. He couldn't remember the last time he'd shed a tear. A car honked as it drove by him, making Jimmy sit up. After considering the road ahead one more time, he turned toward the pond.

He drove into the clearing, made a right, and idled the truck to the end of the road, where it dead-ended into a wall of cypress trees. The pond didn't look much different from what he remembered. Now, the white boulders on the other side of the water were covered in green slime and a snowy egret walked along them, methodically taking pieces of the green film off the rock, into its mouth, and then spitting them back out. A few feet of grass and a picnic table now covered the area where white pebbles the perfect size for skimming across water once lined the shore. Jimmy turned the truck around so that the back fender rested over the edge of the grass. He climbed out, dropped the tailgate, and sat on it. His hand shook as he lit a cigarette and smoked three back to back, blowing small round *O's* in an effort to calm himself.

He heard a cough and looked over to his left where a blond boy whose hair was cut short on top with a rat-tail falling down the back of his white T-shirt climbed from under the picnic table and tossed his line into the pond. The kid, who looked about nine or ten, glanced in Jimmy's direction for a second, then turned back to the water.

Jimmy could see himself as a boy, about that age, with his mother on the shore of this pond. She would sit upright, stiff-backed, as if under her shirt there was an ironing board strapped to her back, on an overturned five-gallon bucket with a beer buried two inches down into the dirt between her legs. Standing a few feet away, Jimmy would hold his fishing pole and watch her look out into the water. Her green eyes and strong chin would shine in the sunlight. He never knew what she saw out in that water, but she always caught more fish than he did.

Whenever she had a fish on, she would let out a "whoa" as she jerked back on the cane pole. After pulling the catfish onto the shore, she'd smile at Jimmy and say, "Not bad for a girl, huh?" He'd walk over and put his right foot on the barb that extended straight up from the catfish's back, pressing it down so that it bent flush with the gray, slimy coat. Then he'd hold the two side barbs tight with one hand while pulling the hook out with the other. His mother would smile at Jimmy and kiss him on the forehead, hug him, smelling of beer and cigarettes and sweet perfume. The sweat on the top of her chest, right where the curve of her breasts started, would wet his lips with the taste of salt. And before long, she would smile at Jimmy again in a way he knew meant that she was ready for him to pull another beer from the cooler in the back of the car.

Jimmy heard the boy yell and turned in that direction. He was jumping up and down and yelling a quick succession of *shits* and *damns* together with an ease that surprised Jimmy. At first he thought that maybe the kid had taken a catfish barb in his hand or maybe he'd stuck a hook through a finger. He took a few steps toward the boy who threw the skinny pole at his bike.

Jimmy said, "You okay?"

"Fine."

"What's wrong?"

The boy looked up at him with an expression of annoyance: his cheeks flushed, his eyes tight, and his breathing hard. He picked the pole up and began wrapping the line around the base of it. The slight early morning breeze had all but vanished and the oppressive heat seemed to be coming on fast. Red-winged black-birds and blue jays yelled back and forth at each other, while a mockingbird echoed the sentiments of both parties. The kid said, "My hook. I lost my last hook."

Three dead bream lay like the points of a triangle at the boy's feet. A loud popping sound came from behind them; Jimmy and the boy turned to the settling pool in the center of the water thirty yards away. The boy said, "Shit."

Jimmy said, "I got a tackle box in the back of my truck."

"That's okay."

The boy climbed onto his bike and held the pole in his hands across the handlebars. Jimmy said, "Wait, what about those fish?"

The boy turned and glared at Jimmy as if that question could have been the stupidest thing he'd ever heard and said, "I don't eat them fish." Then he turned onto the road with the cane pole bouncing across the handlebars like a loose antenna. Weird kid, Jimmy thought. Maybe he had to be somewhere, maybe school, but he wasn't dressed for that.

Jimmy looked at his truck and then back toward the picnic table and the fish. The tiredness he felt earlier paled in comparison to how he felt now. He couldn't think straight. He needed sleep. After standing there for a minute with his eyes half open— seeing nothing but water and green brush all around him— Jimmy walked over to the fish. He bent over and one at a time picked them up by their tails and tossed them gently back into the water. But it did no good; they all floated on the surface and moved with the slight wind to the other side of the pond.

Truman sat back down in the chair. He held the gun out and fired the remaining five bullets into the base of the tree. A thick stream of sap dripped down, bumping and passing over old holes until it reached the ground where hungry ants ran back and forth bathing in it. Truman set the gun down at his feet and looked across the yard at the corner of the driveway where Jimmy had gone. Slight tufts of dust still danced in the air. *That boy has gotten tall,* he thought, *almost as tall as his mother was.* He laughed a little as he remembered the look on Jimmy's face, but stopped when he felt a sudden urge to piss.

He took a couple steps to the end of the porch and undid his zipper and pulled out the old, useless piece of flesh with his right hand, wrapping his left around the porch rail for balance, and aimed at the yard.

The pressure in his bladder increased and the urge came and went. He squeezed somewhere deep inside of his pelvis for relief. A lizard ran along the warped hardwood edge of the porch and jumped into the grass. Truman squeezed some more. His left arm started to shake and his legs felt wobbly. Sweat formed on his forehead. He heard someone breathing deeply and looked up. Covered in sweat, Angie walked around the corner, stretching her arms above her head. For a moment, with the sun behind her, a good three inches of her belly were exposed, and Truman thought her damp, pale skin was about the most beautiful thing he'd ever seen. The muscles of her arms and legs pulsed, and her slight breasts pushed against the shirt. Then the pain came back into his bladder.

He kept watching her, waiting for her to notice him. When she did, she paused for a moment, gave him a hard look which turned to fright as she seemed to realize he was in trouble. As she started to walk toward him, his arm shaking like the strings of an untuned guitar, she said, "Are you all right?"

He said, "I can't go."

Next to him, she was still breathing hard from her run. He looked down and saw spots of browned blood on the end of his uncircumsized penis. She said, "Come on," and grabbed his left arm, "let's go inside."

He pulled away and said, "No, goddamn it."

She ran into the house. He could hear her going through the cabinets, slamming drawers, then she was back outside behind him, stretching a glove onto each hand. She undid the buttons on the overalls, and they fell to the floor. He hoped it wouldn't take long; the last time she'd had to do this the relief was almost instant.

He heard her spit a couple times, then she spread his cheeks with one hand while inserting a finger of her other hand into his asshole. He tightened at first, let out the slightest cry, and then relaxed somewhat. She was inside of him, moving, trying to locate it, massaging back and forth, then he felt his prostate spasm against her finger. A moment later, he saw the steady stream of yellow and red urine puddle on the empty black dirt that circled the porch, and felt the relief he needed.

Davis pulled in behind the wrecker in the back lot of the police department. Three cruisers were parked single-file over by the high chain-link fence. The missing girl's Honda sat in the center of the lot with yellow police tape wrapped all the way around it like a ribbon.

He peeled the tape away from the door. The car's roof was hot to the touch. He looked around the outside, not a dent or scratch anywhere. No signs of forced entry: the windows weren't broken, the locks hadn't been tampered with. There was a new FSU student parking decal on the rear fender. On the inside of the windshield was a sticker for an oil change, due in another fifty miles.

Lifting his hands to the driver's side window, Davis cupped them against the glass and shielded himself from the reflection of the sun behind him. Specks of white flint spotted the dashboard where they'd dusted for fingerprints. Nothing on the car's interior suggested foul play. He wished there were something, anything, a place to start. Maybe he was getting too old for this. He'd planned to retire in four or five months and had hoped it would be a quiet, easy ride out, but that didn't seem to be the case now.

From behind him, Davis heard a long hard growl. Inside the fence, over by the dumpster, about twenty yards away, a pair of pit bulls, a brindle and a white one, were mauling a pile of trash. The brindle one lunged at the white one, who jumped back defensively. Though it looked vicious, Davis didn't think any damage was being done. It was mostly just bumping teeth.

The brindle pit turned and walked away, out a hole in the fence. The white pit watched him go and then began to attack the pile of trash. There were a few dogs that hung around the station, but Davis hadn't seen this one before. He yelled at the dog, told it to get. It turned at the sound of his voice and bared its teeth. Davis felt the heat on his face and neck. The dog took a couple steps toward him; pieces of trash and what looked like blood covered the white around his mouth. Davis turned all the way now. He wasn't sure what the dog was going to do, since he was probably already pumped up from wrestling with his buddy. He put his hand on his holster, clicked the safety off his service revolver with his thumb. Just in case.

Then, as if the dog sensed that he was ready, it charged. It was all thick-muscled legs and red-suckled jowls bouncing around a mask of teeth as it ran. Davis pulled the gun, backed up against the Honda. Turning left and right, he could focus on nothing. Then he heard it—the low, serious pumping of its breath, the rapping of claws on pavement. The gun felt light, feather-like, in his hand. He squeezed the trigger and it looked as if the dog had run into a brick wall, the way it stopped, rolled twice, and then lay there whimpering for a second.

Davis looked around again. The fence seemed long and thick and barbed with rust. He felt a pain in his shoulder that held for a few seconds and then went away. The dog's chest stopped its steady rhythm. Davis couldn't believe nobody had heard the shot. For Christ's sake, it was in the back of the police department. He squatted by the dog and saw where the bullet had entered in the center of its chest and that the red around the dog's mouth was a darker red than blood, as if he'd had his face in barbecue sauce. The pain in Davis' arm came and went and was followed by a squeezing pressure in the center of his chest. He tried to breathe nice and easy. He pulled a nitro from the little metal vial he kept on the chain around his neck and set it under his tongue.

He took a few deep breaths, told himself to take it easy now, let the nitro do what it was supposed to. The heart doctor in Tallahassee had told him that the medicine usually took effect right away but that it could take up to five minutes before he felt complete relief. The man told Davis that he had blockage, two major vessels, and recommended surgery, but Davis hadn't wanted to do it until after he retired.

Behind Davis, a door opened. "Sheriff, are you okay?" It was Ellen Hewe with her dome of white hair. She'd been the secretary at the office for as long as he could remember, back when he was a boy and his father was in charge.

Davis said, "Fine, I'm fine."

Ellen spotted the dog and raised a hand to her mouth. She said, "Oh, mother of God."

"I know. Don't look." He tried to stand in front of her, to block her view, as the pressure in his chest began to subside again.

"What happened?"

"The dog charged me."

"My God."

"Go on back inside and call the vet. Tell him we'll be bringing a dog over. Tell him it's already dead."

After she went back inside, Davis noticed that the blood which had flowed from the small hole had stopped or congealed, and a palm-sized circle of the stuff lay on the ground, an inch from the dog's chest.

The man from the wrecker walked out the back door. He said, "Damn, Sheriff, I've been looking all over for you. I need you to sign for the car." The gray pad with a small pink piece of paper on top looked to Davis like a ticket book.

"What were you going to do if you didn't find me, wait around here all day until I came back?"

The man said, "Yes."

Davis shook his head and started to walk away, thinking, *Goddamn idiot.* The Honda was between him and the door. He marveled at how spotless, new, untarnished it looked, especially now in the wake of what had just happened. He had made it the door and had it half open when he heard the man say, "Is that dog dead?"

Davis didn't answer but went inside and got a sheet to wrap the dog in so that he could do what had to be done with it.

Bobby climbed the porch steps and dropped the bike up against the tankless propane grill, which rested against the dull green, block house, and then leaned the pole across the bike. He unlocked the front door and entered. He heard his father's voice, steady and threatening, "Lock that door, boy." Bobby did.

The TV played a cartoon he didn't recognize right away—a talking cat laughed at its own joke. Past the living room, his father sat at the kitchen table. On one side of the table lay a basketball-sized mound of marijuana and on the other side a box of plastic sandwich bags. Darren, Bobby's father, looked up at him with beady, brown eyes, nodded a quick hello and then went back to work. "Where you been?"

"Went fishing."

"Catch anything?"

"Little bream."

"You going to school today?"

"Should." Bobby wondered if his father knew that he had missed the last two days of school.

"Well, go on then."

Bobby sat at the table, across from his father who was dropping finger-sized amounts of marijuana into the bag like someone portioning ingredients for a special dinner. He filled it until he was satisfied with the amount, a height of two fingers—about an inch—and then sealed the bag and put it into a brown backpack on the floor, by his feet. Bobby said, "Did Mom call?"

Darren didn't look up. "No. I told you to stop asking about that."

"I know."

"She'll call when she calls."

Bobby hadn't heard from his mother in over a week. He hadn't seen her in a month. He was supposed to go to her house every other weekend, but lately she'd been busy, working two jobs. The last time she talked to him on the phone she said that she would make it up to Bobby, but so far she hadn't. And he had wondered, more than once, if he would ever see her again.

Bobby said, "Can I help?"

Darren stopped for a second. "You gonna fuck it up?"

"No."

"You did lock that door?"

Bobby nodded, then walked over and stood to the right of his father. The smell of coffee and the old-sweat scent of the marijuana filled his nose. He ran his fingers through the tallest part of the mound.

Darren said, "Stop fucking around with it."

Bobby pulled his fingers out of the mound as his father continued to sort the marijuana with an agitated expression across his face. A deep gash in the shape of a lightning bolt scarred the center of the table.

Darren said, "Just fill the bag till it gets about as high as, well, let me see." He grabbed Bobby's hand and measured his fingers against the boy's. "Make it three of your fingers."

Bobby picked the marijuana up and slid it into the bag. He liked the greenness and brownness and the bits of black on the leafy material. He didn't understand why his father called it grass or pot. It seemed a name like stinky dirt would be more fitting.

Darren said, "You eat breakfast?"

"No, I'm not hungry."

"Well, I don't want to hear no shit later about how hungry you are."

"You won't."

"Better not."

Bobby said, "What's the biggest fish you ever caught?"

"Shit, boy, I'm working here." Darren dropped another plastic bag into the backpack.

"I saw a huge bass today, huge." Bobby opened his arms wide. Darren shook his head and rolled his eyes and then drank from his mug of coffee.

Without speaking, they continued to work for a few minutes. The size of the mound diminished at a slow, even pace. Then the quick, passing wail of a police siren stunned them both. Darren lunged for the marijuana. Bobby ran to the window and looked out, but the car had already passed. He craned his neck a second time for a chance to see, but it was no use. He liked the sound of sirens and hadn't seen or heard a police car in a few days. They were for catching bad people, or at least that is what his teachers in school had told him. His father called the police "fucking scumbags" and said that if young Bobby ever got the chance to shoot one he should. His father hated some people for reasons Bobby didn't understand, though he was pretty sure it had something to do with his mother leaving; everything seemed to be about that. Before she left, his father had worked as a mechanic instead of working at home and he had more hair on the top of his head and didn't have such a big belly.

Bobby thought his dad was wrong about police officers. Davis, the town sheriff, had always been nice to him, sometimes even offering him rides to school. Bobby liked the sheriff and he liked the free rides, but he wished the man wouldn't always ask him so many questions about his father. He knew that what his father did was illegal. Bobby had asked him about it last year after Davis visited the school and talked to all the kids about drugs and how they were bad for you and that you should report any you see. When Bobby asked him about it, his father admitted that, yes, what he did was illegal, but he said the only reason that was so was because the government wanted a piece of the pie and they weren't getting it. He said that it was easy money and he was helping people, giving them what they wanted. He also said that he and Bobby needed the extra money since his mother had left them. Bobby didn't know about the government and taxes and stuff, but for a while he had thought his father was a smart man since he was working less and making more money and helping people. But eventually this image faded and it was just his father's job, something he wasn't supposed to talk about.

Darren said, "They gone?"

"Yeah."

It was after ten and Bobby decided to watch some cartoons on TV for a while. He would try and call his mother after his father left. Maybe later he would go do some more fishing just before dark, when the day started to cool off. As he headed for the living room, his father loosened his grip on the brown bag and fell back to measuring two fingers at a time.

Jimmy opened his eyes and stared up at the web of branches above him. His face felt warm from the sun, despite the slight shade the trees provided. For a moment, he couldn't say where he was. But when he sat up on the picnic table, he saw the fish popping on the surface of Miller's Pond and felt the hot, Portisville air.

Briefly, he considered pulling out the fishing pole and tackle box he kept behind the seat, but instead smoked two more cigarettes without pause and reviewed his options. He could climb into the truck and drive back to North Carolina, but he didn't think he could stay awake for the drive, even with the hour-long nap he had just finished. He could get a hotel: take a shower, sleep a few more hours and then go on home. Staying with Dan was another possibility.

Lighting another cigarette, he heard Truman's words again: "It ain't like you never killed anybody before."

The man's name was Gary Warsaw and Jimmy had been sleeping with his wife, Helen, for over a year on that day Gary came home and found them in bed. Jimmy was seventeen at the time. Helen was in her mid-thirties and worked as a teacher with his Aunt Carly. Jimmy remembered that it was a summer day. The curtains were drawn. He didn't hear the man come in the room, only felt someone pull him off of Helen. Then she was screaming as the man broke her nose with a single punch and began to strangle her. Jimmy hit him in the back of the head with a large glass vase. The single blow killed him. Self-defense is what Jimmy's lawyer argued and the jury agreed. Helen had told Jimmy that her husband beat her and would show him bruises on her arms and legs to prove it. Jimmy's lawyer told him after the trial that it was photos of those bruises and two prior reports of domestic violence that kept him out of jail.

At the time, Jimmy had convinced himself that Gary Warsaw's death was no great tragedy, that he deserved to die for what he had done to Helen, that he would have in fact killed them both that day, but now he wasn't sure how he felt about that man. It was something he had pushed so far back into the recesses of his mind that he had no real opinion of it, felt no real connection with the memory or events. It was as if that had happened to someone else, an actor in a movie scene years ago, the young Jimmy Wills, a person that was hardly recognizable to him. And the last time he had spoken about it was twelve or thirteen years ago when he told Merrilee, a woman he lived with for a couple years in his early twenties, in one of their late-night, confess-it-all sessions.

He shook his head and climbed back into the truck and drove to the intersection where the road leading to the pond met the highway. As he was about to pull out, he heard a horn and looked up as two cars drove past at a blinding speed.

Jimmy tapped his cigarette against the outside mirror of the truck, and turned on the radio and caught the tail end of a Travis Tritt song. Then a stern male voice spoke to him across the airways: "*Special report. A gray Honda Civic was found on the side of the road early this morning off Highway 144 in Portisville. Authorities say the car belongs to a twenty-year-old college student named Teresa Martin who has been missing for five days. Anyone with information about the car, or the girl, who is described as being five foot three with blond hair and blue eyes, is asked to contact the police immediately.*" The voice transported Jimmy to the night after his mother disappeared. He was staying at Dan's and had been playing cards with his father's friend when a man's voice spoke through the radio, asking for any information on his mother. Dan had jumped up and tried to turn the radio off before the message was completed, but Jimmy had heard all of it.

Jimmy then thought about what he'd been trying desperately not to think about—perhaps because it was a thing he didn't want to know the answer to—the fact that his father had been charged with his mother's murder but had been found not guilty. There had been a time while living with his aunt that she'd made it clear, without coming out and saying so, that she believed Truman had something to do with it. So, for a while, he had thought that it was possible, but he couldn't say for sure now if he believed it or not. He had never seen his father strike his mother or even raise his voice to her; it always seemed to Jimmy that his father followed her around like a puppy. All he knew for certain was that he had been awakened one morning and told his mother was gone. Three days later, they found her buried in a shallow grave between two pine trees, in the woods, a couple of miles from the house, a single bullet in her head.

During the murder trial, Jimmy had lived with his aunt. Afterwards, he came back home to live with Truman. A year later, during a drug deal, one of the federal agents pursuing Truman was killed. Truman went to jail for vehicular manslaughter and a handful of drug charges. It was then that Jimmy was sent back up to North Carolina to live with his Aunt Carly for good.

When Jimmy focused on the radio again, a song was playing about friends in low places. He stared at the inch of metal, which served as the volume knob, sticking out from the side of the truck's stereo and wondered for a second if he'd heard right. If there'd been a special report at all, or if he'd imagined the whole damn thing. Turning the radio off, he remembered the police cars he'd passed earlier on the side of the road and felt certain it must be real.

The two racing cars drove past Jimmy again going the other way. He figured it was probably a couple of boys out getting their races in before the police finished breakfast and started moving through the streets of this town.

Truman pointed the cup of coffee at his Cadillac, an old tub of a car with a white vinyl roof peeling away in spots and walked toward it, kicking the dirt as he advanced. Another fine day, he thought, Angie having to stick her finger up my ass just to take a piss and eating the charred scrambled eggs she made for breakfast. Oh, it's fucking paradise. If Jimmy would have just done it, this would all be over. But Truman was sure he'd be back. He took two more sips of the strong coffee, had a brief coughing fit, then tossed the cup toward the side of the house.

He ran his right index finger along the eddy between the car's hood and front panel and then caressed the grille before walking to the driver's side door. The first car he'd ever owned was a two-door Ford he'd bought after a stint in the army. The day he got back he had walked straight to Hale's down at the corner of Highland and Woodlawn, and paid cash for the car. He had always felt more at home behind the wheel than most places, but now he wasn't even allowed to drive.

He lifted the door handle, felt the pull against his fingers and the heaviness of the door as it opened. He climbed in and rolled the window down as his ass, which was still sore, sank into the cream-colored, cracked leather bench seat. Twenty-five-year-old memories of him and Dan and Davis on a dirt road driving deep into the woods to the cabin they shared, splitting money they'd made, filled his mind. The three men passing a bottle of whiskey back and forth as the car chugged along, up and over deep crevices in the road with animals scurrying about from their blind path.

Truman honked the horn to a steady slow rhythm in his head: one and two and three and four and . . .

Angie yelled, from the front porch, "Truman, knock that off."

Her voice and presence surprised him as if he'd been in another world, or had forgotten that anyone existed outside the confines of the car. She stared out at him with her hands on her hips. Her panty lines were visible beneath the thin shorts and he wondered how hard it might be to get them off of her. As far as he knew, she hadn't had any since she'd been here. Actually, she didn't leave the house much, except for her daily jogs and when she worked a few days a week over at the retirement home.

He climbed out of the car and said, "What?"

She said, "All that noise." Then she disappeared into the house. The screen door rattled for a second or two.

Truman muttered, "Shit," and looked up at the porch, focused for a second on the motionless rocking chair as he slammed the car door. Damn, she could annoy him, but he knew that she really wasn't that bad. He was sure glad she had come upon him earlier on the porch when she did. And she had treated him good when he was really sick, spooning him chunks of ice and wiping his lips clean.

She had even cleaned the inside of the house up. It still wasn't much to look at, not that he particularly cared since he spent most of his time on the porch and didn't have many visitors, but it was better than when she first got here. The coffee tables alone had been covered with foot-high stacks of magazines, old cups, browned playing cards, and boxes of his bullets. Clothes were draped across the couch. She had packed it all up and deposited it into boxes she stacked in the spare bedroom closet. One time, he walked out into the living room, after she had cleaned the place and, for a moment, stood there puzzling over whether or not he had drifted into some stranger's house.

He figured cleaning the place gave her something to do and it kept her out of his hair. It wasn't until she started cleaning out the bathroom closet and asking about a wife, because she found a bunch of Dot's old packages of tampons and some of her razors and a couple old dresses in one of the drawers, that he told her to leave things alone.

The tabby kitten jumped up on the hood of the car. Truman petted it behind the ears, and the kitten leaned into his hand and purred. Truman farted and laughed and decided to go for a walk, giving Angie some time to clear out, so they wouldn't have to talk and she wouldn't ask him if it was getting harder to urinate or some such shit he didn't want to answer.

Truman started down the two-foot-wide path just to the right of his favorite bullet-hole torn tree. The long branches of the pine trees bent around the path and every once in a while he'd have to push a spider web full of lifeless bees and yellow moths out of his way. It was hot and muggy in the woods and low hanging branches from the pine trees and elephant ears hung across the path like an archway. He wished he had worn a shirt but did not feel like going back for one now.

A yellow snake slunk away into the thick carpet of pine needles a few feet to his right and Truman saw the eyes of what he took to be a deer staring out at him from behind a bush and imagined what he must look like: a sloppy man walking, panting, waving his arms, fanning the air for relief from the dive-bombing mosquitoes and wall of gnats.

He felt certain Jimmy was still here in town, somewhere close. He wouldn't come all this way and then turn around and drive home. They had unfinished business. He wondered what he might tell Jimmy to make him do this thing he wanted done. He could offer him money, though he wasn't sure that would be enough.

Truman kept on steady, cussing when he ran into a spider web he hadn't seen. He kicked a pinecone and stepped on a beer bottle buried beneath the pine needles; the bottle shattered under his weight. From far off, he smelled the faint odor of smoke. He felt dizzy and reached out to a tree for balance. He took short breaths, exhaled through his open mouth. The trees around him wobbled and closed in on him. He shook his head and spat at the ground. Leaning against the tree, he told himself not to panic. The dizzy spells had been coming more often, but if he just stood still and took a few deep breaths they usually went away pretty quick.

Truman didn't want to keep on living like this and didn't want to end up in the hospital again with all those damned tubes in him and those gray walls everywhere he looked, and those fuckers standing around talking about him when he was too drugged up to say anything back. In a few minutes, when he started to feel better, Truman turned in the direction he had come, heading back toward his house, telling himself that he would never go back to the hospital.

Jimmy turned onto Main Street. The pine trees and palmettos of the highway disappeared and gave way to downtown Portisville. A fifty-yard stretch of blacktop, flanked on either side by rows of one-story stores and cars parked along the curbs marked the strip. There were a half-dozen benches spread out evenly along the sidewalk and in front of every third store a freshly planted oak tree shot up from a metal grid. On his left, he passed a hardware store with lawnmowers displayed in the front window, a TV repair shop, a health food store and a pharmacy. On his right, the twirling red, white, and blue barber pole of Bob's Chop Shop reminded him of once-a-month haircuts with his mother. She would sit in one of the metal chairs against the window, peeking up from magazines and winking at him or stepping outside to smoke a cigarette.

He parked at the end of the strip in front of the Winn-Dixie. Directly across the street, a park stood in the foreground of the old, white City Hall building and the police station. The Portisville Diner was right next to the Winn-Dixie and it occurred to him that he should eat something, but he wasn't really hungry.

He climbed out of the truck and walked toward the grocery store and noticed the bright orange flyer on the telephone pole. It said MISSING in big black letters. Under that was a photo of a young blond girl. He figured that must be the girl he heard about on the radio and whose car he had passed on the drive in to town. Reading the poster, he learned that her height was 5'3". She weighed 125 pounds and had a mole on the right side of her neck. He heard a car horn and turned but couldn't find the source. Above him, a white banner hung across the street with large yellow ropes. The banner read: SEPTEMBER 16-18, ANNUAL PORTISVILLE FAIR. And under that: PORTISVILLE—THE NEW SOUTH DOWN SOUTH.

Jimmy remembered going to the fair with his mother three weeks before she had disappeared. Each year, his parents would take him, but that final time his father had been away on one of his trips. Jimmy and his mother rode every ride that unseasonably cool night. There were so many people there he'd thought every person in town must have come out. Atop the Ferris wheel, his mother swung her arms in the air and yelled as they reached the highest point, her always-present cigarette glowing against the black sky. The music thrummed in their ears and pounded in their chests, so loud that Jimmy thought his eardrums might burst. All the fair workers smiled at his mother and watched her walk by. This was something he'd gotten used to. Men always watched his mother, and he remembered how one worker—a bearded man with filthy jeans—threw her a creepy wolf whistle. If the man lived in this town, and knew his father, Jimmy had felt sure he wouldn't have done that.

As Jimmy and his mother stood by the concession stand sharing a stick of pink cotton candy, a man with a sunburned face walked up and touched her gently on the right shoulder. Jimmy knew who he was, a local fishing guide named Rick Brown who had taken Truman and his friends out a couple times, and Jimmy could tell that he'd been drinking, his walk full of false confidence. He remembered how his mother turned around and smiled at this man and for just a second her face lit up. She said, "Rick," before she turned back to Jimmy, calling the man Mr. Brown after that. She gave Jimmy two tickets to ride the tea-cups. As he climbed onto the ride and felt it start up, his stomach churned as it always did when he rode rides without her. Then as he began to spin faster and faster, he could see his mother and this man laughing and talking. As Jimmy climbed off the ride, the man walked away into the night crowd.

In the Winn-Dixie, Jimmy felt the cool A/C wash all over him. A row of ten registers moored the front of the store. He knew in grocery stores beer was usually kept on one of the sidewalls. His mother would take him shopping at the Kash N' Karry on Friday nights. The first thing she'd do was go to the beer section and get a twelve-pack of Busch and toss it into the cart Jimmy pushed behind her. Sometimes she'd even open one of the cans, sipping on it as they walked through the aisles, hiding it behind her oversized purse. If she didn't drink one in the store, she would definitely have it open and turned up before they were out of the parking lot. Jimmy's job was to make sure she left no empty beer cans in the car for Truman to find.

Now, carrying a twelve-pack of Miller Lite, he started back to the register and considered his options again. He didn't want to stay at the old house but he didn't want to stay at a hotel either. Maybe he could just go back there, take a nap, go out and get something to eat, spend the night, then leave in the morning. He didn't think his father would mess with him anymore after what had happened earlier. He had made it clear he wasn't going to do what the old man wanted. Jimmy considered staying and not doing what Truman asked, just to spite him. Plus, he felt he needed to set the record straight about that man he killed. It wasn't as if it was cold-blooded murder. It wasn't something Truman had any right to bring it up.

Only two of the registers were open. The one closest to him was the X-press lane with a single customer in line, an old guy in a pink shirt. He pulled a package of steaks, pre-made salad and a bottle of red wine from a handcart and placed them on the counter. Picturing the man having himself a nice evening with his wife of fifty years, Jimmy tried to recall the last time he'd shared a couple of steaks and a bottle of wine with a woman. It had been a while.

He forced a smile at the cashier, an older woman wearing a pair of reading glasses. She didn't smile back and he figured he didn't look so good: middle of the morning and he was standing here with a twelve-pack. She looked familiar and he tried to place her but couldn't. It seemed possible to him that every person he came into contact with was someone from his past.

Jimmy turned to the other open register, one row away. A customer pulled groceries from her cart as the cashier ran item after item after item over the scanner. The cashier was about his age, slim, and had shoulder-length blond hair and small lips. Jimmy knew that under different circumstances, if he were looking, he would have said that she was an attractive woman.

As if feeling his stare, the cashier looked toward him and then away. A man coughed behind Jimmy. Though he tried, Jimmy was unable to turn away from this woman. He felt certain he knew her. Maybe she reminded him of somebody from North Carolina. When the coughing man nudged him forward with his handcart, Jimmy told him to go on ahead.

Jimmy walked to the other register, still trying to place this woman. As he set the beer down, he read her nametag: CAROL. *Carol Binder,* he thought. She had moved to town the year he had started eighth grade and was in his class, though they weren't really friends. The girls all said she had the most beautiful hair they'd ever seen. It reached the back of her knees, but one day, halfway through the school year, for reasons nobody knew, during lunch hour, she had taken a pair of scissors out of the teacher's desk and cut her hair to just below her ears. When she walked into the cafeteria, everyone stopped eating and watched her move through the food line as the tears ran down her face, before one of the teachers led her by the hand out of the cafeteria. She didn't come back to school for a week after that. That summer Jimmy had left Portisville for good.

She looked up again, trying to place him, and it didn't take long before her eyes lit up in a smile of recognition. He smiled back as she finished ringing up the lady's purchases. In Carol's eyes, he could see a hurt or sadness. He knew the phrase "the eyes are the window to the soul" but didn't consider himself the kind of guy who'd waste time trying to figure out what somebody's eyes meant. Still, she had the look of a woman who'd once been beautiful but had fallen in love with the wrong man, one who had told her for so long that she was worth nothing that she'd started to believe it. He wondered if it had begun back there in school, if she'd cut her hair because she didn't think it was beautiful and didn't deserve the attention it provided.

Jimmy searched her hands for a wedding or engagement ring but saw none. On her right hand, at the low knuckle of her ring finger, were two dots of red acrylic paint.

Two high school boys walked in the store, laughing and bumping into each other and made it to the customer service counter before Jimmy saw them. The taller of the boys was muscular and had a tattoo on his right shoulder of Cupid with bow and arrow poised to fire. He smiled at the girl behind the counter, reached across and took her hand in his, then brought it to his lips and kissed the back of it. She blushed as the boy winked at her and walked out of the store. Jimmy shook his head and couldn't help but smile as he squinted over at the girl whose hand the boy had kissed.

Carol said to the customer, "$20.37." The lady handed her a check and turned to leave. Carol said, "Good luck with the baby."

Jimmy hadn't noticed until then that the woman was pregnant, but now he could see that she was. The striped shirt stretched across her round belly and black stretch pants.

Then Carol and Jimmy stood face-to-face. Her register buzzed between them. Jimmy said, "You never grew your hair back."

Carol touched her hair where it ended, on her shoulders. She seemed to take a second or two to understand what he meant, then smiled at Jimmy and said, "No."

Overhead, somebody called for a price check on a bag of 200-count cotton balls.

She said, "Is he dead?"

"Excuse me?" He wasn't sure he had heard her right.

"Truman, is he dead? I couldn't see you coming back unless he was."

He had heard her right, thought it an odd question, but discounted it as concern coming out the wrong way. "No, not yet. They say he doesn't have much time. What about you?"

"Am I dead?"

They both laughed.

"No, I meant…"

She touched his right forearm for a second, then pulled away. Her hands felt soft, damp. "I know what you meant. I left for a while. Went over to the university and took some art classes."

"Why'd you come back?"

"My mother got sick."

Leaning in, Jimmy caught a whiff of her shampoo, something earthy and it made him think of oatmeal or some grain you could pick by hand. He considered telling her that she smelled good, but it didn't seem like a thing he could say without sounding like some horny guy at a bar. He wondered if she could smell the beer on him, and just how bad he looked. He ran a hand through his hair, trying to flatten it out. Was she married? Divorced? Did she have any children? These were questions he wanted to ask, but it was none of his business. Yet again he felt that there was something in her eyes that had done and seen a lot. An image came to him of her walking around with a little snot-nosed boy. The boy holding onto her pant leg and asking if he could have a pack of gum or a piece of candy, and Carol tucking him in with a kiss on the forehead.

Behind Jimmy, a middle-aged woman pushed her cart into Carol's lane. The woman said, "You open?"

Carol nodded and slid Jimmy's beer across the scanner. He

pulled his wallet out and gave her a ten. She handed him back his change. "How long you here for?"

"Not long."

"I have a break in about ten minutes if you want to talk or something."

Jimmy said sure.

"The park across the street."

He nodded and walked away, realizing as he stepped on the black tracking for the automatic door that he'd forgotten the cigarettes. He turned back to the register as Carol laughed and said something to the lady. Jimmy went to the customer service desk and told the girl with the freshly kissed hand that he'd like a carton of Winstons. As she reached up and grabbed the carton, Jimmy turned back to Carol and saw that she too was looking at him.

Bobby hung the phone up. He had let it ring twenty-two times, but his mother wasn't home or she wasn't answering. He made a peanut butter and jelly sandwich and slid the sliding glass door open and stepped out onto the back porch. Suzi, a female Rottweiler who had been sleeping in the soft, shaded sand below the porch, crawled out and approached him. The backyard slanted downward for about thirty yards and led to a small orange grove, which hadn't produced for five years now.

The boy petted Suzi's head with his right hand while keeping the sandwich behind his back with the left. The dog licked at his face. Bobby grabbed her by the neck, hugged her to his chest and then bit her ear gently. Suzi fell into him with her head moving against the boy's mid-section. He set the sandwich on the porch behind him, and they wrestled like that for a few seconds before she climbed off and walked away.

Brushing fur from his shirt, Bobby watched the dog finish off the sandwich, all the while not taking her eyes off him. He smacked her on the rear and she turned sheepishly, darted out into the yard, and then went back to licking her mouth with a full, heavy tongue.

Bobby walked over to the rusted horseshoe post Suzi was tied to. He unclasped the lock on the chain, which lay in the dirt between the post and dog. An overturned dog bowl sat off to the side of the post; its contents spilled into the dirt like hard, brown, berries. He said, "Let's go," held onto the chain and the two of them turned toward the orange grove and the trees that bent to the heat of the day.

Bobby wished he had some water, his mouth and throat dry now from peanut butter and white bread. Suzi pulled against the chain. Bobby pulled back hard and this stopped the dog. The two of them crossed the yard, which was littered with dog shit, toward the low chain-link fence. They climbed under a section that had been bent up months before.

The dry, desolate scent of dirt hung in the air. The orange trees were set straight back in thirty rows with thin dirt roads between them. The boy and dog moved through the groves quietly, going down one row for ten or twenty yards and then switching over to the next. On the ground, in the small patches of dried grass and dirt beneath the trees, empty beer bottles sat upright among the decayed fruit, which looked more like old browned tennis balls than oranges. Bobby didn't understand why these trees couldn't grow fresh oranges. The leaves and buds were green and to him they looked like any other trees. Suzi sniffed the ground and Bobby wondered what it was she sniffed for.

They'd gone a few minutes into the grove when Bobby spotted a green pickup snuggled into the aisle between two rows of trees. A strange, low, rhythmic sound came from the bed of the truck. Suzi looked up. They walked closer. Bobby pulled hard on the dog's chain as the sound came again, this time higher pitched and desperate sounding. Then Bobby realized it was the sound of people moaning. The dog whimpered and looked up at Bobby, then back to the truck, then back at Bobby as if searching for a sign of what to do. Bobby pulled Suzi tight to his leg.

Sitting ten yards away, between two trees, they listened as the moans increased, grew louder, and then stopped, filling the dry air with a few moments of silence. A naked man stood up for a moment, then lay down in the bed of the truck, his bare feet visible on the tailgate. The woman stood, thick-legged and naked with long, dark hair. She had scratch marks across her back. They said something Bobby couldn't hear and the woman laughed and glanced around. Bobby's heart froze. He thought she'd looked right at him. The dog made another muzzled sound and Bobby held her tight to him. The lady squatted and lowered herself onto the man as if she were doing some kind of knee bends. Only her head and half of her chest were visible over the side of the truck. As she moved up and down, the longest part of her coal black hair floated off her back for a second, hung in the air, and then landed on her skin. Every so often, he heard a crisp, pingy sound and it took him a minute to figure out that it was a ring on her finger hitting the top ledge of the truck's bed.

The woman smiled and looked down, mouthing more words to the man below her. Bobby leaned forward but couldn't hear what was said. He thought that she was pretty. These two people in the bed of a pickup truck reminded him of his mother and father. That first night in Panama Beach his father had given him two dollars' worth of quarters and told him to go on and play down in the hotel's game room.

After losing the money in twenty minutes on Pac-Man, Frogger, and Galaga, he had walked back to their room. Outside the door, his hand lifted to knock, he heard his parents doing that thing they did in bed. He knew it was called sex, or making love as his mother called it, adults moving together under the sheets. He'd seen them do it before and had heard the steady rhythmic sounds of their moaning on nights he'd woken and gotten up to use the bathroom and their door wasn't closed all the way. Or the other times, on weekend mornings, when he'd walk by their room and the squeaking sound of a bed in motion would call to him. And afterwards they would come out, hugging and kissing and the three of them would watch cartoons together.

But he grew angry now as the sounds from the truck continued, each moan a reminder of what was no longer part of his life.
He felt a rage build in him. Bobby picked up an empty beer bottle
and threw it at the truck. The bottle smashed against the driver's
side door. The dog barked. Bobby turned to run as he heard the
quick gasping sounds of the man and woman.

Jimmy sat on a bench and studied the park's landscape in front
of him and could find no design to the oak and pine trees that
stood scattered among the grass and handful of picnic tables. In
the four years he'd worked as a landscaper, he'd been taught that
there should always be a pattern to the way things were planted:
rows, angles, balance, counterpoint, something. But if this had a
pattern, it was beyond him. He heard a flutter and looked up past
the oak tree's low-hanging moss, which nodded with the slight
breeze, and saw a pair of sparrows dance on a limb and then flit
away.

Despite the nap he had taken at the lake, Jimmy still felt tired
and his head ached. He wasn't sure why he'd agreed to meet Carol
here. He liked how she had smiled at him in the grocery store. *Ah
fuck,* he thought, *what's the point?* He was leaving, and she would-
n't care if she saw him again or not.

Looking to his right, he saw the City Hall building again and
the police station next to it, connected by a green awning. City
Hall was basically a two-story white box with a dome on top. A
wide row of steps led to the front doors. At the top of the stairs, a
man in a blue suit was smoking a cigarette and talking on a cell
phone. Jimmy figured he was probably a lawyer. His father had
been arraigned in that building for his mother's murder, but the
trial had been held in Tallahassee at the state courthouse. One
day, during the year Jimmy had come back to live with Truman,
he skipped school and went to City Hall. He felt the need to walk
through the building, hoping that maybe it would give him some
answers but it hadn't meant anything to him. It was only a build-

ing with shiny wood floors and high ceilings and men in suits talking on telephones.

Now, he turned back toward the store. Carol was crossing the street, heading in his direction. She had removed the smock and her white shirt was tight against her chest. Her breasts weren't large, but reasonable. She wore white Converse Chuck Taylors with pink laces, which for some reason he couldn't name, Jimmy found cute. She hadn't looked at Jimmy yet, but was running her tongue over her lips, as if smoothing out her lipstick. He turned back around. *Just say hi,* he thought, *be polite, and then leave.*

She said, "Hey, little Jimmy Wills."

Jimmy half-smiled at her and scooted over, so she could sit next to him. He pulled the cigarettes from his pocket. "Smoke?"

She nodded, and he pulled one out and held it up for her. As she parted her lips, Jimmy could see a line of whiteness. He placed the cigarette into her mouth. She closed her lips around it and, for a second, before he lit it, the cigarette bounced against her bottom lip like a seesaw.

He said, "You paint with acrylics?"

"How do you know?"

Jimmy nodded toward the spots of paint on her hands.

She smiled at Jimmy. "Very good."

"A man's got to know his paint."

They both laughed a little at that. "How long you gonna stay?"

He said, "I'm leaving in the morning."

"So quick?"

"There's nothing for me here." *Why stay?* he wondered. He didn't care if and when the old man died.

She looked down at the grass, tapped her fingers on her jeans, and said, "What about your father?"

"What about him?"

"Didn't you come back to help him?"

Jimmy's face flushed. He dropped the cigarette on the ground and stepped on it, then lit another one quickly. Birdsong whistled in his ear, a tufted titmouse hungry for food or a mate. "He does-n't need my help."

"Is he pretty bad?"

"I don't know. I saw him and he didn't look that bad. Not what I was expecting, but they say he's dying."

"I guess you can never tell with those things."

"No, I guess not."

"My mother took a year to die. It was awful. She wasn't the same woman at the end." Carol tapped the end of her cigarette; gray ash fell and disappeared.

Jimmy wondered if it would have been better to see his mother like that, rotting away, changing from the always-moving, always-ex-citing woman he remembered. It would have given him a chance to tell her that he loved her. He knew it was a selfish thought and tried to think of a way to change the subject, tried to think of something to say about Carol's mother, but he didn't remember the woman.

Carol smiled at Jimmy and ran her eyes across his face and said, "You look tired."

"I feel like shit."

"I believe it. You don't look much better."

"I drove here last night."

"No sleep?"

"Just a little nap this morning."

The screeching sound of machinery called in the distance. They both looked over toward the ever-forming fair. Carol said, "You gonna stay for the fair?"

"No, I don't think so."

"Come on, go with me. I don't have a date. I'll make you a big spaghetti dinner. We'll drink wine and tell lies about what we've been doing for the last twenty years. Then you can leave this town and we'll never see each other again."

"Your boyfriend won't mind?" As soon as he said it, Jimmy wished he could take it back. It was a stupid way to ask a question he wanted to know the answer to.

She looked away from Jimmy, smiled, and playfully raised her nose like a snotty child. "He's out of town for the weekend." Jimmy figured he deserved that. She started laughing and he laughed too. He felt comfortable around her. Another time, another place, maybe.

She said, "So does this place seem any different for you?"

Jimmy said, "No, not really. Did it for you?"

"No, it didn't. Places don't change, people do."

"Some." Jimmy wasn't sure if people changed at all.

"I'm sorry about your mother. I never got a chance to tell you that."

"Well yeah, thanks."

Carol smiled and touched his arm. She stood up and dropped her cigarette in the dark dirt below the bench and stepped on it. She started to walk away, turned back and said, "Call me. I'm in the book."

It surprised him that she remembered his mother. He wondered if that was the reason he'd agreed to meet Carol, because she was from a time before his mother was killed and his life changed. He wasn't sure. The word *date* sounded in his head. Jimmy didn't want to fall or be in love, didn't want to care about anybody. He'd seen what love could do, the things it could come to, all of its evil varieties. He'd never seen anything good come of it.

Out of the corner of his eye, Jimmy saw movement and turned. There was a brown lizard, perched at the edge of the bench, two feet away. It was raising its head up and down. Jimmy couldn't remember the last time he had seen a lizard. Occasionally, you saw one in North Carolina, but it was rare. More than likely you'd see skinks and salamanders, but these lizards couldn't stand the cold.

When he was a boy, Jimmy loved lizards and would sit on his front porch watching them walk by in the yard or along the porch's rails. One Saturday afternoon, he had counted over fifty. He had even made a lizard farm. After catching one, he'd put it in an old gerbil cage filled with sticks and grass trimmings, paper towel rolls, leaves and dirt and some crickets. Over the course of a weekend, he had captured one hundred and twenty-four lizards. Four days later, he decided to release them and set the cage on the front porch and watched them empty out into the yard in less than five minutes.

When he reached for this lizard at the end of the bench, it jumped off and disappeared into the grass. Smiling, he turned back to the store, but Carol was already inside. Why not go to the fair with her? She seemed nice enough. He could stay at Truman's for an extra day. Maybe they would talk, maybe they wouldn't. *Look at this as a break from your life, a vacation,* he reasoned. It was Thursday and he wasn't due to start another house until Monday. *Shit,* he figured, *what's a couple days?*

Bobby ran into the house and closed the sliding glass door. He shut the curtains and stood there peeking out for a few minutes, his heart pounding, until he was satisfied that the couple was not coming after him. He drank some orange soda from a two-liter bottle on the counter, walked to the living room and turned the TV on to a show where people screamed at each other and every other word was hidden behind bleeps as the crowd howled with laughter. Bobby turned the TV off, then went down the hall and stopped at his father's room and pushed the door open. The bed was unmade and magazines and dirty clothes lay on the floor like undetonated land mines. He didn't know where his father was.

Bobby picked up a magazine and opened it to the centerfold where a blond woman was lying on her back, holding her legs apart, straight up in the air. She had blue eyes like his mother. Her skin was soft white and he could see the dark hair and pink flesh between her legs. He knew that had something to do with what those people in the truck were doing and what his parents used to do. He wasn't sure why people wanted to do it, though his parents always seemed happy afterwards.

Bobby dropped the magazine and walked over to his father's closet. He wasn't supposed to go in this closet because of what was in there: a gun and bags of marijuana. But Bobby didn't want those things, he wanted something softer, something he could put back before his dad got home.

Reaching into the dark closet, he moved his hands through the roughness of his father's old grease-stained work shirts until he felt what he was after. He pulled out one of his mother's T-shirts. It was one of the only things of hers that was still in the house. The shirt was cotton and soft and yellow. Bobby brought it to his nose and inhaled, smelled fresh laundry detergent. He tried to breathe in deeper, to smell her perfume, but he couldn't.

He climbed onto the bed and lay down in the center of it, spread the shirt across his chest like a blanket. He tried to remember what he'd done to make his mother leave. The week before she had left, he forgot to feed the dog one day and the next day he'd missed the bus and she had to drive him to school. Although she didn't yell or punish him for these things, they seemed as good a reasons as any for her to leave.

He stared up at the ceiling and remembered his mother telling him that good people dream. That in dreams we can all have lives that are different from the ones we lead and that is how he should live his life. And with that, he closed his eyes and fell into a dream of him and his mother and father walking across the ocean to a sandbar where everything was white and bright and together they ate peanut butter and jelly sandwiches until they were full and the sand dollars tickled their feet in the ankle-deep water.

Jimmy pulled into his father's long driveway again, not sure what to expect. He felt his heart rate increase as he turned the corner and then was relieved to see that the porch and chair were empty. He knew he would still probably have to face Truman at the door. If so, he'd tell him that he was going to take a nap and that Truman better not fuck with him.

He carried the duffel bag in one hand and the twelve-pack of beer in the other as he climbed the steps. A few bullet casings littered the floor around the chair. Setting the bag down, Jimmy opened the screen door and was about to turn the knob on the old wooden door when he thought better of it. This wasn't his home anymore and that crazy son of a bitch might be sitting in a chair at the kitchen table waiting with that gun for some fool to break into his house. Jimmy knocked, then shut the screen door.

He heard steps on the wood floor and felt himself bowing his chest a little, taking a deep breath, getting ready for whatever might happen. When the door opened, it wasn't Truman but a dark-haired woman with a clear, pretty face. He couldn't help but notice that she had a nice body underneath a pair of jeans and a T-shirt, and it didn't take him long to recognize her as the woman who was jogging on the side of the road earlier.

She said, "Can I help you?"

He said, "Hi, I'm Jimmy."

"I'm Angie. Truman's nurse."

"I'm Truman's son."

The way she scanned his face told him that she didn't know whether or not to believe him. His father obviously hadn't told her that Jimmy was coming, probably hadn't told her that he had a son. She looked past him at his truck and the square advertising magnet on the driver's side door that said WILLS HOUSEPAINT- ING. This seemed to be all the evidence she needed as she opened the door and stepped back. "Well, come in. Come in."

He walked into the kitchen and set the beer on the table. She lifted a red dishrag from the counter and wrapped it around the handle of the refrigerator like a scarf, as if trying to bide time. Jimmy looked over to the living room. There was an upright stereo against the far wall and a pair of knee-high speakers on either side of it, dimly playing a twangy guitar number. Above the stereo, a stuffed bass with a long cylindrical lure dangling from its lower lip hung on the brown paneled wall.

"Truman is either out with Davis or walking around in the woods."

Jimmy said, "Is Davis still the sheriff?"

"Yeah, he comes by every couple days and they go for rides. They're gone all afternoon sometimes."

"Where do they go?"

"I don't know."

Jimmy nodded slowly, as if trying to picture it. He remembered Davis as a tall man with thick brown hair, his idea of a southern lawman.

"Can I get you something? A glass of water, some iced tea? Coke?"

"No, I'm okay."

She rested a hand on the back of one of the kitchen-table chairs. "Do you have any brothers or sisters?"

"No." He walked over and set the beer in the fridge. "I'm the only one. Did he tell you he had a son?"

She hesitated. "No, I'm sorry."

"Don't be, doesn't surprise me."

He could tell this was all a bit confusing for her and that she was trying to work it out in her mind, but he didn't feel like going into it now. A shower, sleep, a bed was what he needed.

She said, "Where do you live?"

"North Carolina."

"Does he know you're coming?"

"Yeah."

"Well, I wish he would have told me. I could've prepared, cleaned the house or made something for dinner."

"It's okay."

As Angie drank from her glass of water, Jimmy pulled out his pack of cigarettes and began to light one. She said, "Do you mind not smoking? The smoke's not good for Truman."

Jimmy said, "Of course," then slid the cigarette back in the pack and his lighter into his front pocket.

"Do you know what's wrong with him?"

"Kind of. Cancer, right?"

"Yeah. He's pretty much eaten up with it. It's in his lungs, brain and prostate."

Jimmy looked past her at the empty counter and clean kitchen floor and remembered a sink full of dishes, his mother leaning against the counter, asking him how his day at school had been. He checked the table and the counter for his mother's ashtray. It was a clear, glass ashtray that she always kept with her regardless of what room of the house she was in. When it was full, she would carry it out to the front porch and dump it over the rail. But now, he didn't see it anywhere.

Angie said, "When you see him, you might be surprised. He doesn't look that bad. But that's how these things are. He was really bad when I came here a few months ago, had to monitor him around the clock, but he got better. Seems to be doing okay now. But these patients seem fine and then all of a sudden it hits them and they usually don't recover like that more than once. That's why I'm here, for when that happens. But for now, I'm pretty much a high-priced maid." She seemed more comfortable now, in her element, using her official "nurse" voice, slow and confident and reassuring.

"I see."

"How long are you here?"

"Not long, maybe a day or two."

"That'll help."

Jimmy said, "I'm pretty tired. You think I could go take a shower, maybe lie down?"

"Of course."

As they headed toward the hall, which led to the bedrooms, they passed the living room and the old brown couch with the tan throw rug on the floor in front of it. Like Truman, Angie wasn't what he was expecting; she was young and cute and obviously not from around here. At the end of the hall, she reached the door leading to the extra bedroom and said, "Did this used to be your room?"

Jimmy was staring at the wood-paneled wall at a framed black-and-white photo of his father and Dan and Davis on a fishing boat, the three of them straining to hold a huge tarpon. Next to this photo was a light-colored square on the wall where an old picture had once hung. Jimmy remembered the fishing photo but couldn't remember what it was that had been here. When he looked up, Angie was smiling at him, waiting for his response. He said, "I'm sorry, what?"

"Did this used to be your room?"

Angie opened the door to a small bedroom with a twin bed in the center. The only other piece of furniture was a pine chest of drawers. He scanned the room, the naked walls. "Yes, I think so. Yes."

"There are clean towels in the bathroom closet."

Jimmy walked into the room and said, "Okay, thanks."

"Get some rest. I'll get some food out for dinner. You like chicken?"

Jimmy dropped his bag on the bed and scanned the room again. He said, "Sure, chicken sounds good."

Davis climbed out of the car, hiked his pants up and started for the store. The sun beat down on him and he was hungry, tired and agitated. Dan sat behind the counter, and looked up from his newspaper and nodded when Davis entered. The sheriff said, "Where you been? I've been driving in circles waiting for you to come back. In the need for some of your special Pepsi."

"This isn't the only place to buy it around here. I went home for lunch."

Davis grunted and headed for one of the coolers at the back of the store, passing shelves stocked with tampons, toilet paper, notebooks, pens, pencils, combination locks, .22- and .25-caliber bullets in old coffee cans, aspirin, cat and dog food, candy bars, gum, potato chips, canned meat, bread, night crawlers, and five different flavors of those new nutritional candy bars. On the back wall of the store was a trio of six-foot frosty coolers. Two of them were filled with beer and the other one contained some of that fat-free yogurt, as well as Pepsi and Coke products in plastic bottles.

He grabbed a Diet Pepsi and turned the cap and drank from the bottle as he made his way over to another cooler and grabbed a couple foil-wrapped hamburgers and put them in the microwave for a minute each. By the time he got to the front of the store, Dan had a fifth of Wild Turkey and a white coffee mug out on the counter. He poured an inch of whiskey into the mug and Davis filled the rest of it with Diet Pepsi before sticking his right index finger in and stirring the contents. After taking a mouthful, Davis held it out to Dan, who accepted the drink.

Dan said, "Saw you on TV."

"How'd I look?"

"Like shit."

"Figures." Davis smiled and lifted the mug and finished the drink off. As Dan poured in more whiskey, Davis remembered going back to the scene after the dog incident at the station. Bird and the boys were out walking the woods with a pair of hounds. There were also a couple of reporters there, but Davis didn't talk to them since he didn't see the point in answering their questions when he didn't know anything yet.

Dan said, "You seem awful thirsty today."

"I am."

"You all right?"

"As a matter of fact, no, I'm not."

"This girl?"

Davis shook his head. "No, not really. I mean, yeah, that's part of it. Plus, I had to shoot a dog today."

Dan laughed. "A dog?"

"It's not funny."

"Rabies or something?"

"No, it charged me."

Dan took a sip of the late-afternoon concoction. "Well, if it charged you, doesn't sound like you had much choice."

"Hell, I don't know." Davis walked back and got his hamburgers out of the microwave, lifted the buns and covered the meat with ketchup. "Haven't fired my gun in four years."

Dan shrugged his shoulders. "It's your job." Davis didn't say anything—he knew what his goddamn job was—but kept chewing on the burger. When the sheriff finished the first burger, Dan said, "So, what's this about the girl?"

"What did they say on the news?"

"Said she was a college student, been missing for five days and her car was found on the side of the road here."

Davis shook his head. "My friend, you know about as much as I do, then."

Dan said, "What do you think happened?"

"Who the hell knows?"

"Maybe she'll show up."

"They usually don't." He thought of the Dobson girl, of Dot Wills, and of the hundreds of girls he'd read about over the years. He knew that for every one they found, there were a dozen they didn't. For each one, there was a killer. He'd done the math; the numbers were staggering. But these people didn't want to hear that. They wanted excitement.

He knew Bird looked at this case as a chance to solve a crime, to catch a bad man, a real live criminal. The local reporters were all worked up about it. It gave them something to do in a town where a missing dog made the news. But Davis didn't want excitement. He wanted the girl to walk out of the back of Dan's store right then with a smile on her face and tell them it had all been a joke and they could forget about her now and get on back to their lives.

The two men stared out the open door of the store. The two vacant gas pumps, the police cruiser, the road and the pine trees across the street all stood quiet, motionless as if they hadn't moved in decades. Davis felt the first hint of a noon buzz and was hoping Dan wouldn't ask him any more questions. He held up what was left of the second burger, about half. "You want some?"

Dan shook his head no, touched his chest, then said, "Guess who I saw today?"

Davis shook his head.

Dan was smiling. "Guess."

"I'm not in the mood for guessing."

"Jimmy Wills."

The last time Davis had seen the boy was when he dropped him off at his aunt's house. "Really?"

Dan nodded.

"No shit." Davis had waved to the boy that day, but he hadn't waved back, as if he had already decided that he was no longer a part of their lives or this town.

"In the flesh, right here a few hours ago. Think he drove straight through last night."

"Truman didn't mention it to me."

"Looks good, he's a housepainter."

"Well, I'll be." He tried to picture Jimmy as a man but couldn't. An image of a tall, thin, dark-haired boy walking beside his mother came to him.

"Says Truman called and asked him to come home."

"Wonder why."

"Why does Truman do anything?"

Davis said, "Good point."

"How is Truman?"

"About the same. You should go by and see him."

"He don't want to see me."

"I guess that's between you two."

"That it is."

Davis said, "Maybe I ought to bring Truman by here and drop him off, lock the door. Let the two of you talk, work out whatever it is you two are so pissed at each other about."

"I'd appreciate it if you didn't do that."

Davis took a last drink out of the mug and turned to leave, tossing his napkins into the garbage. "Goddamn, little Jimmy Wills." He started for the door, feeling much better than when he had first arrived.

Dan said, "You gonna pay for those burgers?"

"Put it on my tab."

"Tab my ass." Davis heard the words and a slim smile spread across his face as he tossed his hat into his car, started it, and then headed out onto the hot blacktop and all the mirages it promised in the supple shimmering sunlight.

Jimmy stood in front of the mirror, running his hands through his hair until it settled wet and flat and dark on his head. The shower felt good and had revived him. He was in need of a shave but hadn't brought a razor and didn't want to use anything of the old man's, but the straight-edge, with the letters TW across the flat silver stalk, was sitting there in a plastic cup by the porcelain sink. Jimmy recognized it as the same one his father had used when he was a boy. He had seen Truman run the razor across his square jaw and chin hundreds of times.

Jimmy lathered his face, then ran the rust-spotted razor across his chin and wondered why Truman had asked him to come home. If he really wanted to die, why couldn't he just shoot himself? Or pay one of these good old boys around here a couple hundred bucks? They'd do it without asking questions. But maybe Truman wanted to see him before he died, maybe tell him something. Jimmy couldn't say for sure but believed that must be the case. He had never really understood his father, had always been closer to his mother, and it seemed to Jimmy that his father was always gone, working, and when he was around he'd rather spend time with his mother.

On the last downward pass of the razor, he felt the nick at the tip of his chin and looked into the sink as the trickle of blood mixed with the running water. Jimmy said, "Shit," as he rinsed the razor off, set it back in the cup, and held a piece of tissue to the cut.

His mind moved to Carol and her cute shoes and her blond hair. Jimmy tried to imagine what she would look like now if she still had long blond hair, pictured it falling over her red work smock. Why had she been so eager to see him again? Maybe there weren't a lot of men around here to choose from. Maybe she just wanted some company. Maybe she was horny. There were a lot of maybes.

He imagined the two of them walking around holding hands, lying together in bed, her smell across his chest. The soft spots on her body and the way he would move his hands and mouth across them. He could see the two of them shopping for groceries, putting up a six-foot wooden fence that would surround the house they'd live in.

Outside, in the living room, a telephone rang. He shook his head. *Jesus, Jimmy,* he thought, *getting a little carried away, aren't you?* It wasn't the first time he'd done it. He knew he had the tendency, whenever he met a woman with the possibility of a romantic future, of fantasizing about their life together. He tried not to, but his mind would always wander. Two weeks before, he had picked up a thin redhead named Jill at a bar and later that night, after the rough, name-calling sex, as she showered and he lay in bed, he pictured the two of them driving to the coast, renting a boat and doing some fishing. When she walked out of the bathroom, fully dressed, and he'd brought up the possibility of seeing her again, she'd responded, "Naw, it was good but not that good."

Back in his bedroom, Jimmy got dressed in a new pair of jeans and a T-shirt. He ran his hands across the smooth-surfaced top of the dresser that had been his as a boy. He pulled it away from the wall and saw where he'd scratched his name into the back of it with one of his father's knives. Jimmy opened the first drawer and looked inside, nothing there but dust and tiny splinter-sized shards of chipped wood. In the second, third and fourth drawers he found nothing. But when he opened the bottom one, he remembered the secret shelf, a thin piece of wood paneling that covered the floor of this drawer. You could lift the wood and hide things under it. As a boy, he had often hidden his treasures there: favorite baseball cards and birthday cards. He tried to recall if he'd left anything on the day he went to live with Aunt Carly but nothing came to mind.

Jimmy wedged his knife into the corner of the drawer and lifted the thin sheet of wood. An old, yellowed manila envelope with the word *Dot* written in blue marker lay in one corner as if it hadn't been touched in years. Jimmy's mother's name was Dorothy but everybody called her Dot. Jimmy figured his father must have put it there.

Sitting back on the bed, he opened the latch on the back of the envelope and pulled out a black-and-white 8 x 10 photo of his mother. She stood wearing a black gown, her hands folded across her waist. In the lower left corner of the photo was a small gold '58 sticker. He thought it must be from her high school graduation. Jimmy studied the features again: the small nose, the strong chin, the green eyes and the straight black hair. She was smiling and Jimmy could see her white teeth; one of the front lower ones was turned in a little.

He pulled out another photo. This one was an 8 x 10 from his parents' wedding. His mother and father stood side by side, smiling, in front of a huge oak tree, with Dan and Davis on his father's side and two blond women Jimmy didn't recognize at his mother's. Jimmy noticed how Davis and Dan were squinting from the summer sun. His father looked handsome and strong in a white linen suit. And his mother looked beautiful in her summer dress that showed off the tan of her chest and shoulders. Three inches of the photo's top left corner had been clipped an angle, so all that remained were the letters VE. He realized then that this was the missing photo from the hall, next to the fishing shot, the one he had walked by hundreds, if not thousands, of times in his youth.

Jimmy felt something else in the envelope. As he turned it up, a gold chain fell out, onto the bed. A thin wedding band was attached to the chain. He picked the jewelry up as he heard the door open. Truman walked in, staring at Jimmy and said, "What do you got there?"

Jimmy stood and closed his fingers tight around the necklace and ring in his right hand as if to hide it. But he knew it was too late for that. "It's hers."

"Not anymore it ain't."

Truman took another step toward Jimmy and his gaze rose from Jimmy's hand to his face. Smiling unkindly, he pulled the gun out of the side pocket of his overalls and held it out, handle first. "Let's go." He spoke calmly.

"Fuck you, old man."

It happened so fast that Jimmy didn't have time to react as the cold handle of the gun connected with his chin. He fell back onto the bed, catching himself with both hands. Glaring up at Truman, hard and hateful, Jimmy thought, *Just fucking kill him. Nobody would give a shit, not a single soul.*

Truman lurched forward, holding the gun between them, and said, "Come on boy, do it."

Jimmy stood, curling his right hand into a fist. "You're not worth it."

"Maybe not, but I'm your father."

The jewelry felt cool against Jimmy's palm. His jaw stung, and he smelled the liquid-like thin scent of the gun's oil across his chin. The room shone white and bright around him. He wondered if he'd chipped a tooth, tasted his mouth for blood but found none.

Truman motioned toward Jimmy's clenched fist and said, "You're not taking that stuff."

"The fuck I'm not."

"Kill me and it's yours."

The two of them were a foot apart, spittle dangling from Truman's lower lip, when they heard Angie's footsteps on the hardwood floors approaching them. Truman said, "Shit." He shook his head in an act of disgust and then jammed the gun back into the front pocket of the overalls.

Angie stood in the doorway and looked back and forth at the father and son, as if trying to figure out what was going on. Truman straightened up as she stood there. He walked to the door, bumped into her enough to move her from the doorway, then disappeared down the hall.

Jimmy yelled at him, "Hey, watch it."

Angie said, "He didn't mean it. No big deal." She took a step closer to him. "You okay?"

Though he didn't taste it, Jimmy wondered if he was bleeding, if she could see the scars of what had happened. He smiled at her, doubting the smile he offered was believable, and said, "Yeah, cut myself shaving."

"You need anything?"

He shook his head no.

"Don't worry about him. He gets awfully moody sometimes." Angie turned and left the room.

Jimmy liked her spirit; it lifted him, dulled his anger somewhat. And he thought it was interesting how Truman had straightened up as soon as she walked in the room and how silly the old man looked holding the gun out like that. Jimmy even repeated the phrase a couple times, *Come on boy, do it*, and with each repetition the words seemed more ridiculous. He slid the photos and necklace back into the manila envelope, and dropped the secret shelf over it. Then he pulled a pair of white socks with a blue stripe around them from his duffel bag, unfolded them, stuck the ring inside, folded the socks back, and placed them at the bottom of his bag where he knew they would be safe.

Bobby opened his eyes when he heard the door of his father's truck slam shut and the dog started barking. He jumped up and tossed the shirt under the bed and ran into the living room. A moment later, his father walked in the front door, leafing through a stack of mail, the brown backpack slung over his shoulder. That was close, Bobby thought. Darren dropped some of the mail onto the table and then looked up at him.

"What are you doing?"

"Nothing."

Darren shook his head and went back to opening the mail. He said, "Make me a drink."

In the kitchen, Bobby pulled the bottles of Smirnoff and Kahlua from the cabinet below the sink and the carton of half-and-half from the fridge. He filled a glass with ice, half with white cream, and the other half an even mixture of vodka and the dark liquid. He stirred it with a spoon until it turned a milky brown. His father had shown him how to make White Russians six months before and Bobby took extreme pleasure in making the drink just like he wanted. He swallowed a mouthful. It tasted like a milkshake or chocolate milk with a bit of an aftertaste he didn't like. It seemed about right. He took another sip and gave it to his father. Darren said, "Why you drinking that?"

"I'm thirsty."

"Well, drink some damn water then."

"All right."

Bobby stood by his father and looked at the mail strewn across the table. Most of it was addressed to Darren Webster but one of the envelopes had his mother's name, Jennifer Webster, on it. Bobby reached up and grabbed it. "Can I open this?"

"What is it?"

"It's for Mom."

Darren turned quick to Bobby and grabbed it out of his hand. He looked at the envelope, shook his head and dropped it on the table. "It's from Sears. It's junk mail."

Bobby picked it back up and said, "I'll save it for her."

When Darren didn't respond, Bobby walked down the hall to his bedroom. From under his bed, he pulled out a small cardboard box and tossed in the letter. There was other mail in there, mostly from stores like Burdines and JC Penney. He planned to give her all the mail the next time he saw her.

Walking back, he passed his father's room. He remembered that he had to put the shirt back where he had found it. He wished his father would leave so he could do that. When he made it back to the living room, his father was reading a piece of the mail.

Darren said, "You hungry?"

"Sure."

"What are you making us?"

"Very funny."

Bobby wondered if his father missed his mother. If so, he never mentioned her. But Bobby believed that he must. How could he not?

When Darren was done with the mail, he asked Bobby if he wanted to go get something to eat. Bobby nodded, forgetting for a second about the shirt and thinking only of the sweet promise of getting to go somewhere with his father.

Davis went in his house, dropped his keys on the oak end-table by the door and turned the A/C down to 68. He could hear Bev working in the kitchen, could smell the meatloaf she was making. She called, "Hey love, any luck with the girl?"

Davis shook his head at another mention of Teresa Martin. It amazed him how all these people were concerned for this person they didn't even know. In his opinion, it was a noble, if misplaced, human trait. Maybe if he wasn't the sherifff, and didn't know the things he knew, he'd be more hopeful. *But hell,* he thought, *I am the sheriff.*

"No, nothing yet."

After changing into a pair of shorts and a T-shirt, he came back to the kitchen where Bev was pulling the pan of meatloaf from the oven. She smiled at him. "You hungry?"

"Yeah, some food might do me good." Davis made a strong toddy and lifted the glass to his lips and thought that might be just what he needed. Then the telephone rang in the living room and he listened to the message. It was Bird, saying how the folder on the missing girl had finally arrived and that if Davis wanted, he'd bring it over tonight. Davis snatched the phone from its receiver. "Bird, Bird."

"Sheriff, you home?"

"Just ran in the door."

"Well, anyway, like I was saying I got this folder and could bring it over."

"That won't be necessary, son."

"It's no trouble, on my way home."

"No, I'll get it in the morning."

Bird hesitated, then said, "Okay, see ya then."

When Davis hung up, Bev handed him a plate filled with meatloaf and green beans. There was a circle of ketchup on top of his meatloaf, just how he liked it. He grabbed his toddy and they went into the den and sat on the white, leather couch. Davis lifted the remote and scanned through the channels, settling on the national news, turning the volume low, not once looking up at the screen as he ate. They didn't speak and Davis was grateful for the silence. When his plate was empty, save for a few smears of ketchup, he set it on the table next to him and slid down a bit on the couch to a position he found comfortable.

A couple minutes later, Bev turned the TV off and said, "You okay?"

"Sure, fine."

"I don't believe you."

He turned and tried to smile and then rubbed his chin, the scratchy beginnings of a new day's beard already evident. "Is it the girl?" Bev asked.

"I don't know, kind of." He felt the swell in his chest.

"What is it?"

"I can't stop thinking about Dot and her murder."

Bev took a long pull on her glass of wine and waited for him to say more. He knew how she felt about the whole thing, that she had never really cared for Truman. She had told him she didn't think Truman had anything to do with Dot's murder, but he wasn't sure if he believed her.

"When I got the phone call this morning, that was the first thing I thought about. Where we found her car was only a mile or so from where we finally found Dot. Out looking for her today, we may have actually walked over the spot where Dot had been buried."

"Do you think it was the same person?"

"No, nothing like that. I don't think the connections are real, not literally. It's hard to explain. I just got a bad feeling about it as soon as I hung up the phone this morning, like I did about that case. Something told me then that we wouldn't find Dot alive and something is telling me the same thing now about this girl. If that's not enough, guess who came into town today?"

Bev shook her head. "I don't know."

"Jimmy. Jimmy Wills."

"Really?"

"I guess he came home to see how Truman was doing."

"What's he like?"

"Don't know, haven't seen him."

"Well, maybe this girl is okay. Maybe something good happened and not bad." She leaned forward and kissed his cheek.

"Bev, I wish I could believe that. I really do."

"Maybe you should."

He smiled. "You're right. Maybe I should." He leaned over and kissed her on the cheek, then lifted his arm and wrapped it around her shoulder, and she scooted over so that they were about as close as they could get without being in each other's laps.

Bobby and his father sat in their truck in the Wendy's parking lot, eating hamburgers and fries. The fear of his father discovering that he'd been in the closet had made him forget about what he'd seen earlier until now.

Bobby said, "I saw some people in the groves today."

"Who?"

"I don't know. They were in the back of a truck having sex."

Darren turned to him quick. "Sex?"

"Yeah, isn't that what it's called when people do it?"

Darren laughed. "That or fucking. But you don't need to worry about that yet."

"Why do people do it?"

Darren lifted the drink from between his legs and sucked on the straw until it made a loud slurping sound. "Christ, Bobby, what has gotten into you?"

"I don't know."

Darren set the drink back between his legs, looked out the window for a long moment and said, without turning to the boy, "It's in people. Makes us want to. It feels good."

Bobby believed his father that it probably felt good, but he wasn't ready for all that. He figured it was one of those things that were the difference between kids and adults like driving a car or getting a job.

A muffled cellular phone rang and Darren reached past Bobby and opened the glove compartment and pulled the palm-sized phone out. The thick scent of meat, ketchup and greasy fries blanketed the truck's interior. Behind Bobby, there were two small holes, like the bright eyes of a deer, in the truck's back window.

Darren stuffed fries in his mouth as he spoke into the phone. "Yeah, what time?"

Ten yards away, at the drive-through window, somebody ordered two cheeseburgers, large fries, and a medium frosty. A frosty sounded good to Bobby. He hadn't had one since last weekend.

Darren said, "Sure, in a little while," then dropped the phone back in the glove compartment and pulled at the floor mat by Bobby's feet. The mat made a tearing Velcro sound. He pulled three sandwich bags of marijuana from under a pink towel and tossed the bags below his seat, sat up and looked at Bobby and then back out at the road where cars moved by in dull flashes of red and green. Darren studied his watch, then turned to Bobby again. "You want anything else to eat?"

"No."

"A frosty?"

Bobby shook his head and searched with his hand for a stray fry or two at the bottom of the bag. He knew his father was thinking about something. He had that faraway look in his eyes. Maybe he was thinking about fucking, but the way he had put those bags under the seat and the phone call meant he had some work to do. That was okay with Bobby, because he wanted to get back to the house and put his mother's shirt in the closet. Darren said, "You want to go for a little ride?"

Bobby didn't think his father was really asking him. He'd already made up his mind; he tended to do that. Bobby said, "I don't care."

After stuffing the hamburger wrappers and cups and large box of fries into the greasy bag, Darren tossed it into the back of the truck where it landed between a pair of worn tires, on top of the empty handle of an ax.

Jimmy smelled the fried chicken as he walked out of the bedroom. On the TV, a man's voice said, "Ain't much hope if you don't believe."

Angie was at the stove, stirring a pan of mashed potatoes. He admired her body again, that nice round ass in her jeans. He turned away, figuring she didn't need that from him since she probably got enough of it from his father. He said, "You need any help?"

"No, it's just about ready. Have a seat." She motioned with her free hand toward the table. To Jimmy, it seemed odd how this woman he didn't know was playing hostess to him in his old house, a house he had already started to feel comfortable in.

Angie said, "You live up by Charlotte?"

"A few hours west."

"I have a sister in Charlotte. She's also a nurse."

"That's a big city."

"Yes, it is."

Jimmy walked over to the fridge and pulled a beer out, then sat back down before realizing that he hadn't offered her one. He went over and lifted another bottle off the top shelf. "Would you like a beer?"

She stopped stirring the potatoes and turned back in his direction. "No, thanks. I don't usually drink."

During the silent pause between commercials, Jimmy heard the squeaky rhythm of the chair outside and went over to the window. Truman was staring out past the vehicles, into the woods. The tabby kitten walked along the porch's rail a few feet and then jumped onto Truman's lap.

Jimmy wanted to go outside and have a smoke before dinner, but he didn't feel like putting up with any of the old man's shit. He wondered what his father was thinking, if he was thinking anything at all. Truman pinched the cat's tail and ran his hands along its back, under its chest, and then wrapped its ears between his fingers, like someone lifting hair to cut it. Truman turned back in Jimmy's direction. Jimmy stepped away from the window and finished his beer in a long mouthful.

Now at the table there was a plate stacked with shining, golden pieces of chicken. Three paper towels between the meat and plate sopped up grease. On one side of the chicken was a bowl of mashed potatoes dotted with pepper, and on the other side some corn on the cob.

Angie rifled through the fridge for something to drink and after straightening up, holding a pitcher of water, looked from Jimmy to the table. "You think it looks okay?"

Jimmy said, "Great."

"Can you call your father in?"

Jimmy hesitated and went to the door. As he opened it, he told himself to take it easy, try to be decent. The cat looked up at Jimmy, jumped off Truman's lap, and ran to the side of the house.

"Dinner's ready."

Truman stared forward and spat out across the porch's ledge, into the dirt.

Jimmy sat down at the table as Truman grabbed the fifth of Wild Turkey from under the sink. Truman sat at the other end of the table, opposite Jimmy, and poured two inches of bourbon into a clear glass. Jimmy said, "I'll take some of that."

Truman said, "Come and get it." The words rang like a challenge.

Angie said, "Knock it off," then picked the bottle up and set it on the counter. Pouring them each glasses of water, she said to Truman, "You need to stop drinking that stuff."

"It's a new form of chemo." Nobody but Truman laughed at his joke.

Angie said, "Poison is what it is."

Jimmy drank a mouthful of water.

"I hope you two are hungry."

Truman grunted something. With that, they each started for the food and filled their plates. Jimmy bit into the small piece of chicken breast. It was good and moist and burned his upper lip.

Angie said, "It was nice of you to drive down here."

Jimmy nodded at her as he continued to eat. Truman farted. Jimmy and Angie looked up at him, and he smiled and shrugged his shoulders. Angie closed her eyes and said, "Truman, don't do that."

Jimmy said, "Have some damn respect." Truman kept his head down, working at a mound of mashed potatoes on his plate.

Jimmy turned to Angie. "Is that your cat outside?"

She shook her head. "It's his."

Truman raised his eyes and then lowered them.

Angie said, "The two of them are inseparable."

Jimmy couldn't imagine his father owning a cat. He had never even really liked the dogs they had when Jimmy was a boy.

Truman said, "It's not my cat."

Angie said, "Davis gave it to him."

"I just feed it. It's not mine."

There was a bulge in the chest pocket of Truman's overalls and Jimmy realized that he still had the gun there. He wondered if Angie could see this, and didn't know how she could possibly miss it. He said, "So old Davis is still the sheriff, huh?"

"Yeah."

"Only in this town. He still solving crimes?"

Truman said, "About the best he can."

"Yeah, I bet."

Angie said, "Did you hear about that girl that's missing?"

Jimmy said, "Yeah, I saw her car when I was driving in, heard something about it on the radio."

Angie said, "I hope they find her."

Jimmy said, "Yeah."

Truman stood up and walked to the counter and retrieved the bottle of Turkey. He said, "They won't."

Angie said, "They won't what?"

"Find her."

"How do you know?"

Truman shrugged his shoulders.

She said, "You're so negative."

"Somebody probably raped and buried her. Shit happens all the time." Truman said the words without emotion, as if giving directions to Timbuktu.

Angie said, "Why do you have to talk like that?"

Jimmy said, "Don't listen to him, it's just stupid prison talk."

"Got nothing to do with prison. It's life."

Angie turned quickly from father to son with a questioning look on her face, and Jimmy knew then that the mention of Truman serving time was news to her. In an obvious attempt to change the subject, Angie turned to Jimmy. "How long has it been since you've been back here?"

"Close to twenty years."

"Did you miss it?"

"No, nothing for me here." Jimmy scanned his father's face for reaction, but the old man kept his head down like a dog over a full bowl.

Angie spread more butter on her corn and took small bites of it. She looked back and forth from father to son. Jimmy could tell that she was thinking of something to say or ask, trying to fill the silence.

Angie said, "Does your mother live in North Carolina?"

The two men looked up at her and then at each other, blankly. Jimmy waited a second to respond. He wanted to see if Truman would say anything. When he didn't, Jimmy said, "No, she's dead."

Angie sat back. "Oh, I'm sorry."

Jimmy stared at Truman, but the old man wouldn't lift his head now. "It was a long time ago."

Truman glanced up at Jimmy, shook his head ever so slightly, and went back to eating.

Jimmy said, "This is a really good meal."

"Well, thank you."

Then they both turned to Truman, as if waiting for him to respond. He must have sensed it, because he said, "It'll make a turd."

Angie threw Truman a mean look.

Jimmy said, "Why do you have to be like that?"

Truman said, "Like what?"

"You know what. You didn't used to be like this."

"How do you know what I used to be like?"

Jimmy wondered if prison had changed his father. He couldn't remember him acting like this before. After his mother's murder, he had been quiet, reserved, but he hadn't been rude and mean like this. Now, he just seemed like a bitter, old man.

A few minutes passed where the only sound between them was the scraping of forks and knives against the china plates, then Truman said, "This corn ain't bad."

Jimmy was pleased when Angie didn't acknowledge Truman's

half-assed compliment. Instead, she stood, as if she'd had all she could handle of this dinner conversation, and dropped her plate and silverware in the sink. She said, "I made the meal, you two can do the dishes."

Truman picked at his teeth with a toothpick and shook his head as if to say *There is no way in hell I'm doing that.* Angie went into the living room and plopped down on the couch, grabbed an issue of *TV Guide* from the table and leafed through it.

After finishing off his last piece of chicken, Jimmy dumped the bones and scraps of meat into the garbage can before dropping the plate into the soapy water. At the table, he picked up the bottle in front of Truman, took a long hard pull and then carried it over to the counter.

Truman said, "Bring that back over here."

"No, come and get it."

Smiling, Truman said, "I just might."

Jimmy said, "You want to wash or dry?"

Truman grumbled something unintelligible, walked over to the sink and tossed the plate in, splashing water high over the edge, onto the floor, by Jimmy's feet.

Jimmy said, "Keep it up."

"And what?" Truman picked up the bottle and headed for the door.

Angie said, "What are you doing?"

"I'm going outside."

"Not until them dishes are done."

Truman glared at her, then at Jimmy, then back at her. He said, "Ah, fuck it," as he started for the sink.

Jimmy scooted over and washed and rinsed the dishes on one side of the double sink and then handed them to Truman who dried them and set them on the counter. They didn't speak as they worked. An old musky scent, some uneven mix of alcohol and sweat, came off the old man. Jimmy couldn't recall ever washing dishes with his father, but he could remember doing them with his mother: her taking sips of beer as he put the dishes away, trying to keep up; the way she would flick the water at him, laughing, singing along to Creedence or Janis, using a butter knife for a microphone, her wet hand tapping against the counter for a drum.

Truman nudged over, pushing Jimmy with his hips, taking him out of the memory. Jimmy pushed back with his own hips. Truman said, "Knock it off, boy."

"You started it."

"Bullshit."

Truman threw the towel down on the counter and walked outside. Angie came over and cleaned off the table with a wet dishrag. She said, "I'm sorry about bringing up your mother."

Jimmy said, "Don't worry about it. Did you know that he had been in prison?"

She shook her head no. "What did he do?"

"He was in a wreck where some people were killed."

"Was he drinking?"

"No, well, I don't think so. He hit a car and it went off a bridge. There were two cops in the car. They had been chasing him for hours."

"Chasing him?"

"He used to run drugs up through Georgia and South Carolina and Tennessee."

She said, "Oh," and crossed her arms over her chest, then filled a glass with tapwater and drank it down quick. "Was Davis the sheriff back then?"

"Yes."

"Did he know that Truman dealt drugs?"

Jimmy hesitated. He wasn't sure how much he should tell her, but he'd already told her a lot. "Yeah, he did. The two of them and a man named Dan used to be in it together. Of course, that was until Davis' father, who happened to be sheriff, found out and said the only way he wouldn't throw all three of them in jail was if Davis became his deputy and the other two stopped dealing. Six months later, Davis' father died and Davis became the sheriff."

After putting the last few dishes away, Angie said, "And the three of them kept dealing?"

"Davis stopped, but the other two kept at it." Jimmy wanted to change the subject, so he said, "Why are you here?"

"What do you mean?"

"Why with him, now?"

"It's a job."

"I don't know how you can stand it. The way he treats you."

"Oh, I've had meaner patients than him."

"He wasn't always so mean."

"They never are."

Outside, Truman launched into another coughing fit. Jimmy turned to Angie. She said, "He's okay. It happens. His lungs."

Truman coughed one final time and spat. Angie went back toward the bathroom and Jimmy stood in the kitchen for a moment, not sure of what to do next. He could go out to a bar and maybe shoot some pool or throw darts, but he didn't feel like running into anybody else he used to know.

Bobby eyed his house's porch light as they rounded the corner and hoped again that his father would go out for the night. They hadn't spoken on the drive and Bobby had spent the last couple miles of it thinking about what had happened earlier as he was waiting for his father to come out of the blue house where they had stopped. He had been sitting in the truck when he heard the grumble of an engine and turned to see an old white car pull up next to him. A short lady, about his mother's age, climbed out, smiled at him and said, "Who are you?"

"Bobby."

"What are you doing here?"

"My dad." He pointed toward the house.

The lady looked in that direction and then back at Bobby. The smile left her face as she said, "Son of a bitch, buying that shit again." As she headed toward the porch, Bobby didn't know if she meant he was a son of a bitch, or if his father was a son a bitch, or what exactly she was talking about. A moment later, his father walked out the front door and passed the woman on the steps. Backing out of the yard, they heard yelling come from the house, which for some reason Bobby didn't understand, made his father laugh.

Now, Bobby and Darren pulled into their driveway. What looked like a hundred moths flew around the porch light, as if it were an energy source and they were in great need of what it offered. Suzi barked viciously in the backyard, something she always did at the sound of a vehicle in the driveway. Darren yelled at the dog, told her to shut the hell up.

In the house, Darren went back to his room and Bobby stood in the living room, leaning against the couch, waiting to see what would happen. Maybe his father wouldn't notice that the shirt was missing. Maybe he never looked in that part of the closet. But Bobby felt certain he would get caught and didn't think there was much he could do about it now. What would the punishment be? Maybe his father would ground him, not let him go fishing for a week. Maybe he would make him pick up the dog shit in the backyard. The punishments had been so infrequent since his mother left that there was no established pattern. Bobby considered telling his father just to see what would happen.

Darren came back down the hall, carrying his backpack. Bobby said, "You going out?"

"Trying to get rid of me?"

"No."

Darren laughed. "Yeah, I got to take care of some stuff."

Bobby's heart slowed. He thought he might just be out of the woods.

"If I'm not back in the morning, you had better go to school. We don't need no truant officers coming around here, you hear me?"

"Yes."

Darren pulled a ten from his pocket and dropped it on the table in front of Bobby, then ruffled the boy's hair with his hand. "That's lunch money."

Touching the edge of the bill with his thumb, Bobby said, "I know."

"You need to be getting to sleep."

"All right."

Darren picked up his backpack. At the front door, he turned around, looked at Bobby, then down at the carpet. He seemed about to say something. His lips moved but no words came. Then he shook his head and was gone. Bobby stood by the front curtain. When the truck's taillights were nothing more than tiny red dots in the night, he ran into his father's bedroom and put the shirt back where he'd found it.

Jimmy carried one of the chairs from the table out to the porch and placed it a few feet to the right of Truman's recliner. They didn't say anything for a good while, just studied the woods turning from dark to black as Jimmy smoked a cigarette. Behind them, in the house, Angie watched TV. Truman and Jimmy passed the bottle back and forth every few minutes, using grunts or an extended arm to signal they were ready for some. The cicadas hummed and purred so steadily that to Jimmy it became one line of noise, a hundred million miles long.

Jimmy considered asking his father about prison, about his mother. He wanted to hear the story of how his parents met. He had a vague memory of something having to do with Truman seeing his mother in a high school play and falling for her. He knew they'd started dating while she was still in school and married a month after she graduated. But he couldn't recall what play it was or why Truman was in a high school auditorium when he had never even finished school. Why had they waited seven years before having him? Had Truman ever thought about him in the years that had passed? Maybe he tried to call, but Aunt Carly wouldn't allow them to talk. There were so many questions he would have liked to have answered, but they were here together now and the words weren't coming.

Truman took the last mouthful and set the bottle at his feet. He said, "Why don't you go get another one of those. Under the kitchen sink."

Jimmy stood a bit too quick, had to grab onto the porch banister to steady himself, then slowly walked into the house. Angie sat in front of the TV watching a movie with a young and greasy Dustin Hoffman falling down a set of stairs. It looked like *Midnight Cowboy* and Jimmy wondered where old stud-boy Jon Voight was these days.

Angie said, "You two catching up on old times?"

"Something like that. You okay?"

She smiled at Jimmy, said that she was.

He walked back out with a half-empty bottle. Truman said, "Check her out." By the porch steps, the kitten had some small animal, a field mouse or baby rat, on its back and was mauling it, clawing. The injured animal let out a shrill cry and the cat hissed.

When Jimmy turned back to Truman, the old man was holding the empty bottle out and said, "Throw this up in the air, do us a little skeet shooting."

It was an old joke between his parents. When she finished a beer, and the gun was nearby, Truman would say, "Dot, let's do a little skeet shooting." She would throw it up in the air, out by the woods, and Truman would shoot it, rarely missing.

Jimmy walked to the edge of the porch, glanced back at his old man, who held the gun straight out toward the woods. "You ready?"

Truman nodded that he was. Jimmy threw the bottle high into the air, out into the yard, and Truman squeezed the trigger. A moment later, the bottle exploded and glass showered the hood of the truck. Jimmy smiled, then caught himself, and tried to blanken his face as he turned back to his father.

Truman said, "I can still do some things."

Jimmy sat back down in the chair. Bats darted in and out of the woods and skittered overhead like black crying stars. Jimmy tried to follow their paths, but they were too fast and he lost them in the trees and dark clouds. A car's horn rang out on the highway. *Twenty years,* Jimmy thought, *and all we can do is shoot at empty flying bottles of whiskey.*

Truman stood up and tried to hand him the gun.

Jimmy stepped back, kept his arms at his side. "I'm not gonna shoot you."

"No shit. You've made that clear." Truman set the gun down, then walked over to an old bucket on the far porch ledge, reached inside, and came out with a handful of bullets, poured them in his pocket. A few fell to the porch floor and rolled away.

Jimmy ran his hand over the gun's handle, traced a finger over the barrel. The thin, oily scent which had hung around his nose since he'd been slapped in the bedroom came back to him, strong now. Truman said, "Take a shot at that pine tree."

Jimmy looked to where Truman was pointing, out across the yard, past his truck and the Cadillac. Darkness and the distant outline of trees were all he saw. "Which one?"

Truman pointed straight ahead as he sat back down. "There's a quarter nailed to that tree."

Jimmy tried to focus on it, but the more he stared the less he saw, just lean shadows like lines in a drunken man's vision of paradise. He held the gun up high and fired; the soft sound of a thud came back to him. Jimmy said, "Got it."

Truman said, "Bullshit. You hit the tree, but not the quarter."

"How do you know?"

"If you hit it it'll make a pinging sound, like a rock thrown onto a tin roof, and the bullet hitting the quarter will cause a spark."

Truman lifted his hand and Jimmy gave him the gun. He aimed at the tree and fired, a ping and the flashing light of silver came back. Then Truman did it again.

Jimmy took the gun and aimed. He could see the silver now,

like the smallest dot in the center of the blackness. He squeezed the trigger twice, but there was no ping or flash of light.

Angie opened the door and said, "I'm going to bed. Please try and keep it down."

Jimmy said, "Okay, good night." Then he sat with his back against one of the porch's posts, facing Truman.

Truman said, "Practice is what you need."

The light in the living room dimmed. The one in Angie's bedroom lit for a few minutes then darkened. Against Jimmy's back, the post felt nice and hard. An owl hooted and cried in the night. Jimmy said, "How did you find me?"

"Private investigator, took him two days. Not hard to find somebody when they own their own business."

Jimmy nodded, then rested his eyes for a second. Truman said, "Did you like living with your aunt?"

Surprised at the question, Jimmy said, "She's a good woman, treated me well."

The cat walked past Jimmy and jumped up on Truman's lap. He petted her. Jimmy noticed the specks of blood across her chest. Truman said, "Doesn't much care for me."

"A lot of people don't much care for you."

Truman laughed. "I thought the whole world loved me."

"Ran into Carol Binder at the store today."

Truman grunted and the cat jumped down and ran to the opposite end of the porch.

"First thing she asked is if you were dead. Seemed a little disappointed when I said not yet."

Truman spat into the blackness of the night. "Well, she's no prize, now is she?"

"Seemed nice enough to me."

"She's a whore, boy."

Jimmy stood up, wondering why it had to be like this.

Truman smiled and said, "Got your hair up a little, don't you? What, did she already let you put it in her this afternoon?"

Jimmy turned away from him and walked to the edge of the porch and looked out into the blackness, dizzy from the Turkey. He hoped movement, any kind, might be enough to change the subject.

But Truman kept on: "Yeah, she's about fucked every man in this town."

Jimmy held onto the banister and said, "Shut up." He wasn't sure if his father was just trying to piss him off, or if maybe he did know something about her. She did seem eager to go on a date with him. He wanted to let it slide, Goddamn he did, and it still seemed possible that he could if Truman would just shut up.

Truman said, "I heard she moved away so that she could get some fresh meat."

Jimmy turned and took a quick step toward Truman and punched him in the nose. His head rocked back a second, hitting the pillow sewn to the chair's headrest. Cranking his arm back, ready to punch again, Jimmy wanted him to say one more thing, one more word after so many years without any, about his mother or about Carol or about anybody. Blood started to flow from Truman's nose and he touched it, looked down at his hand, and smiled at Jimmy. He pulled a dirty handkerchief from his pocket and dabbed his nose. He said, "Glad to see you still got a little Wills blood in you after all."

Jimmy's hand stung and his knuckles burned. He was surprised that he'd actually hit his father. He felt hollow, dazed, as if the punch weren't real, as if it were something he'd wanted to do his whole life and now that he'd done it didn't feel damn near as good as he'd imagined it would. He fought against the desire to reach for his father's face and pull the handkerchief away and see if his nose still bled.

Truman must have sensed the concern on Jimmy's face, because he said, "Come on boy, don't get all soft on me now."

Jimmy said, "Shut up." He wanted his face to look angry, to scare the old man, but he knew that it didn't. He walked off the porch with no clear destination in mind, only the need for distance between himself and his father and what he had just done. Breathing hard and heavy, he made it only as far as the old Ford before he stopped and leaned against the bed of the truck, his foot resting against the tire. The air was wet and thick and a bug of some sort buzzed at his head and Jimmy swatted at it, missing. He expected Truman to say something, to taunt him, but he didn't. And after a minute or two, Jimmy calmed somewhat and his breathing became regular again as he turned back to the porch.

His trepidation fell away and he felt better as he began to climb the steps. It wasn't so much that he'd hit him, but that he'd stood up for something, even if it was a woman he didn't really know much about. Jimmy picked the gun up off the porch floor and pointed out toward the tree and squeezed the trigger but there was no ping, no spark. He looked over at Truman who shrugged his shoulders, still dabbing at his nose. Jimmy held the gun out toward the tree, squeezed the trigger, and again it was only the thud of copper slicing through wood. Aiming harder, straining his eyes, he pulled the trigger again, but the gun was empty. Truman laughed behind him and Jimmy thought, *Fuck you, old man.*

FRIDAY

DAVIS TURNED the patrol car into Truman's driveway and parked behind the Cadillac and saw the two men sleeping on the porch. He poured some coffee from a Thermos into an old white mug, then set the Thermos back on the floor. He rolled the window down and stuck his hand out and felt the slight breeze lift the hair on his forearm. Early mornings were his favorite part of the day: empty roads and the way the sky filled with blueness and how starting early allowed him to be home by four, so he could help Bev out in the garden. These thoughts were soured by the realization that with everything going on right now it would probably be a while before he had that privilege again. A black bird flew down in front of his car and then disappeared into the upper reaches of the trees behind him.

He stepped out of the car and slammed the door, hoping to wake this family of two. Truman stirred, coughed and spit blindly off the porch before looking out toward Davis. After running his clenched fist over his face and across his eyes, he said, "Sheriff."

"Morning, Truman." Davis climbed the steps and held the coffee mug out toward his old friend, who shook his head no at the offering. Davis said, "It's good stuff. Colombian." He spotted the dried blood on Truman's upper lip, the swelling at the crown of his nose, the gun on the floor between his feet. "You boys doing a little father and son camping and wrestling out here on the porch?"

Truman glanced over at Jimmy, then smiled at Davis and yawned. He stood and walked to the end of the porch and pissed over the side, laughing as the stream rose in front of him, letting out a long, cool, "Ahh."

Davis turned to Jimmy. He looked like he was in pretty good shape, tall and wiry with thick arms. When Davis heard Truman zip back up, he said, "What's he doing back here?"

"Came back to visit his old dying father. Called me out of the blue. I guess he missed me."

Davis said, "Yeah, I bet." But maybe the boy did want to see his father, though Davis seriously doubted it. He had asked Truman, about a year ago, while visiting him in jail, if he had ever heard from Jimmy and Truman had said no. If he remembered correctly, Dan had told him yesterday that Jimmy said Truman called. Maybe Dan got it wrong or maybe Truman was just confused with the sickness and all.

Davis said, "I saw that girl you got working for you out on the road, jogging, a few minutes ago."

"That's all she does. Run, run, run."

"Some people like to exercise. Maybe you ought to try some?"

"Shit, why? I'll be dead soon."

Davis dumped the rest of the coffee out over the porch rail. "I wish you wouldn't talk like that."

Truman eased himself back into the chair. "I'll tell you what, she does have some nice, thick legs."

Davis said, "I didn't notice."

"That's right, Mr. 'I've Been Happily Married Thirty-Three Years To The Same Lady.'"

Davis was tempted to correct him, thirty-four, but didn't. "Anyway, I'm sure you've heard about this missing girl?"

"They were talking about her at dinner, said they'd heard it on the radio."

"State police are gonna be coming down here this morning."

"Why you telling me all this? Think I care about some girl?"

Davis said, "How long we known each other?"

"Thirty-some years."

"That's why I'm telling you."

"Well, I don't know anything about her. Don't have the energy for women anymore."

Davis said, "I hope that never happens to me." He turned to Jimmy, who hadn't moved the whole time he'd been there, then back up at Truman who was licking at his upper lip, trying to get rid of the dried blood. "He's a mighty sound sleeper."

"Up late. They don't make 'em like they used to."

Davis said, "You want to go for a ride?"

"Where to?"

"Just down the road. I got a call—they found a pair of jeans that seem to match what that girl was wearing, not far from where they found her car. Was on my way there. Thought I'd swing by, have a look, then go into town and get some breakfast."

Truman said, "Sure, I'll go for a ride. Let me go get my teeth." He stood again and went in the house, while Davis started toward the cruiser.

Truman counted four squad cars on the shoulder of the road and assumed it was the entire police force of Portisville. Pulling in behind the last cruiser, Davis took off his sunglasses and slid them on the dash. The sun came in the front windshield, already thick and permanent, a few minutes past eight. Bird met them as they climbed out of the car, his smile fading when he saw Truman. "Morning, Sheriff." Bird handed Davis a manila folder. "Here's that folder on the girl."

Davis set it on the dashboard without opening it. "Thanks, who found the pants?"

"Charlie Simmons. Said he just got out of his truck and walked into the woods to take a piss when he saw the jeans hanging from a branch."

Bird and Davis began walking away from the car, toward the clearing. Truman hesitated for a second, not sure if he was supposed to follow or not. But he figured if Davis had invited him along then he should be able to, so he followed them over to the two men and the little opening in the woods. Bird turned back to Truman and stared unkindly at him for a second as if willing him not to come.

Charlie Simmons, who was one of the town's five lawyers, was wearing an orange vest and camouflage hat and leaning against his Jeep, talking to a pair of deputies, smoking and laughing. When he saw Davis, he straightened up and threw his cigarette down and stepped on it. Davis said, "You know there's a fine for littering, don't you?"

Charlie lowered his head toward the ground, as if a child being scolded. Truman thought it looked like he was folding in on himself. Everyone else looked at Davis, who kept his face blank and straight, staring forward. A breaking stick echoed from somewhere deep in the woods. Davis said, "So, Charlie, you found the pants?"

"About fifteen yards in." He pointed at a small footpath, which was visible from the road. Five yards into the trail it made a sharp right so that from the highway it looked as if the trail lasted only that short distance before you hit a wall of pine trees and scrub. In Truman's opinion, it was not a trail a stranger to this town would follow.

Davis said, "You usually piss with your hunting vest on?"

Charlie's face flushed red and he turned again toward the ground, stuffed his hands in his pockets, and dug his boots into the dirt as if taking root. Truman thought, *You dumb shit*, and was impressed by the way Davis handled the situation.

Davis shook his head and turned to Bird. "Did you check the pants out?"

"We didn't touch them. Thought you should have a look first."

Davis said, "Let's go have a look, then."

Davis and Bird, along with Truman, started into the woods. Bird said, loud enough so that Truman could hear, "Sheriff, should he be coming with us?"

"Yeah, he's fine."

Truman stayed a few feet back from them, his right knee aching as he walked. He could feel the other two deputies behind him now, leaning up against their cars and talking shit on the other side of the brush, wondering the same thing Bird had without the balls to ask.

From the road, the dense line of trees and shrubbery looked like every other patch of woods in Portisville. Truman's house was two miles north, but he knew that you could walk from here to there without any problem, if you knew when to turn left and right. He doubted that any of these deputies knew the way but Davis sure did. They'd walked it together many times before. To his right, on a dead branch, a gray owl stared down at him. It seemed possible to Truman that same owl was in the woods over twenty years ago when they'd walked the same ground looking for Dot.

Truman, Davis, and a deputy named Franklin had canvassed the woods for five hours that first day. It had rained three days straight, and their boots sank an inch or two with every step they took, ripping and burying the wet leaves below them. The men poked at bushes and low-hanging branches, moved back and forth past the hole they would eventually find her in two days later, covered in a blanket of pine needles and the thick green brush of palmetto branches.

But that first day, Truman had seen her face in everything. It smiled at him from the branches of trees and the long leafy folds of elephant ears as he stumbled along and could only think of one thing, *before*, their wedding day: honeysuckle and crimson and ham and beer, small gray birds diving down at the birdfeeder in his backyard and a white-tailed hare that had sat below the feeder munching on clover as the hulls and bird droppings showered him. And as Truman and Dot made love, later that night, with her on top of him, her dark hair hung past her shoulders, partially covering her breasts, her nipples appearing now and then as if the small dark eyes of a child peeking through blackened fingers. He lifted his head and took them one at a time in his mouth, pulling, biting, sucking. The white skin of her belly and the words she said, over and over, her eyes aglow in the candle light, staring down at him, "I am yours now, Truman. I will love you forever."

"Here they are."

The words scratched at the roof of Truman's mind. He wasn't sure of the source, the time. He opened his eyes and saw that the ground below his feet was solid and dry. A wave of grief, of loss, moved through his chest and chin and finally settled across his trembling lips. Then he saw the jeans draped over the branch of a pine tree as if drying on a clothesline.

Davis stepped to within an inch of the jeans and lifted his head as if trying to smell them. "All right. Take some photos before you move them, rope off the area and we need to do another full search around here."

Bird said, "Yes, sir." The deputy took a step toward Davis and the pants.

Davis said, "Look, I got that meeting and I'm gonna run Truman back home. I'll see you in a couple hours, give me a call if you find anything." The deputy nodded an okay.

"Sheriff, do you want me to arrest Simmons for poaching?"

"Naw, just get a statement about what he was doing out here. We got bigger fish to fry."

Davis and Truman started for the opening, not speaking as they walked. In the clearing, Davis walked over and spoke to the deputies while Truman headed back to the car and climbed in. He felt a burning in his chest and coughed hard three times. He opened the door and spat out the window; yellow phlegm mixed with blood soiled the ground.

Davis patted one of the deputies on the shoulder and walked slowly to the car. He turned the key and a fuzzy voice spoke from the CB. Davis turned it down, eased back onto the highway, nodded at his deputies and did a wide U-turn in the center of the road.

Truman said, "Think you might have something?"

"Who knows. It could be anything."

Behind them, in the rearview mirror, the diminishing figures on the roadside mixed with the blacktop and trees into one undistinguishable mass.

Jimmy rose and went into the house and was pleased to see that Angie had started coffee before leaving. He poured himself a cup, added a bit of milk, and stirred it with his finger, not quite sure how to gauge the conversation he had heard between his father and Davis, though it did seem friendly enough. He walked back outside and stood with his knees leaning against the porch rail. As he looked out into the yard, a dull headache sounded somewhere in the back of his head. There was glass all over the hood of his truck from last night. The trees were thick except for the thin path by the quarter-adorned tree. He didn't feel a breeze, nothing, and thought about when he was a child, how mornings like this were all he had known until he moved up to North Carolina. About how sometimes the cool mornings up there would make his teenaged eyes water.

He needed to figure out what to do today. If he did stay and go with Carol tonight then he might take a drive around town, see what he could see, maybe even go do some fishing. He'd call her in a little while, see how she sounded on the phone, see if she still seemed interested. His father had said a lot about her last night and he had no idea whether or not any of it was true. Either way, it made him curious about her. He would take a quick lay if that was what she was offering, but something told him it was more than that.

Jimmy went back inside for a second cup of coffee, his headache starting to fade. He looked around and took in the old light-blue wallpaper in the living room. There was a tan throw rug with one burnt corner in front of the couch. His mother had dropped a cigarette on it and stood there laughing, too drunk to do anything, as he stomped it out. There was also an egg-sized hole by one of the rear legs of the couch a pet gerbil of his had made. He hadn't noticed much about the house last night, and thought it was probably because of everything that had happened yesterday. But now, all around him some vast library of memories was coming forth.

He walked over behind the couch and ran his hands along the top of it. It was scratchy there but the back of the couch was smooth and easy to the touch. His mother would sleep there in the afternoons with a row of beer cans on the coffee table, the ashtray full of cigarette butts. One day, after school, he had sat on the floor while she slept, watching the way her chest rose and fell beneath the half-buttoned white shirt. He moved a finger across her nose and then down the center of her chest until it settled on her exposed navel where he traced the soft dark hair that circled her belly button. He did this for a minute before she opened her eyes, laughing when she saw him, the freckles by her right eye dancing as she smiled. She pulled him up on the couch, and he lay next to her, unable to sleep but loving her and smelling the cigarettes and beer that lingered over every inch of her body.

The sound of steps on the porch outside pulled Jimmy from the memory. Angie, covered in sweat, walked in the front door and smiled at Jimmy. "Good morning."

Jimmy said, "Morning," back and went over to the table. "Have a good run?"

Pouring tap water into a glass, she said, "It was tough this morning."

"I'm sorry about all that noise last night."

"It's okay, I'm almost used to it."

Jimmy smiled, not sure if she was serious or not.

"Where is your father?"

"He went out with Davis."

After finishing her glass of water, Angie said, "Excuse me," then went back to her room.

When she came back out, the wet running shirt was replaced with a dry, white T-shirt. Her bangs were stuck to her forehead from the dried sweat. "Did you want breakfast?"

Jimmy said, "No, I'm okay. I was just about to get in the shower. Then I was gonna go for a drive."

"Yeah, I've gotta go to work for a few hours."

"You have another job?"

"I do four hours in the morning—Monday, Wednesday, and

Friday—over at the retirement home. It gets me out of the house. When he needs more help I'll quit, but now there isn't much for me to do."

Jimmy said, "That makes sense." He'd had a hard time trying to figure out what she did at the house all day with Truman and figured she probably just tried to stay out of his way.

Angie filled a glass with orange juice and dropped a couple of pieces of bread into the toaster.

Jimmy said, "I hope I didn't scare you last night."

"What do you mean?"

"Telling you all that stuff about him going to jail."

She shook her head. "No, I was just surprised. I guess I still don't quite understand how Davis and your father are such good friends, especially if he put Truman in jail."

Jimmy said, "He didn't have much of a choice. It was an open and shut case."

Angie pulled the toast from the toaster and sat down at the table.

Jimmy said, "How did you get this job? How did you meet him?"

"I had been working for the same doctor in Brunswick for three years and wanted a change. I wanted to get out of that office and do something different, a chance to get out of town, so I applied for a job doing home health care. He is actually my first patient."

Jimmy said, "Lucky you."

Angie laughed. "Yeah, lucky me."

Bobby stood on the side of Highway 144 and watched the occasional car speed by. He wished he could stay home and go fishing every day. But he had promised God that if He made it so his dad didn't find out that Bobby was in his closet, then he wouldn't miss any more school. He didn't think God was someone you should break a promise to, though He still hadn't brought his mother back, something Bobby had asked Him to do many times before.

Kicking the dirt under his feet, Bobby unearthed an empty can of Skoal. He picked it up and tossed it off into the trees. It looked like a miniature Frisbee or spaceship sailing through the air. He wasn't sure what he'd tell Mrs. Floyd, his homeroom teacher, about missing the last two days of school. Maybe he could tell her that his mother was sick and he had to stay home with her.

The patrol car came around the corner and with the screech of tires, stopped in front of Bobby, making him jump back. It was Sheriff Davis and some old man Bobby didn't recognize in the front seat. Davis rolled down his window. "Hey, Bobby."

He walked over to the car and leaned against the door. "Hi, Sheriff."

"You on your way to school?"

"Yeah."

"Come on, let me give you a ride. We're heading that way."

Bobby looked back in the direction of his house, glad that he had cleared the corner so that his father couldn't see him, and climbed in the back of the cruiser. The man in the front passenger seat was staring at him in his sun-visor mirror. Leaning forward, Bobby said as quietly as he could, his right hand cupping the side of his mouth, "Sheriff, is he under arrest?"

Davis smiled at Bobby in the rearview mirror. "Yep."

"Shouldn't he be in the back seat?"

"Naw, that is only in the movies."

Sitting back, Bobby settled into the thick black vinyl seats. He'd never sat in the back before. On the silver grille, between the front and back seats, there were a couple spots of dried blood behind the prisoner's head.

Davis said, "This is Truman Wills."

The name Wills seemed vaguely familiar to Bobby. He thought his father might have mentioned it before, but his father mentioned so many names he couldn't be sure. Bobby said hi and Mr. Wills nodded back without saying anything.

Davis said, "How's your father doing?"

"Good."

"He still working at home?"

"Yeah."

"What exactly does he do?"

"I don't know."

"Well what does it look like?"

"I don't know."

"How is your mother doing?"

"Fine."

A red Camaro was parked along the side the road. A man in jeans and a T-shirt leaned over the hood, working on the car. Davis pulled over and stopped. "Let me just make sure he's all right." Parking ten yards in front of the car, Davis climbed out and walked back.

Bobby hoped that he wouldn't be late for school. Mr. Wills stared forward. On the side of the road, the grass was spotted with dew. Bobby said, "You live here?"

"Yes." Truman stuck his head out the window, as if to hear what was being said at the car behind them.

"Do you know my father?"

Truman turned back and faced Bobby. "Yeah, I know him."

"You're not really under arrest, are you?"

"Why do you say that?"

"No handcuffs."

Truman smiled. "Not today."

"Have you ever been to prison before?"

Truman nodded. "Lots of people go to prison."

"My dad's never been to prison."

Truman looked hard at Bobby. "Not yet." Davis' belt rattled as he walked toward the car. They both looked up at him.

"You two ready to go?"

Truman said, "Yeah, let's go. I'm hungry."

Bobby said, "He all right?"

Davis said, "Yeah, just a busted water hose. Said somebody was bringing one out for him."

They drove the rest of the way in silence, passing other kids walking to school. Bobby was pleased that the sheriff didn't stop to pick them up. It made him feel different, special. When they pulled into the school parking lot, Bobby heard the early bell ring, indicating he had ten minutes to get to class. Climbing out of the car, he said, "Thanks, Sheriff."

"Anytime, son."

Bobby looked back over at Mr. Wills as if about to say something, then turned back to Davis. "Sheriff, could you do the siren?"

Davis smiled and winked at Bobby. He hit the red switch and the car's siren wailed and kids stopped walking into the building and watched and listened to the police car as it pulled away. Bobby smiled, felt lifted somehow by the siren, as if it was as sweet as the sound of his mother's voice waking him in the morning.

Davis and Truman didn't speak for some time, but stared forward, watching the stretch of tree-lined blacktop that seemed to surround everything in this town. The pine trees stood tall and overgrown alongside Highway 144, swaying with the soft breeze as if waking slightly dazed, surprised by the sun that was upon them again. The occasional plastic bag on the side of the road lifted into the air when they passed as if caught in the squad car's slipstream. Crows leaned forward on fence posts like some kind of feathered trapeze artists and though Davis couldn't hear them over the hum of the engine he could see their beaks open and imagined their harsh, repetitive caw.

Davis wondered what his friend saw in all those trees. He suspected prison might make you appreciate being out amongst nature again, though thus far Truman hadn't mentioned anything remotely like that. As far as he could tell Truman hadn't changed much except for his sickness but now he was starting to look good again, his face rounder and his eyes clearer.

Truman said, "Why were you questioning him like that?"

"I wouldn't call it that, just making conversation."

"Whatever."

"His old man is dealing. Darren Webster, ever heard of him?"

"No."

"Well, he's been in it about a year and a half now, from what I can tell. Started off slow, caught him selling a dime bag about a year ago, but we didn't press for all the charges. Maybe we should have. His wife had left him and he had custody of the boy and we hoped it was a one-time thing. I think he's moving up, though, and when he does he'll go down. He's driving in and out the state, trafficking, which, as we both know, makes it a federal offense.

"Close as I can tell, he started because his wife left him. About two years ago, she moved into an apartment ten miles north of here, outside the county line. He took it hard, quit his job over at Guseels Auto Body. I don't know for sure but hear he has a cousin up in Georgia who got him into it. I guess after she left, he lost the will to be good."

"What's 'to be good' mean?"

"I forgot who I was talking to."

"Don't forget you used to be not so good yourself."

Davis said, "Trust me, I haven't forgotten. If I wanted to, you wouldn't let me."

"You think it was really his wife leaving that got him into it?"

"Yeah, I do. Like I said, first offense. Why else would he start?"

Truman said, "Why did we?"

Davis paused before answering, not sure he wanted this conversation to continue on the path it had taken. He hadn't thought about their old business in a while and knew that it was a question he didn't want to answer. Finally, he said, "Because we were dumb and young and thought we were outlaws, thought the law couldn't touch us."

"Don't forget the money. Plus the fact that your daddy was the sheriff made it interesting."

Davis turned to Truman, who smiled back at him. "Well, maybe for you. But it left me in a perpetual state of scared shitless."

"But hell, it was fun, man. The three of us driving all over the place. Pulling into a town with wads of money and having anything we damn well pleased. You and Dan in the back seat, counting or sorting, my heart jumping when we crossed another state line. I felt alive then. Felt like I was part of something. It probably sounds stupid, but I figure it was like being on a great baseball or football team for one season when everything clicks and it's moving like a machine that can't be stopped, like it's the right thing and everything else is wrong. Fuck what the law says."

Davis hadn't seen Truman this excited in a long time. A part of himself had enjoyed those years, enjoyed the hell out of them actually, but he would not give Truman the satisfaction of agreeing with him. A herd of Herefords seemed to bow at them as they passed. Davis said, "Jimmy looks good."

"I guess. He's tall." Truman's excited tone disappeared and he was back to his normal monotone.

"Just like his mother."

"She was tall, wasn't she?"

"Tall and beautiful. How long is he here for?"

"I don't know. A day or two, I guess."

"Couple days will be nice."

Truman said, "Let me drive."

It was the first time Truman had asked that question since his release from prison. When Davis visited him in prison and asked how he was holding up, Truman said that the thing he really missed was driving. He had asked Davis a few months before he was released if he would let him drive, and Davis had said yes because no other answer seemed right at the time. On the day he drove Truman home from prison, Davis expected Truman to call him on the favor, but he hadn't. He had only sat against the passenger side door, staring out the window, looking somewhat defeated, or numb, instead of free.

Even after they stopped at the diner and ate a lunch of hamburgers and fries and Coca-Cola, he still didn't ask. That first day, other customers stared at them as they walked in the door and took a pair of stools at the counter. It didn't take long for the whispering to start, the turned heads, and he knew what they were all thinking: son-of-a-bitching sheriff hanging out with his buddy Truman "the criminal" Wills again. But it didn't matter to him what they said or thought, as he had promised Truman on the day he drove him to the state pen that he would, in turn, drive him home. His keeping of that promise and their friendship so far outweighed what these people had to say or thought, that to Davis they were invisible, a non-factor. He could tell that Truman enjoyed it though, the way people looked sideways at him as if meeting his eyes could melt them into soft motes of flesh. After they had ordered their food, Davis told Truman that he hoped the Braves made it to the World Series again because a cousin of his was working for the team and might be able to get a couple tickets. Truman said that sounded good to him and they spent an hour talking about baseball and the minor and major beauties of hitting a little white ball as far and wide as possible.

As time went by, Davis stopped worrying about Truman asking Davis to drive, but now here it was in front of him, and Truman's feet were pressed into the floorboard, as if he were pressing pedals, accelerating and braking when necessary. "We don't have time for that and breakfast. Got that meeting with the fellas from the state."

"Fuck breakfast."

When they stopped at a blinking red light a few miles south of downtown, Truman said, "So, what do you say?"

"No, another day, Truman."

"Aw, come on."

"No.

Truman opened his door and climbed out, smiling as he crossed in front of the car and thumping the hood with the palm of his hands. A pickup truck passed going the other way. The driver honked and when Davis looked up, Truman was at his door, smiling down at him.

Davis said, "I could get in all kind of trouble for this. You don't have a license anymore."

"So what, you're the law."

"Don't do this to me."

"Don't it sound fun?"

Davis said, "No." Then he thought a thing he would never say to his friend, *What about the last time you were behind a wheel,* and regretted it. Without speaking, perhaps for the guilt of that last thought, Davis undid his seat belt and climbed out of the cruiser and walked over to the other side and got in. "Put your damn seat belt on."

"No."

"You want to drive, then you're gonna put it on." Davis slammed his door shut. It frustrated the hell out of him how Truman always got his way, as if he had some power, something Davis couldn't name, a tenacity or will that always seemed to overpower those around him. Davis felt a pull in the center of his chest but couldn't say for sure whether it was cardiac or not since it seemed to vanish as quickly as it had come. "And don't go downtown."

Truman said, "Shit," and clipped on his seatbelt, then shifted his balls with his left hand and gripped the wheel with the other. He started out slow, tentative, like someone who had fallen from a horse and was not going to let it happen again. Soon, Truman began tapping the steering wheel with his thumbs—left, right, left, right. Davis checked his watch and knew he didn't have time to be screwing around like this, but the look on Truman's face, all smiles with the tip of his tongue sticking out a little as he drove, made Davis decide to let him have a few more minutes.

Truman turned off the highway and went up a little two-track out into a segment of woods that cut back and then ran parallel to 144. The dirt road was barely wider than the car and branches fanned the doors, scratched at the windshield. On his side of the road, twenty yards into the woods, Davis could see a pair of men in white coveralls, working a couple of hives, smoking the bees out. As he picked up speed, Truman began to tap his thumbs quicker, da-da-da-da. Davis hid his smile from Truman and relaxed into the seat, despite himself.

After rolling down the window, Truman stuck his hand out so that the branches slapped his bare hands and wrist and he started to hum a song, deep and throaty. In a matter of minutes, it seemed like they had fallen back thirty years and were driving out into the woods on one of the trips up north for the deals which had started their friendship, which over time had helped it grow. And that is how they would travel: Truman driving, effortlessly with one hand on the wheel and the other out the window, Davis in the passenger seat, and Dan in the back, or other times they were both in the back. Davis wished Dan were with them right now, but his two best friends hadn't spoken in so long it didn't seem like they would ever speak again. Although Davis never really knew what happened between them, as neither would say, he always assumed it had something to do with the fact that Dan had distanced himself from Truman during Dot's murder trial, as if the idea of Truman going to jail was a wake-up call. After Truman was cleared of all charges in Dot's murder, Dan stopped dealing and bought the country store. He wasn't with Truman the night of the wreck. As far as Davis knew, Dan had never visited Truman in prison.

But back then, the three of them were as close as brothers and damned lucky they didn't get caught. Davis had responsibility now, had people who counted on him, but he squeezed his eyes tighter and felt the blood pumping in his neck and told himself, *A few more minutes,* as he let himself be driven by Truman again.

Truman hit a hole in the road and Davis felt the lift and fall in his stomach and then the jarring slam as the front of the car came down. His head jerked back and Truman laughed as the car leveled out. Davis wondered if Truman was thinking about that night of the wreck. When he had pulled up to Truman's, an hour later, he was sitting on the porch waiting, freshly shaved, not even trying to get away. The two men had drunk a glass of whiskey together before Davis drove him in. He remembered what Truman said, "Almost got away with it, didn't I?"

Now, the opening in the trees and the wide clearing, which forked at the road, was in front of them. As Davis was about to say, "Okay, I'll take it from here," Truman spun the steering wheel hard right and was on the highway again. Up ahead, Davis saw the turn-off into Truman's yard and, for a moment, he didn't think he had ever been so happy to see anything in all his life.

Bobby scratched a *B* into the desk in front of him. The edge of his pencil dug deep into the old wood, alongside messages left long ago—*Phil Was Here, Party, Boogie Woogie, Eat Me, Florida Sucks.* He could barely hear Mrs. Floyd at the front of the class, her voice a dull, soft thing that he was able to block out as he considered how lucky he was to get a ride from the sheriff. He thought again about what that man had said about his father. He didn't want his father to go to jail but he did want to live with his mother again. If his father went away, then his mother would have to let him live with her, right? Somebody had to take care of him. Maybe his father would like jail. Maybe it wasn't so bad there.

"Mr. Webster." Bobby heard the voice and at first discounted it as more of her rambling, this time just some words that struck him as familiar. Then something deep inside of him, a solid dread, a thing he couldn't name, made it clear that she was talking to him. He pushed the pencil down harder and the lead broke, spun there and then rolled down the desk and fell to the floor. "What are you doing?"

He lifted his head and she was a few feet in front of him, old enough to be any of these kids' grandmothers in her green dress and white hair. He turned back toward a boy with glasses, but it did no good. The kid stared forward, blank-faced, unwilling to offer what Bobby needed.

She was over him now, standing there, peering down with mean, beady brown eyes. "What are you doing?"

"Nothing."

"You were writing on the desk."

"Was not." His face felt like it was on fire. He hated her for making him feel like this. It wasn't his fault. Other kids had done it. If she said something he cared about up there in front of the class instead of talking about what the capital of North Dakota was he wouldn't have been so bored. In her eyes, he caught sight of some fright and looked to where she was staring. His right hand was balled into a fist with the broken tip of the pencil pointing at her. He let go of the pencil and it dropped into his lap.

"I want you to go to the principal's office, right now." She turned and began to walk to the front of the class. Bobby felt angry, so angry he thought he might cry, but he told himself not to, not in front of all these other kids. He knew that at lunch Nick Malis would surely run and tell everyone from their homeroom class last year. He didn't want that. He wanted to punch Nick, actually, wanted to make the blame, or attention, slide away from him, onto some other boy, a boy who had probably been doing the same thing he had.

Mrs. Floyd straightened up, then turned to the rest of the students, letting her long neck scan the classroom from left to right, like a bird searching the shore for a bite to eat. "Who wants to escort Mr. Webster to the principal's office?"

Bobby didn't look up to see who had responded, could tell somebody had because of the shuffling of a desk, but kept his head down, staring at the mottled one below him and read a message he hadn't noticed before: *Heather Is A Ho.*

"Miss Stein, thank you for volunteering."

Bobby hated the way she called all of them Mister or Miss. They were kids. They weren't adults. Didn't she know anything?

Mollie Stein was cute and wore a tan dress and had pink barrettes in her straight blond hair. She stood at the door waiting for Bobby, her hands on her hips. As he stood, the pencil fell from his lap. He made a move to pick it up, then walked on, realizing he had no use for that now. Mollie Stein smiled at Bobby, but he didn't smile back as they started out the door. He felt like an un-handcuffed prisoner being led by a guard to his captor.

As they moved past the first row of gray lockers and the match-ing tile below, one part of Bobby wanted to push Mollie Stein down and run over her back and out the door and another part of him wondered how long it would be before she was out in the back of a pickup truck in a dusty orange grove, on top of a naked man, her hair flapping in the non-existent wind doing that thing that everyone said felt so good.

She said, "Have you ever been to the principal's office before?"

"Yes, of course I have."

Turning back to him, she said, "Don't get mad at me."

"Well, don't ask stupid questions."

They had better get to the office soon or he would have to hit her. He could tell his father that they made a mistake and that it was somebody else who was doing it and the old lady got con-fused and called the wrong student. Here it was the third week of school and he was already in trouble. His father had told him that he better be good as they didn't need any teachers coming by the house, messing in their business. He wanted to be good and knew that he had to if he wanted to get his mother back, but there al-ways seemed to be something between him and that other boy, the good one, the one he wanted to be. Try harder is what he would have to do.

"There it is."

Bobby looked up. The door at the end of the hall was made of wood but there was a square of glass in the top half. In the center of the glass, the word PRINCIPAL was stenciled in big black let-ters. On the other side of the door, Bobby could tell there were people in there because he saw shadows moving around but the blurry glass made it hard to see anything clearly. Above the door a red, rectangular sign said NO GUM.

When Bobby turned to tell Mollie good-bye, she stuck her

tongue out and ran away back down the hall. Bobby stuck his tongue out too, but it was too late. She was already gone, around the corner, out of his view.

He approached the door slowly, put a tentative hand on the brass handle and turned it. A small wall of voices came back to him as the door opened. Then he realized that this wasn't actually the principal's office, but the waiting room like in a doctor's office. There was a woman, about the same age as his mother, in a yellow dress, behind the desk. She was talking on the telephone. The nameplate at the edge of the desk said her name was Wendy King.

She smiled at Bobby and nodded him toward a seat and continued to speak into the phone. There were framed photos on her desk and he wondered who was in the pictures. Did she have a son like him? Would she be leaving him soon? Did all mothers do that?

She hung up the phone and said, "What can I do for you?"

"I have to see the principal."

"What did you do?" She was animated when she spoke, seemed kind and patient unlike Mrs. Floyd. She pulled a piece of paper from a drawer in her desk and looked up at him as if waiting for his response before she began writing.

"I wrote on a desk."

"With what?"

"A pencil."

"Well, why did you do that?"

"I don't know." He could feel the blood pumping in his neck and was tired of all these questions.

She threw him a scolding look. "That wasn't a very good idea."

"Shut up, you're not my mother."

She turned quick, any hint of a smile gone. "No, young man, I am not. But something tells me it won't be long before I meet her."

She stood up and went to the other door, turned back to him and said, "Wait here," then disappeared inside. She wasn't nice, none of them were.

His feet seemed to twitch, and his hands drummed the plastic seat he was in. He could hear voices on the other side of the door and imagined they were discussing ways to punish him: paddling, suspensions, standing at the blackboard writing *I will not write on desks* hundreds of times. When he could stand the waiting no more, Bobby stood and ran out the door. He passed rows of blurred lockers, water fountains and the class he had just come from. He passed the stairway that lead to the boys' locker room. He passed the door to the cafeteria. Then his hands were on the double doors leading outside and the heat hit him quick, made him gasp a second and then he saw through blurred eyes a wall of trees across the street and ran for them.

Truman sat on the porch in his rocking chair, eating a bowl of cereal, sweat dampening his arms and chest. The cereal tasted good to him, the milk nice and cold. He had forgotten how good it felt to be driving fast and free. It was strange that the doctors told him he was dying, considering how he felt now. But he didn't know much about medicine, or the body, and Angie had told him that he would probably feel fine for a while, after that first bout of sickness and then he'd go downhill fast. *Fuck it,* he thought, *there is nothing I can do about it.*

He closed his eyes and imagined he was back behind the wheel, turning corners, moving fast up and over bumps in the road, his foot against the gas pedal. The look on Davis' face was priceless too; the old boy looked like he might shit himself. Truman wondered if it was really his time. If he was going to turn around and if so, should he continue with his plans to end his life? But he had made up his mind and could not go back on his word, even if he was the only person that would know he had.

Now, by his feet, Truman saw a couple bullets on the floor, resting up against the bottom of the banister. He thought of being out here on the porch with Jimmy last night, of how it felt good to shoot with someone even if the son of a bitch did end up punching him in the nose. Truman had only brought Jimmy here with the idea that if he pushed hard enough, the boy would do what he wanted. But, the truth is, it was good to see him; he looked like he was doing all right for himself.

He remembered the first time Jimmy had fired a gun. He was six, maybe seven, and Truman had driven him and Dot out to a piece of property, a hundred and fifty acres of thick woods, he owned with Dan and Davis. A single dirt road plowed through the center of a pine forest leading to a small cabin with an old rusted truck out front. This cabin was where the three men would meet and make plans. It was furnished with a cot, an old pine table with three chairs, and a Styrofoam cooler that was normally full of beer cans floating in melted ice.

That day, the middle of summer, Dot sat on the back of the then-new Cadillac sipping ice cold beer, dripping condensation falling off the cans onto her thin, revealing T-shirt. Truman lined six beer cans in a row on the truck's hood and stood a few feet from his wife and son, shooting the cans one at a time, moving from outer to inner. Dot had told Truman that she didn't want Jimmy anywhere near his guns, but had said nothing that day as the boy sat against the fender, between her legs, and the two of them watched Truman target shoot.

As Truman reloaded the pistol, Dot walked out into the woods, behind the cabin, to pee. He called Jimmy over and held the gun out to him, handle first. "You want to take a shot?"

Jimmy smiled up at Truman and nodded that he did. Truman wrapped Jimmy's finger around the handle of the gun. The boy stared wide-eyed at the weapon in his right hand, then turned around so that his back was against Truman's chest. Together they squeezed the trigger and Truman felt the boy jump back against him with each shot; his head hitting Truman's chest as the bottles fell. The crisp sound of shattering glass and laughter filled the dense, hot air around them.

Dot walked out of the woods and yelled, "Truman."

At the sound of his mother's voice, Jimmy let go of the gun and ran back to her. Truman smiled and walked over and kissed her. She tried to turn away, but he held her face to him and after a second or two she gave in and kissed back. Later that night, as they made love, all Truman could hear between his wife's moans of pleasure was the sound of the gun going off and Jimmy's laughter.

Truman thought that Dot babied the boy too much and after months of trying to convince her that he needed to toughen Jimmy up, she finally agreed to let him take Jimmy hunting, three weeks after his ninth birthday.

Truman woke at four the morning of their planned trip and walked into Jimmy's bedroom and stood over the boy for a few minutes; the white sheets curled just below his chin. The boy's features were similar to his mother's: the sharp chin, the pug nose, and the same black hair. Jimmy stirred in his sleep and woke, staring up at Truman who said, "You ready? It's the big day."

In the kitchen, Truman found Dot standing in front of the stove, wearing a blue robe, smoking a cigarette, as she ran a spatula into a black frying pan full of scrambled eggs. The smell of toast, coffee, and eggs filled the room. Truman walked up behind her, hugged her and kissed the back of her hair, which smelled like cigarettes, and cupped her breasts. After a bit of fake moaning, she turned around and hugged him.

When Jimmy walked into the room, dressed in the green-and-brown camouflage shirt and pants Truman had bought him for his birthday, she smiled and said, "My little hunter." He sat at the table, next to his mother, and started eating the plateful of eggs and toast she had set out for him. Truman sat on the other side of Dot, sipping coffee. Looking back on it now, everything seemed at that moment to Truman as good as it would ever be.

After loading the guns and cooler into the back of the pickup, Truman stepped back onto the porch and watched Dot hug Jimmy and then kiss him on the cheek. Jimmy walked past Truman toward the truck. As Truman hugged Dot, she said, "You make sure he's okay."

"I will."

"Truman, he's my life. Take care of him."

"I know. He'll be fine. We'll get a deer and eat venison for a week."

Later, as they moved across the empty dark road, Truman turned to Jimmy. The boy was looking out the window of the truck, watching the endless row of dark woods that forever lined their lives. Truman said, "You sleep okay?"

"Yes, sir."

"You feel lucky today?"

"Yes, sir."

After leaving the highway, they drove a half an hour on the narrow dirt road through the slash pines and palmettos, before dead-ending into a locked gate marked with the bright orange sign: NO TRESPASSING. Truman climbed out of the truck, walked to the gate and undid the lock with a key he pulled from his pants pocket. After reaching the cabin, they walked down a wooded trail with Truman leading the way.

Truman thought of what Dot had said, "He is my life." And though he knew it wasn't right, he had felt that there was a wall between him and the boy and that wall was their shared love of this woman who only had so much love to give. He hoped that them being together like this would start to break down that wall and their family would be closer for it. Something that, he knew now, had never really happened.

They weren't in the stand five minutes when Jimmy grabbed Truman's shirt and said, "There's one." Jimmy pointed to a small clearing where the eight-point buck stood, tan and fat with his head buried into the base of a palmetto bush. Truman's heart beat quick. He felt light-headed. He always felt like that on seeing the first deer of the season. He said, "You want this one?"

Jimmy shook his head no. This didn't surprise Truman. When he was a boy, hunting with his father, he would be nervous and want his father to show him the way it was supposed to be done. He looked back at Jimmy, smiled and raised the gun to his shoulder. In that moment, everything else faded away. All he saw was the deer's thick neck and chest in front of him through the scope and heard his son's quick breathing behind him. He remembered actually thinking about not shooting the deer, wanting this moment to stretch out and last as long as possible—father and son together with this thick, peaceful animal walking around below them. He'd almost decided to do that when the deer looked up in their direction and Truman squeezed the trigger out of instinct.

The deer fell quick and with ease, as if it had been held up with some thin un-seeable fishing line which somebody had cut at the same moment he squeezed the trigger. Truman's blood pounded in his head as he stared, through the scope, at the thick green bush where the deer had been standing. Then he heard Jimmy's voice: "You got him."

When they reached the deer, Truman saw that there was a small hole in the center of its neck. A thin, steady stream of blood flowed from the hole, pooling amongst the brown pine needles. The only sign that the deer was still alive was the slight movement of its eyes, which darted from side to side, and the shallow rise and fall of its chest. Truman looked at Jimmy, could see the horror in those young eyes, the gloss that always preceded tears. He wished this one, the first kill Jimmy would ever see, could have been a clean one—simply a deer falling over dead, like magic— but it hadn't been. With the two of them standing over the deer, Jimmy said, "He ain't dead."

"I know."

Truman turned to his son, who had begun to cry softly. Truman thought, *Die, just fucking die, you dumb-ass deer.* They stood like that for a few more seconds, before Truman said, "This is part of it boy, toughen up."

The deer looked up at the two of them and moved one of its front legs back and forth as if to let them know he wasn't dead, but didn't try to stand. Truman said, "When something's almost dead like this you gotta go through with it. Put it out of its misery. No reason making it suffer. We're here to kill, not wound."

Then he raised the gun to the deer's head. He looked back at Jimmy and said, "It's the only decent thing to do." With that he squeezed the trigger of the gun and felt its weight push hard against his right shoulder.

Now, Truman pointed his .38 at the tree and fired three times, all three shots sending a quick *ping* back to him. He lifted the gun to his right temple and felt the warmth of the barrel there against his flesh. His finger inched along the trigger, rubbing it back and forth. In prison, he had heard about men who tried to shoot themselves in the head but had missed or the bullet hadn't entered the brain but had been deflected by the skull into other parts of their neck or body. He'd heard about men who had blown their faces off, had gone blind or been paralyzed. Worse off than when they'd started.

Truman stuck the gun into his mouth. He could feel his chest rising and falling, his heart beating quick and thick down there. The barrel touched his tongue and Truman pulled it back an inch. He tasted oil and heat and permanence. He closed his eyes and opened them. It felt like he had stuffed something in his mouth that he couldn't chew. Then his hand started to shake, a little at first, but then more. The barrel bounced from his upper to his lower teeth. He pulled the gun out and shot the remaining three bullets toward the tree before spitting a wash of blood-stained saliva out over the porch's rail.

Jimmy sat on the tailgate of the truck, his legs dangling, a cigarette in his hand, and spat at the ground. The graveyard, a square plot of land no bigger than a basketball court with various-sized gravestones and obelisks placed in rows, some even, others rearing back and forth, as if about to fall like dominoes, was to his left. Beyond the graveyard was a field of flat grass flowing into more pines, as if the space for this cemetery had been cut out of those trees. To his right, a pair of mockingbirds skirted in and out of yet another wall of pine trees. There was something about these tall, thin trees all around him that he found comforting, as if they served as a buffer to the outside world.

Taking a final hit of the third cigarette, he threw it at the white dirt. He had been sitting there for five minutes, had told himself that he would smoke a cigarette and then go see her stone. It wasn't that he didn't want to see her, or the plot of land where she now rested, but he didn't like to think of her as dead and gone, which the stone symbolized in an undeniable fashion.

He lay back in the truck's bed, telling himself, *One more minute,* snug between a ladder and a couple cans of paint, smelling the familiar paint fumes. Above him, a single cotton-ball-shaped cloud blew through the otherwise clear sky and then drifted away. Closing his eyes, he remembered coming here every Sunday in the year following her death. He would walk the three miles to the cemetery, carrying a brown bag with a sandwich and a drink and sit at the gravesite and tell her stories about what he had done in school that week or how his father was doing.

After the food was gone and the stories told, he would lie down and put his head to the dirt, listening for anything, any sign. He didn't believe that she was alive, only that by doing this he was closer to her in some way. Davis had found him sleeping by the stone a couple times and drove him home, dropping him off on the side of the road by the house, never telling Truman as Jimmy had asked him not to.

Now, Jimmy heard the crush of tire over gravel and listened as it came closer, was aside his truck and then past him. He sat up. The car was ten yards down the road, an old brown Buick with Georgia plates. A man got out, smiled and nodded at Jimmy and then walked into the field of headstones with a bushel of flowers in one hand, the pinks, greens and yellows a stark contrast to the drab stones that surrounded him.

Jimmy wished that he would have brought some flowers, but he hadn't known he was going to come here. He had left the house with no real destination in mind, only a couple hours to kill before he met Carol for lunch. He hadn't stopped at the school, but driven by, as it was a normal school day and teeming with kids and teachers, just the kind of place a man in a truck didn't need to be sitting, staring into the schoolyard, whether lost in memories or not. He'd driven past the sign for the cemetery twice before finally turning in.

After depositing the flowers and saying a few words to someone from his past, the man walked back to his car, climbed in and drove away. He didn't bother waving to Jimmy as he passed. Jimmy pulled the pack of cigarettes out again, brought one to his lips, but didn't light it and instead put it behind his right ear. He couldn't be sitting out here all day long. It was getting hot and he had places to go.

Jimmy lifted the tailgate on the truck and started for the gravestones. A red-winged blackbird called out, and Jimmy felt comforted in being able to identify the bird by sound alone and silently thanked Aunt Carly for the skill. It had been so long since he had been in this cemetery that it surprised him how his feet seemed to take him to where he needed to go with little effort. He passed familiar names on the stones: Thelma Wengs, Cole Rolland, Charles Whitmere, and knew he was on the right path. He had read these names so many times that they had become a part of his mother's life, of his past, even though he had never met these people. On days when he had talked to his mother and did not feel like going home yet, he would lie on his back, stare up at the sky and imagine what her neighbors did, or used to do, for a living. He could think of no real job for a woman named Thelma but pictured Cole a farmer and Charles a businessman of sorts. Once, much later, in his mid-twenties, he had a customer named Cole and spent a couple days atop a ladder painting the man's brick house frost white and trying to remember whom he had known with that name. It wasn't until a week after the job was completed, sitting in a bar and working on his third draft beer, that it dawned on him that it was Cole Rolland, one of his mother's gravesite neighbors.

About thirty yards in, he saw her stone:

DOROTHY VALERIE WILLS
In Loving Memory
January 15, 1940–May 12, 1978

It looked just like he remembered it, gray and glinting in the sunlight. He was happy to see that it wasn't weather-damaged or vandalized in any way. Kneeling on the ground in front of it, Jimmy ran his finger along the letters of her name, slow arcs over the *D* and *T*, quick tight little *O*'s. The tears came without warning and he put his head to the dirt, and the grass tickled his face again as it had long ago, a soothing tickle that he had come to associate with his mother. He kept it there for a short time, listening, hearing nothing but the soft sway of a random tree and feeling the hot air settling over him.

Bobby walked along the side of the road, kicking the dusty shoulder. He didn't know what would happen with school, if he would be able to walk in the doors Monday and go to class as if nothing had happened, or if maybe they would be standing there waiting for him, ready to snatch him up and drag him away before he could get in the building. The latter seemed possible, very possible.

His house was only another half-mile up on the right and it occurred to Bobby that they might be waiting for him there. They would take him back to the principal's office and that Wendy lady would hold him down as the principal spanked him with a paddle, probably the one he had heard about that had shiny nickels inlaid in the wood. But that wasn't the worst of it; really, what really scared him was that his father would know what he had done. He'd been lucky yesterday with the shirt and closet but didn't think his luck could hold much longer.

There were no cars, or his father's truck, in front of the house.

The fishing pole leaned against the porch, next to the bike. The top part of the pole bowed as if it had a small bream on the line. Looking around sheepishly, like a burglar making sure all was clear, he climbed the steps, grabbed the bike and started back down the road. The dog barked in the backyard and Bobby wished he could take her along, but knew he couldn't. If his father came home and the dog wasn't barking then he would surely know something was going on. Then Bobby wondered if he would notice that the bike was gone. He didn't think he would.

Bobby hopped onto the seat and turned the bike back in the direction he had just come from. Soon the dog's barks grew quieter, more distant. He lowered his head and started to pedal, feeling the thick air wash across his body like a blanket. Pedaling along the side of the road, he looked down at the grass to his right, and though he couldn't see them clearly he could feel the green-and-brown line of trees. Occasionally he heard a bird cry out but he didn't know the names of birds or why they would make such noise. Not that he particularly cared, considering how those stupid birds had stolen his worms yesterday.

He turned onto Highway 144 and passed the school and then he crossed the old railroad tracks and kept going. He heard the sound of a vehicle coming up behind him. His first thought was that it was his father or a truant officer or that Wendy lady and the principal. He squeezed his handlebars and cussed and looked over at the trees, mapping out some impossible escape route. It wasn't them, though, just some old white pickup truck. He stayed on the road leading to his mother's, pedaling, pushing forward, and in no time a thin sheet of sweat began to appear across his back and legs, so that he could feel his shirt sticking to him like another layer of skin.

Jimmy opened the heavy glass door to the sheriff's office and entered. He didn't have much time before he was supposed to meet Carol for lunch, but he wanted to stop in and say hi to Davis. An

old lady with white hair sat at a desk, working on a crossword puz-
zle. Soft music played from a little radio by her phone. She looked
up and smiled at Jimmy. "What can I do for you?"

"Is the sheriff around?"

She opened the top drawer of her desk and slid the crossword
in there. "Do you want to report a crime?"

"No, I just wanted to say hi."

When she didn't respond to this, he said, "He's an old friend."

She picked up the phone and rested it on her shoulder.
"What's your name?"

"Jimmy Wills."

Titling her head, she studied him closer, as if she didn't believe
him. "Truman and Dot Wills' boy?"

"Yeah."

"Huh." Then she dialed some number and spoke into the
phone, saying that Jimmy Wills was here. "Take a seat. He'll be
right out."

Jimmy turned back to a strip of mismatched plastic chairs. On
the wall, above them, was a large map of the state of Florida with
Portisville highlighted in blue. Before he could sit down, he heard
Davis' voice, "Say it isn't so."

A smile crept across Jimmy's face and then Davis was on him, a
big friendly hug, bathing him in a mild cologne that could have
been Old Spice. "About time you came to see me. So how the hell
are you?"

"Good, good, can't complain." Jimmy couldn't help but notice
that the sheriff's hair had whitened and he had the beginnings of a
potbelly.

"Doesn't do any good."

"Sure doesn't."

They walked back into Davis' office. The sheriff sat behind an
oak desk in a squeaky chair. Jimmy sat across from him. There was a
white-curtained window behind Davis that Jimmy thought probably overlooked downtown. A gun rack, stocked full of rifles, stood

against one wood-paneled wall and a few framed photos lined the other. Most of the photos had Davis shaking hands with important-looking men in suits. Politicians, Jimmy figured. There was also a row of pictures of Davis' father in uniform. The resemblance was striking: the extra flesh at the dimpled chin and deep wrinkles on the outside borders of their eyes.

"So what do you think of your old hometown?"

Jimmy said, "Not much." The words came quickly and he hoped his tone wasn't too strong. Davis had done nothing to him.

Davis smiled. "Oh, come on now. It's not that bad. What about your old man?"

"He's still a pain in the ass."

Davis laughed. "No, that hasn't changed. He is looking better than he was a couple months ago. I thought we were going to lose him."

"I heard."

"It was nice of you come back to see him."

Jimmy said, "Yeah, well he called me."

"But still you came back."

Jimmy resisted telling him the details of Truman's initial phone call and the requests to kill him. What difference would it make if he told Davis? Why not tell him? It wasn't that he was trying to protect his father, but he didn't have the time to go into all of that now. Plus, some part of Jimmy still wondered if that was the real reason Truman had called him home.

The telephone rang and Davis winked at Jimmy and then answered it. As he spoke into the phone, Jimmy remembered when the sheriff drove him to North Carolina that final time, after Truman had been arrested for the wreck. On the long drive much was said, promises to stay in touch and possible visits, but what Jimmy remembered now, most clearly, was Davis saying, a few miles into South Carolina, "Boy, people will disappoint you every day of your life if you let them."

Davis hung the phone up and shook his head. "It's a mess."

"What's that?"

"This missing girl."

Jimmy said, "Saw some flyers for her, reminded me of Mom."

Davis offered a pained smile. "Yeah, me too."

"Anything on her?"

Davis said, "Not really."

"Sheriff, let me ask you something."

"Sure, shoot."

"It's about Mom's murder."

Davis shifted in his chair and leaned forward so that his elbows rested on the desk. "What about it?"

"Do you think he did it?"

Davis said, "Truman? No, I don't. Why do you ask?"

"Then why did it go to trial? I mean, you're the sheriff. You pressed the charges, arrested him. You didn't have to."

Davis rubbed his forehead a couple times real hard. "Look, Jimmy, you were just a kid then. You don't know how it was."

"I don't understand what you're saying."

"I'm saying that we all have to do things we don't want to do. We arrested him because we had nothing else, no other suspects. Your mother's family wanted someone to blame. The town wanted a Band-Aid so that they could sleep at night and not have to worry about it happening to them, which I can understand to a point. It's a natural reaction. The prosecutor was young—it was his first big case—and wanted a conviction for murder under his belt. He seemed to have a hard-on for your old man from the start. He knew that Truman dealt. He also knew that we were friends, so he didn't listen to me when I told him we didn't have a case. The whole thing was a big mess. It shouldn't have gone to trial. Only evidence we had was some circumstantial stuff that didn't amount to much. You may have also heard that I didn't try hard enough, let an old friend get away. That's bullshit. You can't convict somebody of a crime they didn't commit. Truman was out of town that night. He had an alibi. He told me he didn't do it, and I believed him."

"Why did people think he did it?"

Davis leaned back in his chair and smiled at Jimmy. "You see, the thing is Truman was always an outsider, even if he did spend most of his life here. He did his thing and went about his business and didn't like people who wanted to know more about him. Hell, half the trouble Truman has, no, more than half, he creates for himself. People expect certain things—I'm not saying it's right—but they do. He didn't act like they thought a grieving man should. He didn't cry at the funeral. Never visited the grave after she was buried. People have different ways of dealing with death. But instead of making it easy on himself and doing what people expected, your old man gave them the finger every time he could."

Giving them the finger, Jimmy thought, *sounds like Truman.* "Did you visit him in jail?"

"Every other week."

"You kept the house up, too?"

"Yeah, I did what I could."

"Why?"

"Because we were friends, like brothers."

Jimmy looked down at his watch. He only had five minutes to get over to the diner. "I better be going."

"You got plans for lunch?"

"Yeah."

"You gonna be around long?"

Jimmy stood up. "A day or two."

Davis stood as well. "We'll see you again before you go."

After a quick handshake, the two men headed for the door.

Davis told Ellen to hold his calls, then locked the door to his office. He looked out the window and saw Jimmy crossing the street, heading toward the diner. Sitting back down, Davis heard Jimmy's question again and wondered what the chances were that he would come home at the same time as this girl showed up missing. Pretty damned slim, he guessed. Dot's case had, of course, stayed in the back of his mind, only popping up occasionally, like when the Dobson girl was killed. Now though, it was right here in front of him.

He shook his head and walked over to the file cabinet. At the back was Dot's file, an inch-thick manila envelope with her name in the upper window. On the front of the envelope were three stamped red lines. Each line contained a different title: DATE REPORTED, ARREST DATE, DATE OF CONVICTION. The first two were filled in but the conviction line was still empty.

As he sat back down, Davis dropped the folder onto the center of the desk, atop the one Bird had given him on Teresa Martin. He looked down at Dot's folder again and hesitated before opening it, wondering what good could come of looking at it now. But something inside of him, that same something that had driven him for more than two decades to ask the why and when and how of crimes, both petty and large, had to at least look again.

The first thing he saw when he opened the file was a photo of Dot in the woods where they had found her. She was wearing one of Truman's pajama tops that stretched down to her knees. Her eyes were open in the photo and there was a small bullet hole in her forehead. Around her the ground looked like a solid sheet of pine needles. He rifled through another set of photos of her, all taken at the gravesite from different angles, all showing a beautiful woman dead. Then he came across a pair of photos of Truman, a side and a front shot. The scratches on Truman's neck and shoulder were circled in black ink. The two on his right neck and one on the left neck didn't look too bad—no more than what a stick would cause if you brushed by it—but the one on his left shoulder looked deeper.

Davis read the official report he had filed. Truman said he came home around six and noticed a couple spots of blood on the kitchen floor, which he figured, at first, were from an accident her or Jimmy had the night before. Then he saw that she wasn't in their bed, so he woke Jimmy up and asked him if he knew where she was and the boy said no. After telling him to go back to sleep, Truman walked around the house, inside and out, seeing nothing unusual. Her purse was on the kitchen table, and her car was in the front yard with the keys in the ignition like always. It looked as if she had simply vanished. At 6:30, he called Davis. Davis got there by seven and Truman was sitting on the edge of the porch, smoking a cigarette, his hair wet with sweat. Again, they woke Jimmy and asked if he knew where she was, but he said he didn't know. The last time he had seen her was the previous night.

Davis and Truman walked the woods around the house for an hour, calling her name but to no avail. After Truman drove Jimmy to school, he came back and called all of her relatives but none had heard from her. By noon, Davis had all five members of Portisville's police force searching for her—some were out in the woods while others went from house to house on Highway 144 asking if anyone had seen or heard anything. Three days later they found her in the woods, buried in a shallow grave, less than a mile from the home. Lab results later proved that the blood on the floor was indeed Dot's.

So those were what Davis believed, at the time he filed the report, were the facts of the case. He had always assumed the killer was a drifter passing through. A long-haired man, wearing an army jacket, had made a scene downtown, refusing to pay for a meal, the day before she was killed, but that was the seventies and everybody had long hair and army jackets. Needless to say, they never found that man.

The prosecutor tried to convict Truman with circumstantial evidence—most of it very circumstantial, Davis thought. Dot was shot with a .38. Truman owned three that Davis knew of. He kept one under his car seat, one under the sofa and another in the freezer. But .38s were common enough handguns and most people in town bought the bullets for them from the same place. Truman's guns were confiscated a week after the murder, but the prosecutor argued that any evidence would certainly have been removed by then. There was also no sign of forced entry but Truman claimed that it wasn't unusual for them to leave the door unlocked. Truman's shoe prints were found at the gravesite, but so many pairs of shoes had walked across it during the search that Truman's lawyer said to focus on one pair was ludicrous. The biggest issue dealt with the scratches on Truman's upper body and the corresponding tissue found under Dot's nails.

The prosecutor said that because Dot was shot at close range it was very likely that she put up a struggle, just the kind of struggle that could produce the scratches on Truman's neck and shoulder. Truman's claims of sex the previous afternoon held up in court as the lab technicians could only date the flesh under Dot's nails to within twelve hours of her death.

Davis remembered a couple small things he had left out of the file, things that had seemed to him to be more circumstantial evidence. One of them had to do with Jimmy. Truman had said that he woke Jimmy up after getting home and before calling Davis. The day they found Dot's body Davis asked Jimmy again if he remembered anything else about that night and the boy said no. The only thing he remembered was the next morning when his father and Davis woke him up. Davis asked if he remembered his father alone waking him up before Davis got there. Jimmy said no. This, Davis figured, was just a sleepy, tired kid's story. At the time, Davis was willing to give Truman the benefit of the doubt. He also didn't want the prosecutor to get ahold of the boy.

The other thing had to do with Dan. Dan said in his original statement that he and Truman got back just before five while Truman said it wasn't until six. In subsequent interviews, in the days that followed, Dan changed his time to six. Again Davis figured Dan was just tired that first time he'd asked about it, so he didn't push it.

A month after they discovered her body, the prosecutor told Davis to arrest Truman. The prosecutor, knowing he didn't have a strong case, was hoping, Davis believed, that the local need for someone to blame this on might be enough to get a conviction. He spent much of his time portraying Truman as a violent outlaw, a lifelong criminal. He'd had a pair of arrests for assault years earlier and three minor drug charges. All these were small things, but according to the prosecutor, just the kinds of things that would eventually lead to a man murdering his wife in a violent rage. Dot was portrayed as a woman who drank to excess, who had been arrested twice for DUI's in Tallahassee. These portraits of the Willses led, in the prosecutor's argument, to a wild couple that were due to blow up one day. The jury didn't buy it; they had plenty of reasonable doubt. There simply wasn't enough evidence, nothing that put Truman there at the time of her murder, and nothing that was concrete enough for those dozen people to send him away.

It was soon after the murder and trial that Truman seemed to change. He had never been Mr. Nice Guy, but it was this cantankerous nature that Davis had always found somewhat charming. But a certain hardness seemed to come over him, a meanness that Davis had never seen in him before. Davis thought it was his way of grieving, but if so, he had never come back around.

Davis knew that time tended to have a way of helping you see things a bit more clearly. He was hoping that would be the case here. At the time, he had only briefly considered the possibility that Truman might have something to do with the murder. He was a young sheriff and his friend was grieving and it didn't seem right to push him. Now though, looking at the case again, he did see a few questions he would have pursued. He still didn't believe that if given the same set of evidence today he would run out and arrest the man, but it was enough to leave a kernel of doubt there.

Maybe when this was all over with the missing girl he would look more into Dot's case. But what good would that do? He couldn't try Truman again and didn't really want to know if his friend was involved in this thing that had been clouding his life and this town for the last twenty-some years. What bothered him most about this case was not that it was the one smudge in his otherwise pretty good run as the sheriff, but that he was unable to serve justice of some sort to a woman he had considered a friend.

Bobby rode his bike along Highway 144. Every few minutes, a car or pickup would speed by. Thankfully, it wasn't his father or anybody he knew. He passed gravel driveways, every hundred yards or so, each one leading to a house. They all looked alike—small white houses with leaning porches. The sameness to them made him wonder if they were sold that way, bent and ready to deteriorate. An old black man sat on one of the porches with a cane across his lap, rocking and bobbing his head slightly as if to some rhythm only he could hear. Bobby imagined the man standing up and carrying a pitcher of ice cold water out to the road and handing it to him, or maybe a little white Dixie cup like he'd seen those people on TV give to bike riders in road races.

He didn't know how far away his mother's apartment was, how many actual miles, only that it usually took about twenty minutes when his father drove him over there. He had only ridden his bike to her place once before. That time it had taken him over an hour. His mother had yelled at him, told him that it was a dangerous road and that he didn't need to ever do that, but Bobby had been trying to call and she wasn't answering. He knew that if he told her what he had done at school she would be disappointed. But he didn't care about that. He wanted to talk to her. He needed to see her.

There was a gas station on the side of the road and Bobby almost passed it before he made a sharp right and turned into the parking lot. The lot was empty and Bobby set his bike against the bench in front of the store. On the window was a poster for a missing girl. She had blond hair and was smiling. Bobby thought for a moment about how his mother seemed to be missing from his life.

Inside the store, the A/C felt good on his arms and he thought he might like to stay in here for a couple minutes and just rest and let the cool air cover his body and dry him out. His father had stopped here the last time he had dropped Bobby off at his mother's, so he knew where the Coke box was in the back of the store.

At the counter, he paid the man with change from his plastic bag. The man shook his head and gave up on counting the pennies and just waved Bobby out of the store. Sitting against the curb, Bobby turned to a field across the road that had been stripped of trees so that it looked dirty and old, filled with mud and tire tracks of some sort. There were big yellow tractors and field-plowing machines but there was nobody working. Bobby thought it must be fun to drive one of those things, sitting high above everyone else. The Coke tasted good and cold and the shade from the store made him feel good, too. He then decided that this was a fine day, that it was much better than being in school. No matter how much trouble he would get in, he had come this far while the rest of those fools were stuck in class learning capitals with old beady-eyed Mrs. Floyd.

The counterman came outside and lit a cigarette. Bobby looked back at him and the man blew a thin wall of smoke up into the sky, then lifted his foot and stuck it into a garbage can, pushing the trash down. He had shorts on and white socks and black shoes. He sat down on the curb, a foot or two away, and said, "Hot day."

Bobby said, "They're all hot."

The man laughed. "Truer words were never spoken. You supposed to be in school, Einstein?"

Bobby said, "No."

"Why not?"

"Got out early."

"Don't bullshit me. It's barely one o'clock. School doesn't get out early on Fridays."

"Mine did." Bobby wondered if he was some kind of undercover truant office that was stationed at this store, waiting for boys just like him to come in for a break from some long journey so that he could bust them.

"Where do you go?"

"Portisville Elementary."

"A county back."

"I know."

"Where you on your way to now?"

"Fleetsville."

"A couple more miles down the road."

"I know."

"What are you going there for?"

"Gonna see my mother."

"The road is dangerous on a bike." The man finished his cigarette and threw it at the ground, then lit another one. Bobby stared at the discarded cigarette, which had landed not far from some spilled gasoline out by the pumps. He hoped it didn't light up the whole damned lot. After a minute, Bobby stood up and stepped on it. The man laughed. "Think of the insurance money you just cost me."

Bobby avoided the man's stare and turned back to the road. "Not much traffic so far."

"It's bound to pick up."

"I'm almost there."

"I can get you a ride."

"No, I'm okay."

Then the telephone rang and the man stood, said, "Shit," took a couple quick puffs of the cigarette and then threw it down. When he was inside, Bobby jumped up and stepped on that cigarette and started to ride out of the lot. He had gone a good twenty yards past the store before remembering that he forgot his Coke, but he wasn't going to go back for it now.

Unfortunately, the man was right because once Bobby got back on the road traffic did indeed pick up. He wondered if maybe it was because there weren't as many trees like they had in Portisville and people drove faster when there weren't any trees around. Maybe trees made people think that a deer could jump out at any minute. His father had hit one at the beginning of the summer, and Bobby remembered helping him wash the smelly blood off the front bumper of their truck.

Soon, the trees all but disappeared and were replaced by stores on the side of the road and McDonaldses and Burger Kings and a big shopping center with grocery stores and the Eckerd's where his mother had worked after first moving out of their house. He passed a series of large, white apartment buildings and then saw the sign for hers, WATER OAKS LANDING, and turned in to the parking lot and rode under the big oak tree with the low-hanging limbs. His mother had told him they had to build the parking lot around the tree because it had been there long before they'd ever considered apartments. He rode past two pink buildings until he got to the last one; the one she lived in.

Jimmy walked in the diner and scanned the room but saw no sign of Carol yet among the busy lunch crowd. Opposite the front door there was a counter with swivel stools. On the back wall was a large, rectangular hole where he could see a tall black cook working. A row of booths, to his right, lined the wall and there were a dozen square tables in a single row separating the booths from the counter.

An older woman in jeans and a ketchup-stained T-shirt walked by, holding in each hand a plastic yellow plate full of fries and a sandwich, and said, "Seat yourself."

Jimmy decided on a booth, mostly so that he could he see out the window and catch Carol as she came in. The crowd around him spoke in multiple conversations, the chatter of voices up and down, cut by the occasional call from the kitchen that an order was up. He tried to follow a conversation on the benefits of leasing a car over buying but then someone let out a laugh, distracting him. The place smelled of coffee and grease and fried meat and cigarettes and didn't seem to have a No Smoking section as people lit up in all corners of the room. Jimmy wondered if he'd been here before, thought he probably had but could not remember. That was fine with him. He'd about had it with all the memories the town had given back to him in the last couple days.

The lady with the ketchup-stained T-shirt walked over and sat across from Jimmy in the booth and let out a big breath as if her ass hitting the seat had caused air to be expelled from her lungs. "Lunch time is too busy to sit alone at a booth."

"I have a date coming."

She said, without looking up, "What can I get you to drink, then?"

"Iced tea."

"And for her?"

"The same."

"The special is a barbecue pork sandwich." Then she was gone toward the counter, refilling coffee for a man in a flannel shirt and red baseball hat.

Date? He hadn't thought of it really as a date. Just something to do, someone to talk to. The word had just come to him, but now it made him question his subconscious, and the signals given and received. What if she thought of it as a date? Hell, he told himself, it didn't matter one way or the other.

He looked out the window and saw again the posters for the missing girl. They made him think of the conversation he had just had with Davis. He was glad he'd asked him about his mother's murder, about his father's possible involvement. It cleared up a few things for him but not everything. Not that he didn't believe Davis, but he and Truman had been, in the sheriff's own words *like brothers*, and Jimmy wondered just how much Davis would be willing to do for Truman. He didn't think he would be willing to lie in a court of law.

Outside, cars continued to pass slowly by, an occasional honk and a driver waving to somebody on the sidewalk. The majority of the cars were not new, as if the latest models hadn't quite made it to Portisville yet. The few people out walking around were older, closer to his father's age, some rough-looking men, a lot of them in overalls and work boots. Although farming wasn't the only kind of work in Portisville and the surrounding small towns, hands-on physical work certainly outnumbered office work.

On the other side of the park, where he had met Carol the day before, the Ferris wheel turned slowly and the pirate ship rose and fell as workers tested rides, getting ready for the first night of the fair. A wave of excitement, a type he hadn't felt in a while, came over him. The fair might just be fun.

Then, across the street, a man walked slowly along, his hands bouncing off store windows. At first, Jimmy thought he looked injured in some way, using storefronts to hold himself up, but he soon realized that the man was in the midst of a middle-of-the-day drunk. One of the shop owners walked out his door, said something to the man, who shook his fist in response and then kept on his way, eventually making it to a narrow alley where he braced himself against a wall and vomited.

The waitress slid the two glasses of tea on the table in front of Jimmy and walked away. When Jimmy looked back at the street, he saw the man head deeper into the alley as the shop owner stood outside spraying his window with cleaner and scrubbing the glass with a white cloth.

He wondered if he should have gotten Carol tea or if he should have even gotten anything himself. Was it rude to drink before the other person got there? It had been a while since he'd been on a date that didn't start in a bar. He shook his head again, acting like a damned kid. He took a long mouthful of his tea, which tasted good and cold.

A cellular phone rang. A large man at the counter in overalls and a dusty T-shirt pulled the phone from his back pocket and spoke into it, laughing at something the person on the other end said. It didn't take long before it became just one more conversation among the others. Jimmy wondered again if he'd been here before. The grease stains on the walls and the smoke stains on the ceiling tiles confirmed that it was old enough, and he imagined himself sitting at the counter, drinking a vanilla shake with his mother, spinning around on the stools and laughing as the cool drink satisfied him after a long day of playing in the sun. But that wasn't what his childhood was like. That was some TV show version of what being a kid in a small southern town was like.

"Hey, Jimmy Wills."

Carol stood in front of him, smiling, in a pair of jeans and a white button-down shirt. Her hair looked freshly combed, her lipstick newly applied and the shirt she wore wasn't tucked in. There was something about this woman wearing an un-tucked shirt that he found downright sexy. He started to stand and said, "Have a seat."

"I'm sorry I'm late. I couldn't get off the register. Fridays are pretty busy."

"Don't sweat it."

She picked up her glass and eyed it. "Iced tea?"

He nodded.

"Great, my favorite."

She took a big mouthful of the tea. They each took additional mouthfuls of the beverage as if it held the secrets to the way their conversation should go. He studied her face, the softness of it, her hazel eyes, her clean, white neck. Carol said, "So what have you been doing today?"

"I went for a drive after I called you, went by the school and then by Mom's grave."

"How was that?"

"I didn't stop at the school, but it was actually pretty good to go by the cemetery." He thought about the fact that the visit had calmed him in a way he hadn't expected and how in a sense the visit had then led him to Davis and those questions.

Carol said, "It always makes me feel good to visit my mother's grave."

"It looked just like I remembered."

"I should probably visit more often."

They smiled at each other until Jimmy turned to the counter where the cook was calling out the number of another finished order.

When Jimmy turned back to Carol, he said, "You still want to go to the fair?"

She said, "Of course. Have you decided to stay?"

"Yeah, why not. I don't have to start another job for a couple days."

She smiled again and put her hands on his, which were resting on either side of his glass, for a second and then pulled them away. "Good, I can't wait."

"It should be fun."

"Tell me about your work. What do you paint, houses or businesses?"

Jimmy crunched the cube of ice in his mouth. "Mostly houses. I work alone and do both insides and out."

"Do you like it?"

Jimmy didn't think he'd ever been asked that before. "Yeah," he said, "I do. I like how you start out with one thing and make it another. Also how you can see your progress daily. Maybe that's a simple way to look at it."

"No, I understand what you mean. That's one of the things I like about painting. You have this white canvas and some image in your mind that you're trying to put up on that canvas to transform it and if you're lucky in the end they match."

Jimmy wanted to also say how he liked the mindlessness of the work. Standing on that ladder with the brush or sprayer in hand you didn't worry about the world or the stock market or what the price of gas was or any of that other shit, just this thing in front of you. How he liked to make something old and tarnished look new again. Like he was covering up some messy past and giving it a fresh start.

He said, "How long you been painting?"

"About seven years. Like I was saying yesterday, I went to Florida

State and studied art there. I paint every day now, a couple hours, usually in the morning before work."

"Ever try and sell any of it?"

She smiled and he thought it looked like she might have blushed. Just then the waitress walked over. "Have you decided?"

Carol looked at Jimmy and smiled, shrugging her shoulders. He said, "We'll take two of the lunch specials with french fries."

When the waitress walked away, Carol said, "What is the special?"

"Barbecue sandwich."

"Chicken or pork?"

"Pork, I assume."

She frowned. "I'm vegetarian."

"Shit, I'm sorry." He waved to try and get the waitress' attention, sending Carol into a fit of laughter. He sat back down. "Let me guess. You're not vegetarian."

She shook her head. "I couldn't help myself."

Despite feeling silly, he also felt relieved in knowing that she wasn't afraid to joke with him. "So, have you sold any of your paintings?"

That shy look came across her face again. "A few. They have some of my paintings in the library here and some at State. There is also an exhibit of my work over at the University of West Florida in Pensacola."

"An exhibit?"

"About a dozen full-sized drawings and a few sketches."

"So you're a real artist?"

She laughed. "I'm a painter. Who knows what makes art? They mostly like the stuff because it has a Florida flavor to it. There's a lot of gators and landscapes."

"Maybe I'll buy one."

"If you're nice to me I might just give you one."

They laughed as the waitress set the plates down in front of them and they began eating.

Bobby lifted his bike into the bike rack. He walked through the hall-way, past the laundry room and into the center of the building. The apartment building was a big, three-story square with the middle cut out. To Bobby, the place looked more like a hotel than an apartment complex. In the courtyard, he walked by palm trees and the fenced-in pool. There was an older lady sitting in one of the lawn chairs by the pool. She had on dark sunglasses and there was a lot of white flesh hanging out of her bathing suit.

He was surprised that there weren't any kids there, since the pool had always been filled with them on his other visits, but then he figured it was still too early and that they were all probably at school. The last time he had been here he played a game of water volleyball with some boys. He remembered how he got to be in the shallow end and scored three points and how he seemed to shoot straight out of the water when the ball came in his direc-tion. He wanted to go swimming now because he was hot but was afraid that the lady would start asking questions about why he wasn't in school.

On the third floor, he walked along the outside hall, passed iden-tical white wood doors with room numbers in gold stickers above the peepholes. Some people had grills outside their apartments and others had chairs. He stopped when he got to her door, number 37. Against the wall, there was a plastic chair with a plant in a basket on the seat. The leaves of the plant hung over the side of the basket, past the chair's seat and arms and rested on the green Astroturf carpet that lined the hall.

Bobby tried to look in the window but the curtains were drawn and he could see nothing. His mother worked nights sometimes and he wondered if she might be asleep. If she was, he didn't want to wake her. He thought he might just sit here for a little while to see if maybe she came outside to go swimming or to get some sun. He lifted the plant from the chair and set it on the ground. Then he sat down and closed his eyes, happy again for the shade, and the possibility that his mother might be a few feet away, just on the other side of the door.

Davis pulled in behind the row of cars on the side of the road. Besides the two Portisville patrol cars that he'd left earlier, there were now three unmarked cruisers with state license tags, a crime scene investigation van from Tallahassee, and a news van. Strips of yellow police tape surrounded the outside of the trees for as far as he could see. He was impressed and suspicious at how fast these men worked.

Davis walked toward them, straightening his belt along the way. A dark-haired man in khakis and a white polo shirt was talking to a reporter. The reporter was a blond woman in her early twenties, who shared a striking resemblance to Teresa Martin. Davis recognized her as the night reporter for one of the Tallahassee stations.

Bird met Davis a few feet away from the reporter. Bird looked tired and sweaty and there was a tear in the left shoulder of his uniform. Davis said, "What's this all about?"

Bird said, "Name's Vince Strane. He's the head investigator for the State Bureau of Investigation."

Strane said something to the reporter and she turned and smiled at Davis. He felt his gut go heavy for a moment and then she was walking toward him, a tall cameraman walking behind her. She offered a manicured hand. "Sheriff Davis, I'm Tammy Sullins, Fox 9 news. I was wondering if you could answer a few questions for me, about the Teresa Martin investigation."

Davis said, "Not a lot to tell."

She said, "That's okay," then applied some shiny lip gloss and told the cameraman she was ready.

"We are here in Portisville, Florida, the town where Teresa Martin's Honda Civic was found abandoned on the side of the road. With me is Sheriff Davis. What can you tell us, Sheriff?"

Davis felt his heart tighten a little as the camera pointed in his direction. Behind them, a dog barked in the woods. *The hounds are working and here we are talking,* he thought.

"Not a lot."

"Do you care to elaborate?"

"No, not at this time."

"Anything else you could tell us about the case?"

For a moment, Davis felt like it was twenty years before and he was standing on the steps of the county courthouse in Tallahassee and a eager young reporter just like this one was asking him about the Dot Wills murder case. He said, "No."

She frowned and looked past him. "How long have you been sheriff here?"

Davis had about enough of this as he could take. "How long you been alive?"

She turned to him quick. "Twenty-four years."

"Longer than you been alive, young lady."

This seemed to stump her because she lowered the microphone for a second. Before she could say anything else, Davis walked on past her, over toward Vince Strane. Behind him, he could hear the reporter. "And so the search continues for Teresa Martin."

Strane smile at Davis. "You have quite a way with the press." Up close, Davis could see that emblazoned on his shirt over the right side of his chest was *Florida Bureau of Investigation.* He also noticed that the top part of his right earlobe was missing. It was not a new wound.

Bird introduced the two men and they shook hands. Davis didn't like the way this man was staring at him, but ignored it and said, looking down at the plastic bag Strane pulled from his front pocket, "What did you find?"

Bird said, "In the back pocket of the jeans, we found a business card from Trim's Taxidermy."

"Trim?"

"Yes, sir."

Strane handed Davis the bag. The card looked like your basic white business card and had a picture of a stuffed duck in the center with the name of the business and phone number printed below it. There was no blood or anything too obvious, just a bent corner, which you'd expect from a card left in a pair of jeans for any length of time. "How about in the woods?"

Bird said, "We've been out here four hours and haven't seen a thing. Covered the distance between here and where we found the car yesterday and a mile in all directions."

"How many men are out there?"

Bird looked back to Strane, who said, "Two of yours and six of mine."

"How much farther you plan on going?"

"We've covered all the trails, but we're gonna keep going over the ground until it gets dark."

"Don't suppose there is too much I can do around here. I'm going to go see Trim."

Bird said, "I'm coming with you."

On the way to Trim's Taxidermy, Davis said, "They treating you okay?"

"Yeah, they're fine."

"All right, I don't want no big shots coming down here taking over on us."

"No, they're okay. Just doing their job. Did you find anything in the folder?"

At first, Davis thought that he was talking about the Wills case, but then he realized Bird was referring to Teresa Martin's folder. "No, nothing really."

The folder included a dozen pictures of the girl, starting at age five up to one taken by her roommate the day before she disappeared. Her room looked just as he thought a co-ed's dorm room would: posters and paintings on the walls, brushes and combs on a dresser, mirrors, and some clothes thrown on a blue bedspread. He'd read a letter she wrote to her mother the week before and seen her grades from last year. All of it leading, in Davis' opinion, to an average twenty-year-old girl.

Trim's Taxidermy was not the kind of place one would just happen upon. There was a sign for it on Highway 144, which led you down Hollow's Grove Road and then you came to another in a se-

ries of signs—old planks of 2 x 4, carved into arrows, some said
TRIM'S TAXIDERMY, while others simply said TRIM or TAXI—all
instructing right turns. These constant turns made it seem as
though you were driving in a circle, or might pop out onto the
highway again at any moment, but Davis knew that wouldn't happen and that they were driving deeper and deeper into the interior
of Portisville.

An old, faded Indian totem pole stood in the center of Trim's
front yard like some decrepit centerpiece. On the front porch of
the house were various pieces of the man's work—a couple of
deer, an owl, and half a dozen raccoons—all startlingly accurate,
shaded by a leaning green tarpaulin, which hung down from the
roof to the totem pole. Davis knew that the stuff Trim left out
front were items customers didn't pick up and usually sold for
half price.

Bird said, "You don't really think Trim has something to do
with this, do you?"

Davis shook his head. "I don't know. It's not likely, but if we knew
for sure then it wouldn't be called investigating. Plus, I don't know
about you but I don't want to be out in the woods with a bunch of
strangers, all of who happen to be carrying loaded weapons."

"Sounds like hunting."

The joke was not lost on Davis, who said, "That's why I don't
hunt."

The two men walked around back where Trim's garage-sized
workshop was located. Trim opened the door as they were about
to knock. He was about fifty and dressed in jeans and a blood-
stained, brown T-shirt and had on a Daniel Boone-style hat with
a raccoon tail hanging down the back of his neck. Tufts of his gray
hair shot out from the sides of the hat. He smiled at his visitors
with a clean-shaven face and said, "Sheriff. Deputy. To what do I
owe the honor?"

Trim started to offer his hand, then thought better of it and
withdrew, as if suddenly remembering what his hand had mo-

ments before been inside. Davis said, "You hear anything about a missing girl?"

Trim said, "No, sir. Can't say I have."

Davis told him about Teresa Martin and how they found the jeans, which he made a point of saying may or may not be connected to the girl, with one of Trim's business cards in the back pocket.

Trim said, "Goodness me. Well, come in here for a second. I got some glue drying that I need to set."

What struck Davis most about the shop, even more than the rank, dried blood smell was how dark it was. The only visible light was one hanging bulb over the work desk. Trim leaned forward, his elbows resting on the desk, and with a forefinger moved the tack-sized eye of a squirrel into place. When he was done, he lifted the animal up and examined its face to make sure the eyes were level.

"Sorry about that. It's just that if I don't get the glue on pretty quick it makes all kind of mess." He walked past Davis and turned on an additional overhead light, which lit the shop up, revealing wall-to-wall shelving filled with a vast menagerie of dead and stuffed animals: more squirrels, rabbits, raccoons, a fox, bear heads and paws, a lone moose head, and a bevy of snakes.

Trim pulled a seat from under the workbench and two folding chairs from a corner of the room and the three men sat in an uneven circle, facing each other. Trim said, "Now, a college girl, huh?" and scratched at his chin. "Not many girls come in here, especially not those that are college-minded."

Bird said, "Well, she wouldn't have actually had to come in here."

"Good point. You say you found her yesterday?"

Bird said, "We found a pair of pants, but we're not sure if they're even hers."

Davis wondered if Trim would continue to parrot their questions back to them, as a man who works alone with dead animals, miles from anyone, probably relished the opportunity for conversation. Davis noticed that Bird was staring at a five-gallon bucket full of what looked like blood mixed with some sort of yellow mucus material. Trim must have noticed, too, because he turned to the deputy and said, "That's my embalming vat."

Bird didn't respond to this, but kept studying the bucket as if it held some secrets he desperately needed to know.

Davis said, "So you haven't had any unusual customers lately?"

"I haven't had a customer in over a week. I do get calls from all over. My cards show up in the damnedest places. A man called me from Tennessee last night, asked if I specialized in fish, which is the one thing I don't do." The ignorance of the man from Tennessee was apparently hilarious to Trim because he fell into a laughing fit.

When the laughing died down, Davis said, "Well, like I said, we just wanted to touch base with you. Can you make me a list of all your clients and all the hunting shops your cards might be in?"

"Sure, Sheriff, of course."

Davis stood. Bird and Trim followed suit. Then the three men walked outside, back into the boiling sunlight. Trim said, "If either of you want, you can have any of those critters on the front porch."

Davis smiled and said, "No, I'm fine. What about you, Bird?"

"No, thanks."

Back at the front of the house, Davis stopped at the Indian totem pole with its washed-out reds and blues. He could remember when it was new, ten or fifteen years ago, and thought, now, that time had sure done a number on it.

Bird said, "What do you think?"

"Like he said, Bird, his cards are all over."

"Did that place give you the creeps?"

"Son, anymore, a lot of places give me the creeps."

Jimmy stood on his father's porch and held the old man's .38 out toward the tree with the quarter nailed to it. The steamy, mid-afternoon Florida air was cut by the call of another red-winged blackbird, a breed he rarely saw in North Carolina. Jimmy searched the horizon but couldn't find the source. He turned back to the tree and stared at that silver dot and fired twice, but all that came back were simple thuds, then the whoosh of birds taking flight.

Jimmy sat back in his father's chair. It was rough in spots, full of lumps that jabbed him in the back, as if the thing had contorted to the old man's body. Lifting his feet up onto the banister, Jimmy leaned back and closed his eyes. Lunch with Carol had been good. There was something about her that made him feel comfortable. He wondered if the reason it had been so easy talking to her was because it couldn't work between them—he lived up there and she was here—which took away many of the usual pressures. But maybe that was why he was back here, so that he could meet her. Maybe it was fate, whatever the hell that was.

Out in the yard a slight gust cut the air and bent the first line of trees in the woods. Then, as quickly as it had come, it was gone and the trees stood there as stiff and upright as soldiers protecting whatever lay behind them.

Any discomfort he had felt in the chair earlier seemed to have disappeared as if it had now contorted to his shape. The day had taken on the feel of a vacation to him: nowhere to be, nothing to do, simply slow down and relax. The old familiar Florida heat reached him on the porch, causing a sheen of sweat to appear across his body. In a couple of months it would be winter. He had never really gotten used to the cold and wondered if it was because he grew up in Florida. This seemed silly, yet possible, to him. He liked the heat, always had as far back as he could remember and summer was his favorite time of the year. Sure, fall was beautiful in North Carolina and spring was lovely with everything in bloom, but it was the summer, working atop a ladder in a pair of cut-off shorts with the sun beating down on him like a slow-roasting oven set at ninety-six degrees, that he lived for. In the winter, nestled in those Carolina mountains, the threat of snow always placed his business and livelihood in jeopardy for three or four months a year. If he couldn't get inside work, which everyone wanted and there was never enough of, he would be faced with either being snowed out or freezing his ass off atop a ladder.

It had occurred to him more than once that he ought to move away from North Carolina. Whenever he would have these thoughts, always in the thick of winter, it was somewhere south that he would think about. Maybe eastern Georgia or the gulf coast of Mississippi or Louisiana. He'd even thought about Florida, somewhere like Orlando or Tampa, big cities with plenty of work that would keep him busy all year long. He hadn't ever considered coming back to Portisville. There was too much here, too many memories, too many things that were better left alone, in his opinion. Plus, there simply wouldn't be enough work for him in a town this size.

But maybe somewhere like Tallahassee or Pensacola, places where there was still a good bit of building going on and lots of older houses in need of fresh paint jobs. He would be close enough so that he could visit his mother's grave whenever he wanted. He could even see Carol again. *Come on Jimmy*, he told himself, *calm down.* He knew he shouldn't be thinking about her like that, hell, they barely knew each other, but he couldn't help himself. Why not let his imagination run wild? Why not take what was here in front of him?

Now, he felt something crawl across his right pant leg, down by his knee. At first, he thought it might be a spider, but it was too heavy for that. A cockroach? He opened his eyes. It was a damned lizard, sitting there, turning its head left and right, its chin bobbing up and down. Jimmy smiled and slowly moved his right hand from his chest to the side of his waist. The lizard didn't move. As Jimmy lifted his hand, the lizard looked up at him. Jimmy blew an easy cool breath, then reached down and grabbed the lizard. It wiggled back and forth, opening and closing its mouth. Jimmy put his right index finger by the lizard's mouth and it clamped down. No pain really, just a feeling of something there like what he imagined loop earrings would feel like. He lifted his hand and the lizard hung in the air, its legs wiggling about madly, its tail slanting and twisting this way and that. When the lizard let go, it fell to the porch floor and ran away. On the tip of Jimmy's finger, you could see three tiny white teeth like splinters. *Yeah,* he thought, laughing, *I could get used to this.*

He stood up and pointed the gun out at the tree and fired but without luck. He closed his eyes and pointed again in the direction of the tree, figuring he'd have about as much luck hitting the quarter this way. A moment before firing, his finger tickling the trigger, Jimmy opened his eyes and saw Truman standing in front of the tree. He lifted the gun out of reflex. The bullet sliced through the wood, inches above Truman's head. For a second, Jimmy couldn't be sure if his father was there or not, if his imagination had taken over, or if all of this—the phone call, being back in Portisville on his childhood porch and firing a gun at his father—was all some sick dream. He shook his head. It was no dream or phantom image, but Truman himself. Jimmy said, "Son of a bitch," as he dropped the gun and stared out at the old man.

Truman said, laughing, "Come on boy, you can do it," and then pulled a quarter from his pocket and held it up to his forehead with his right hand while stretching the left arm out like a scarecrow or some overall-wearing man practicing a cheerleading pose he hadn't quite mastered. Truman held the stance for a few seconds. His lips locked tight into a smile and his eyes shined bright with hurried breath, laughing like he was part of a vaudeville act, as if crowds cheered somewhere in his mind and young, thick-hipped, voluptuous women dropped to their knees at the mere sight of him.

When it became evident that Jimmy was not going to pick the gun up and take another shot, Truman slid the quarter back into his pocket, shrugged his shoulders and said, "Almost," as he started back for the porch.

Davis flicked his turn signal on and then eased into the familiar gravel lot in front of Dan's store. There was a man pumping gas into a beat-up truck. He smiled and waved at Davis who returned the gesture, trying to pull the man's name from the back of his mind, but he could not.

As Davis climbed out of the car, the man called across the lot, "Any luck with that girl?"

Davis stiffened his back. "Working on it."

When he walked inside, Dan was watching TV, laughing at something Davis couldn't see and wasn't curious enough to investigate. Dan turned to the door, offered a quick nod and smile, then pulled the fifth of Wild Turkey from its spot under the counter. Davis retrieved a bottle of Diet Pepsi before meeting Dan at the counter.

As the sheriff fixed a strong one, Dan turned the TV off and said, "So?"

"Don't start."

"Aw, come on."

Davis shook his head. "We found some jeans, might be hers. Something tells me they aren't though."

"Why?"

"It just doesn't make sense. Let's say something did happen to that girl out in the woods. Would whoever was involved leave something as obvious as her jeans on a damned tree?"

"Maybe it's a clue. Maybe he's playing with you."

"He who?"

Dan said, "I don't know. Whoever did this."

"We don't really know if anything has happened to her."

"Come on, Sheriff, people don't just disappear."

Davis said, "I know they don't."

"You hungry?"

Davis shook his head no as Dan cracked open a package of strawberry Pop-Tarts and pulled one out. "Try one of these."

"Not today. You want to play a hand?"

"You got money to lose?"

Davis said, "You pay my wages."

Dan smiled. "Very funny."

Behind the counter, the two men sat at opposite ends of the card table. Dan shuffled and called five-card draw. The first cards Davis was dealt—three sevens and a king and queen—lifted his spirits a bit, but then it occurred to him that he probably shouldn't be sitting here playing cards and having a drink. What if them boys from the State or that reporter stopped in? Hell, there wasn't much he could do. He just wanted a few minutes of normalcy. They had it all covered—had already shipped the pants back to Tallahassee for a bunch of tests.

Davis said, "Jimmy came by and saw me this morning."

"Looks good, doesn't he?"

"Guess what he asked me?"

"I don't know."

"Asked if Truman killed Dot."

Dan looked up at Davis, then took a generous mouthful of his drink. "And what did you tell him?"

"I told him no."

"He didn't do it."

"I know." Davis dropped the king and queen and asked for two cards. Dan took three. Davis got a six and a four. No help there. "I can't blame him. It's not something he can forget about."

"None of us can."

"I guess it would be different if we found the killer."

"I think so."

"So what do you got?"

Dan had two pair, queens and eights, not enough to beat the sheriff's three sevens. Davis began to shuffle the cards and figured that this was as good a time as any to ask about the old case. "Jimmy's question got me thinking, so I looked at Dot's old case file. Do you remember the morning you and Truman drove back?"

"Not really. That was a long time ago."

Davis wasn't sure how much he wanted to, or should, push. He dealt them each five cards. He had no pairs, no matching suits, nothing. Dan tossed three cards down and Davis gave him three new ones. He threw down two of his own cards and took two more, ended up with a pair of fours.

"I just wonder if you're still sure it was six that you guys got back in town."

"Didn't we cover this at the trial?"

"We did."

"That was twenty years ago. I'm sure if I said it was six then it was six."

"It's just that when I originally asked you told me it was five. Just wondering what made you change your mind about the time."

Dan gave him a long look, seemed to be studying his forehead and then the wall above his head. "I don't remember. Hell, I don't remember what time I took a shit yesterday."

"It's not the same thing."

"I'm not saying it is." Dan showed him his cards: a full house; a pair of nines and three aces. Then he got up to make some more drinks. Davis didn't like having to ask his friend these types of questions. He was tired but Jimmy's questions had got him going. There was no reason to be doing this, just pissing Dan off was all it was doing.

Davis dealt again, but he didn't care about the cards in front of him. After playing a hand in silence, Dan said, "So what's this rumor I heard about you letting Truman drive your squad car?"

Davis laughed. "Damn, it doesn't take long for word to travel around here."

"Small town."

"Nothing but."

"So it's true?"

"Guilty as charged."

As Dan went to the bathroom at the back of the store, Davis realized that the slight buzz he had been after had turned the corner into the beginnings of inebriation. In an attempt to combat this, he stood up and walked around the store and ate one of Dan's Pop-Tarts.

Dan came back out and said, "We done?"

"Yeah, I better get going." He walked up to the counter and blew his breath in Dan's direction. "Can you smell it on me?"

Dan said, "That's a first." He fanned the air in front of him. "Just bad breath."

After pouring himself a cup of coffee, Davis headed for the door. Dan called, "You want me to add that to your tab?"

"Might as well."

At the door, Davis turned back to Dan who had already taken his place again in front of the TV. The cards sat face down on the table next to Dan as if Davis could come back in an hour, a week or a month, and they could resume their game. "You going to the fair tonight?"

Dan shook his head. "Past my bedtime. What about you?"

"I don't have much choice."

The door rattled behind him and Davis headed for his car, considered going back by the crime scene again, but decided if they found anything they could call him, plus Bird was sure to give him a full report tonight. What he needed was a nap, something he hadn't needed or wanted in a while, but he didn't really have enough time for that. Maybe a little drive would do him good, give him time to drink his coffee and clear his head.

Jimmy and Truman stood, a couple feet apart, on the shore of Miller's Pond. They didn't speak for some time but held their fishing poles and stared out into the water. It had surprised Jimmy when the old man suggested it after his stunt in front of the tree, since they had only been fishing together a couple times. The sun felt good on Jimmy's back and he wondered what Carol was doing. He imagined her standing in front of an easel, painting alligators with feet shaped like the state of Florida walking through vast and sparse landscapes.

Truman said, "You make good money painting houses?"

"I do okay."

"Truck looks pretty old."

"Runs fine. Just needs a paint job."

"That shouldn't be a problem."

Jimmy laughed. "That's true. Shit, I just need some free time."

"I can give you some money."

Jimmy turned toward his father, unsure of how to read the statement. "That's okay."

"No, I mean a lot of money."

The old man looked at Jimmy once, then back out at the still water where a thin layer of gnats buzzed the surface. Jimmy hadn't thought about his father's money, which he figured there was probably a good chunk of buried somewhere. He didn't want any of it. He had done okay for himself, wasn't rich or even well-off, but he had a house and if he wanted something he could afford to buy it.

Jimmy said, "No thanks, I do fine on my own."

The end of Truman's pole bent forward like the elastic spine of a tent, but before he could even jerk back on the rod, the line fell slack. He shook his head as he cranked the ancient Zebco and the old, rotting line squeaked as it disappeared into the little ball of a reel. After securing another worm to the hook, he cast the line back out into the water, which rippled for a second and then settled as if its stillness hadn't been violated by entry moments before.

Truman continued, "Ten thousand dollars if you'll put me out of my misery."

Jimmy closed his eyes, then looked up at the deep blue sky, which seemed to go on forever. The request no longer seemed real, only comical and lacking malice. Jimmy thought they had made it past that, so that this offer seemed more desperate-sounding than anything.

"Twenty thousand." Truman spoke without emotion. "We'll make it look like a suicide. Just shoot me and place the gun in my hand. I'll write a suicide note. Walk away and never come back."

Jimmy didn't say anything for a long beat, as the idea swam around his mind, surreal and unfathomable. Two days before, the notion of seeing his father again or the two of them standing together fishing, would have never crossed his mind, and now this. He was angry for his father's insistence, his willingness to pull him down, for the fact that he had called him after all these years, not to make peace or see how his only child had turned out but to end his life, as if Jimmy were required to fulfill a promise he had never made.

Jimmy said, "You don't get to pick when you die. It doesn't work that way."

Truman fished in the front pocket of his overalls with his free left hand, pulled out a thick roll of money and said, "Look."

Although he couldn't be sure what type of bills they were, Jimmy figured they were probably hundreds. There had always been stacks of money on the kitchen table when he was a boy and he remembered how his mother would lift the inch-thick, rubber-banded rolls of green cash and fan herself with them.

Truman said, his voice rising now, building up steam, "I'm not going back in the hospital. I'm not gonna die like that, rotting away with tubes stuck up my dick and nose and throat."

"Why don't you do it yourself?"

Truman didn't say anything for a couple of minutes, but stared straight ahead where a turtle bobbed in the water a few feet off shore. When Jimmy thought and hoped his father's rant was through, and he had no intention of countering anything that had been said, Truman continued, "Do you remember that time we went hunting? When we shot that deer and it didn't die, how we had to put it out of its misery? That is what I am asking you to do."

Jimmy considered saying, *Yeah, I remember it, and that is the goddamned reason I have never wanted to go hunting again,* but he didn't. He understood the point Truman was getting at, but he would not do what his father wanted.

Truman folded the money and placed it back into his pocket as if accepting the fact that Jimmy wasn't going to do it. Calmer now, Truman said, "So there's nothing I can do to make this happen?"

Jimmy shook his head.

As they fished in silence, each of them getting nibbles but nothing worthy of attention, Jimmy waited for Truman's next offer. Although he had no idea what it might be, Jimmy expected it to be crazier than the last—mayor for a week, free whores for a year, a hundred thousand dollars, season tickets to the Braves.

When no such offer materialized, Jimmy said, "Went by Mom's gravesite today."

Truman stared out into the water as if he hadn't heard.

Jimmy said, "When was the last time you went there?"

"Cemeteries don't have anything I need."

"What the fuck does that mean?"

"What's the point of standing next to a stone and crying?"

"You could pay your respects."

"I respected her enough when she was alive. A day doesn't go by where I don't think about her."

Jimmy said, "Did you kill her?" He was shocked he'd gotten the question out so quickly. He could not have predicted a minute, or even seconds before, that he would have asked, although he knew the question had been churning somewhere in the back of his mind and had been pushed forward after the conversation with Davis, waiting to be released when all the conditions were perfect.

Truman didn't look at Jimmy but said, without pause, "No, I did not. I loved her."

Jimmy turned to his father, who shook his head no as if answering the question for a second time. Truman walked over to the bushes on the other side of the truck. When he was slow in returning, Jimmy glanced back and saw him vomit and then try to cover the evidence by kicking dirt over it.

"You okay?"

As he made it back to Jimmy's side, Truman muttered, "Sweet as peaches."

Jimmy said, "It was self-defense."

"What?"

"You said I've killed before." It seemed important to Jimmy that Truman know what happened.

"Girlfriend's husband, I heard."

"That's true, but he attacked me, was gonna kill her."

Truman said, "Those things happen when you fuck another man's wife."

Fuck you, Jimmy thought, but he continued anyway. "She was tutoring me and it just kind of started. I don't even remember how. One minute we were talking verbs and the next we're on her couch. We'd been screwing around for about a year and then one day he came home early from work. We didn't even hear him come in the back door. He hit me in the head with something, threw me off her, knocked me out—I don't know how long—and when I came to he was on top of her, strangling her. I grabbed this vase she kept next to the bed full of fake flowers and hit him over the head one time, once. I just wanted him off of her."

Truman said, "I know."

Jimmy felt the tears start to form, despite it being something that had happened so long ago, something he hadn't thought about until Truman mentioned it yesterday. But now each time he remembered that day it was becoming more real to him and less like a thing that had happened to someone else. To quell the tears, for he did not want to let his father see him cry, Jimmy pulled his penis out and pissed into the pond where the bubbles floated on the surface like the tiny mouths of top-water feeders.

Truman said, "Look at this."

Jimmy turned as his father was pulling an old photo from his wallet. The photo was black and white and folded in half. Even with the thick crease down the middle, the image was clear: Truman and Dot sat on their porch steps with ten-year-old Jimmy between them, the three of them sharing a smile. Taking the photo into his hand, Jimmy studied the house and the flowers—

camellias and impatiens—that bordered the ground around the porch.

And though Jimmy couldn't place that exact photo, he appreciated his father's attempt to change the subject. He wondered if more of those types of memories existed. If by trying not to think of his past, he had erased the good with the bad.

Truman said, "I was thinking about planting some flowers like those in the picture. Fixing the place up again."

Jimmy said, "Couldn't hurt."

"You got any extra white paint?"

"Probably."

"How long you think it would take to paint the house?"

"Just the outside?"

"Yeah."

"A couple days."

"Could we do it in a day?"

Jimmy handed the photo back. "What's the rush?"

Truman folded the photo and slid it into a side compartment of his wallet. "You said you had to get back."

Though he wanted to keep his guard up against his father, he could feel it slipping. "We could probably get a quick coat on, sure."

Truman reeled his line in and said, "They ain't biting. Let's go buy some flowers."

They tossed their poles in the back of the truck and climbed in. As Jimmy turned the key, he felt better for the chance to tell his version of what had happened with that man so long ago and because, for the first time, he believed what his father had to say.

Bobby woke when he heard someone splashing in the pool. He sat up in the chair and looked out over the rail's edge as the large woman he'd seen earlier climbed out of the shallow end. She dropped her things into a pink bag and walked out the fence to some apartment across the way. Turning back to his mother's door, he saw that it was still closed and the curtains were still drawn. He wasn't sure how long he had been asleep but didn't think it had been too long because there were still no kids around.

He decided to go ahead and knock on her door and see if she was home. There was no answer and so he did it again, faster and harder, but still nothing. After pushing the chair up against the wall, Bobby stood up on it, trying to see over the top of the curtains. Darkness was the only thing he could see. The window felt cool against his hand and forehead from the air-conditioner inside. He wondered if she could have slipped past him but didn't know why she would do that.

He wasn't sure how long he should stay. He wanted to see her, but if he waited too long then that might mean he would have to ride back in the dark, which he didn't want to do. Plus, he couldn't be too late or his father would start asking questions. Especially if he didn't have his fishing pole with him.

The schoolbus' brakes called out in the parking lot, behind the building. He jumped down off the chair and leaned against the guardrail and waited for the kids to appear in the courtyard. The heat covered him again as soon as he stood up and out of the immediate shade. Below him, they started to appear: boys and girls his age—a few younger, a few older. Soon the yard, down by the pool, was a line of children walking in the grass and then disappearing in different directions, doors opening and closing.

"Hey, Bobby."

He turned and Tony, the boy who lived in the apartment next door, stood there, holding a book bag, working his key into the door. They had played together before, swum in the water, and watched TV as their mothers made grilled cheese sandwiches.

"What are you doing here?"

"Visiting my mom."

Tony said, "Oh, okay." He went into his apartment and left the door open. "You want something to drink?"

Bobby nodded and walked into the apartment. It was like his mother's, a couple rooms with white walls. His mother's didn't have as much furniture as this one did. She only had one couch plus a small folding table, which was where they would eat when he visited. After Tony gave him a glass of water, Bobby said, "Have you seen my mother?"

"Not today, no."

"When does she usually come home?"

Tony shrugged his shoulders as if to say that he didn't know. Bobby noticed that the shorts he had on had holes on the sides and strands of white material hung down from the cut-offs.

Bobby said, "Where's your mom?"

"She gets home at six. You want to play ball?"

Bobby did want to stay, but he didn't know when his mother would be home. He wasn't sure what his father would do if he found out he had ridden his bike this far. He didn't want to find out, either. Then he remembered about the fair tonight that he was supposed to go to.

Bobby said, "No, I better get going."

Tony said, "Do you want me to tell your mom you were here?"

Bobby thought about this a second, then said, "No, that's okay."

Tony shut his door and started walking toward the stairs. Bobby followed a few feet behind, thinking about how good it would be to live here. How he would get see his mother every day, and he could go swimming and play ball with Tony and his friends whenever he wanted.

Then they were down the stairs and Tony walked around the corner and Bobby went over to his bike, jerked it off the rack, spat at the ground and then started the long ride back to Portisville.

Jimmy and Truman drove past the new Walgreen's store. Truman stuck his arm out the window, something Jimmy remembered his father calling "catching the air."

"Got an extra smoke?"

"Should you be smoking?"

Truman said, "Let's call it a dying man's wish."

Jimmy forced a laugh and held the pack out, and Truman took one and then set the pack on the seat next to him. After engaging the truck's lighter, Truman said, "How long you had this truck?"

"Five years. It's a good work truck."

"I bet."

The back of the truck was now filled with even more cans of paint, along with the two six-packs of impatiens and four camellias they had picked up at the nursery. Truman had shown Jimmy the picture again and told him he wanted flowers just like those in the photo. When Jimmy said that the sun might be too much for the impatiens, Truman said that he didn't care; they didn't need to last too long.

Now, Jimmy said, "What was prison like?"

Truman said, "You didn't have to serve time?"

"Just a couple nights in juvie."

"It's time. One day and then the next. Nothing special. Outside in the sun if it wasn't raining and then inside watching TV, listening to men tell lies about how many women they fucked."

"Twenty years is a lot of time."

"You remember when we used to go for drives? You, me, and your mother?"

"Sure." It was obvious to Jimmy that Truman didn't want to talk about prison.

"Driving, driving, driving, all over the damn place. Remember when we went down to the Keys?" Truman smiled when he said *Keys*.

"No."

"You were young, four or five."

Jimmy stared out the window at the trees and the dirt on the side of the road. He remembered driving around with his parents, especially with his mother in the year or two before she was killed, but he had no memory of ever going to the Keys.

"You used to love to ride. When you were a baby and started crying, the only thing that would shut you up was if we loaded you in the car and drove around for a little while. It'd knock you out and you'd sleep all night long. A couple times she didn't even bring you in the house, was afraid you'd wake back up, so she slept curled up next to you in the back seat."

Though he couldn't exactly remember those comforting rides as a baby, it surprised him that his father did. He wasn't sure if he believed him or if this was some further ploy on his father's part. He still couldn't say he trusted the old man. When they passed the billboard, Jimmy turned his blinker on. Through the thin line of trees bordering the driveway, he could see the house and the empty porch. He parked next to the Cadillac and looked closely at the porch for the first time. The ground where they intended to plant these flowers was a foot-wide area of dirt and weeds littered with bullet casings and a few bottle caps. Jimmy figured most people would probably have some difficulty cultivating an image of what the flowers would look like there and how the house would look painted. But he had started jobs where things looked much worse and his experience told him that the place would look good by this time tomorrow.

Jimmy climbed out of the truck and carried the cans of paint over to the porch. Walking back, he saw Truman slip something into the truck's glove compartment. "What are you doing?"

Truman shut the door. "Nothing." He walked past Jimmy, carrying two of the camellias. At the truck, Jimmy opened the glove compartment box. There was a thick roll of money there—the money Truman had shown him at the pond.

Truman said, "Keep it."

"No."

"Just fucking keep it."

Angie walked out the front door and smiled down at them, crossing her arms over her chest. Jimmy could tell from the look on her face that she didn't quite know how to interpret the scene in front of her. She said, "What's going on?"

Truman said, "We're gonna do some work tomorrow. Time to fix the old place up."

Jimmy left the money where it was. He would give it back before he left, but he didn't want to get into it now in front of her. He picked up the trays of impatiens and said, "Plant these and paint the house."

She said, in a tone that suggested she had some doubts about the project, "That'll be good."

Truman got down on his knees and started throwing trash and weeds into a pile. Jimmy squatted next to him and began to pull the impatiens from their plastic packs. He set six of the plants in front of the porch on one side of the steps in an even row of alternating purple, pink, and white flowers as a guide to where they would be planted. Then he placed the remaining six on the other side of the steps in the same pattern. He used the four camellias as bookends: one on each side of the steps and one at each end of the porch.

She said, "Whose idea was this?"

Jimmy said, "His."

"That's a surprise."

Jimmy turned to Truman. Small circles of sweat had already begun to appear on the back of his shirt. "I've got to get going. Let me show you how to work the power sprayer to get the old paint off."

Jimmy pulled the power sprayer from the back of the truck and set it on the ground, rolling the compressor behind him as he walked over to the side of the house. Truman and Angie followed Jimmy and watched him attach the water hose to a hole on the side of the compressor and then turn it on. As it warmed up, Jimmy picked up the spray gun and said, "Hold it like this." He held the nozzle with his right hand and the extended barrel of the spray gun with his left.

Truman grunted and took it in hand. "Like a shotgun."

Jimmy said, "Yeah, kind of, just pull the trigger."

Truman pointed it waist level at the house and squeezed. The thick, heavy flow of water peeled away a line of loose white paint.

Jimmy said, "Remember, you don't have to get every bit of paint off, just go over it easy, get the big stuff that's peeling off. You got it?"

"Yeah."

"And make sure the hose doesn't get kinked."

Truman nodded and squeezed the spray gun's trigger again, causing Angie to jump back. Jimmy wondered if his father should be working like this, especially with the sun still out, even in the fading light, but decided that Truman looked happy and that hopefully he was smart enough to know when to stop. He felt a slight pull to stay and help him spray the house, but it wouldn't take too long, maybe an hour at the most.

Jimmy said, "Don't work too hard." He doubted his father could hear him over the compressor's loud, constant ticking.

Angie followed him to the front of the house. "Where are you going?"

"A friend is making me dinner."

"Been in town a day and a half and you already have a date?"

He laughed. "I wouldn't call it a date. Just going to the fair."

Jimmy left them outside and went in the house and washed his hands in the kitchen sink and pulled a beer from the fridge, then he got some new clothes from the bedroom and went into the bathroom. As he turned the shower on, and the steam began to fill the small room, he tried again to remember his first years, being driven around by his mother and father, so comfortable with the rock and rhythm of a car and their company that he could sleep with no worries. Then he heard the spray of water from outside hit the shower window and jumped back for a second, before catching his breath and laughing.

Bobby entered the house hot and sweaty from the bike ride and saw his father lying on the couch, watching *The Flinstones,* laughing as Fred hit Barney over the head with a Pterodactyl leg. Without looking up at him, Darren said, "How was school?"

"All right." The question made him wonder if his father already knew about what had happened that day and was waiting for him to confess. He didn't think he could know about the ride to his mother's but maybe that Wendy lady and the principal and Mrs. Floyd were lying in wait in his bedroom and his father was helping them. All of it seemed possible except for the last part. He knew that his father wouldn't let anyone into the house, especially not someone from school.

Darren said, looking over the couch at Bobby, "Jesus, boy, you're sweating like a pig."

"It's hot out there."

"Not that hot."

"I was riding my bike."

"Hell, did you ride to Georgia?"

"No."

Bobby walked timidly towards his bedroom. The hallway seemed darker than normal. When he reached the room, he took a deep breath and pushed the door open and was pleased to find nobody there, just a bed he hadn't made in a week.

A few minutes later, coming back down the hall after changing his shirt, Bobby heard his father's laughter again and walked through the kitchen and drank a couple mouthfuls of milk from the carton and then glanced out the sliding glass door. Suzi was asleep, under the tree, with her fat dog-head resting on her paws.

Standing by the end of the couch, Bobby waited for his father to lift his legs so he could sit down. Eventually, Darren looked up at the boy, then at his feet, and lifted his legs. Bobby sat down and his father rested his dirty-socked feet on the boy's knees.

At the first commercial, Darren said, "When do you want to go to the fair?"

"When you're ready."

"After this is over, I'll take a shower."

Riding home, Bobby had realized that if he went to the fair tonight he would probably run into somebody from school. He was certain there would be other kids there, Nick for sure and maybe even that Mollie Stein girl. It wasn't the kids he worried about, but old Mrs. Floyd and that Wendy lady and the principal. The principal hadn't actually seen him, and Mrs. Floyd might not even know he hadn't made it all the way into the deep reaches of the office before turning and running, so he felt okay about them but it was that Wendy lady he would have to watch out for. Maybe it would be safer if they waited and went tomorrow, on Saturday, but he couldn't be sure that would be any better.

He couldn't tell his father that he had changed his mind about going to the fair but wondered what would happen if he confessed about the incident at school today. He didn't know what his punishment would be. Maybe his father wouldn't take him to the fair. And if he did take him to the fair, his father would at least know what happened at school and if he did see one of his teachers there would be nothing they could tell him that Bobby hadn't already told them. He decided his best bet was to tell him about school and see what happened.

At the end of *The Flinstones*, as the credits scrolled across Barney and Bamm-Bamm's faces, his father turned the TV off, lifted a foot inches from the boy's face, and then sat up. Bobby said, "I got in trouble today."

Darren turned to him. "What did you do?"

"I wrote on a desk."

"With what?"

"A pencil."

"Why the hell did you do that?"

"I was bored."

Darren said, "Don't be," and stood, shaking his head, and walked away, down the hall, toward the bathroom.

Bobby sat on the couch, staring at the blank TV, amazed that it had gone so well. Sure he had left out the part about running out of the principal's office, not to mention the trip to his mom's, but he had told him most of it. He knew that his father wasn't real good at talking, not like his mother, and would usually get frustrated and stand up mid-sentence and walk away, but he had thought that this, involving school, would be different.

Davis drove northbound on Highway 144. At the northern edge of town, right before the fork in the road, there was a sign leading to the only subdivision in Portisville, The Pines. The subdivision wasn't much, an island of houses circled by a street and then a wider circle of houses, which backed up to a wall of pine trees. Only half of the thirty houses were occupied. Some of the vacant ones had old FOR SALE signs in their front yards but a few of them were simply empty.

Davis pulled in front of one of these vacant, not for sale, houses and cut his engine. It looked like so many of the others. A small cinderblock house with a paved walkway splitting the front yard in half, a palm tree on either side of the path. Chained to one of the porch's trellises, by the front door, was a red bike. The air had leaked out of both tires and one of the hard plastic handlebar grips was missing. The bike had belonged to the Dobson girl, Vikki, before she was murdered.

Davis turned his car radio off and looked around the neighborhood. A man mowed his yard three houses away. Beyond that, an old couple sat on their porch taking in the waning Friday early-evening sunlight. Since Bird patrolled this side of 144 and Davis took the east side of town, he hadn't been by the house in seven or eight months, not since the night a man in the neighborhood got drunk and started shooting his .25 at the stars above. But Davis had been too busy to appreciate the house that night.

Anna Dobson, Vikki's mother, had moved away after a suspect was arrested for her daughter's murder. She never returned. The last Davis had heard she was living with her sister in Connecticut. He'd heard rumors that she hadn't taken anything. That the house was still full of clothes, the refrigerator stocked, and the sink piled high with dishes. He thought there might still be a key to the place, but he didn't know where it was. Probably in a plastic bag in her case file if he had to guess, but he couldn't say for sure. He couldn't blame the woman for leaving. She had nothing here. Her husband had been killed in a car accident when Vikki was just a baby. Thankfully, she had been smart enough to pay the house off with his insurance money.

Most of what Davis knew about the Dobson place after the murder came from the neighbor, a retired man named Bill Higgins, who occasionally cornered Davis at the Portisville Diner and spoke to him over a cup of coffee. It was because of Bill Higgins that Davis knew that different people in the neighborhood took turns mowing the yard. He had to admit that the place looked pretty good. If it wasn't for the sad-looking bike on the porch you wouldn't suspect that the house was abandoned.

That night, five years ago, Anna Dobson had called Davis a few minutes after eleven. He had lain there for a couple seconds, letting the phone ring, hoping perhaps that it was part of a dream until Bev elbowed him and told him to answer it. Even before saying hello, Davis knew it was bad news. Good news never comes in the middle of the night. Anna told him how she had come home from work at her usual time, a little after six, and Vikki wasn't home. She thought this was strange because Vikki usually had dinner started. Yet, at first, it still seemed possible that her daughter had stopped by a friend's and lost track of time. By seven, she began to worry but decided to wait a little while longer, taking a shower to pass the time. By eight, she started calling all of Vikki's friends. One of her schoolmates said that she had walked home with her, but the girls split at the entrance to the subdivision. Her fear growing, Anna drove around, circling the school and driving downtown. When Anna got home, she called Davis.

Anna was standing on the porch, smoking a cigarette, when Davis arrived. Although he told her that he couldn't actually consider Vikki "missing" until twenty-four hours had passed, they drove by the school, downtown, and up and down Highway 144, driving slowly on the empty road while Davis flashed his spotlight into the woods. Anna told him that her daughter wouldn't run away and that she knew something was wrong. About a dozen children had been reported missing while Davis was the sheriff, but all of these had worked themselves out in a day or two. Usually, they involved a parent taking a child after a fight with a spouse, or a teenager who runs away only to find out that his plans of freedom aren't what he expected. But this was different. He couldn't say what it was — a sixth sense, a feeling of unease, maybe the urgency of the person reporting the missing person — but he knew Anna was right and they wouldn't find the girl alive.

By two, exhausted, they made it back to the house. Anna lay down on the couch for a few minutes to rest her eyes and fell asleep. Davis fell asleep too, sitting at the kitchen table. When the sun came up the next morning, he walked door-to-door, questioning her neighbors even though Vikki still wasn't officially "missing" yet. The eighth door he knocked on belonged to Mr. Lee, the town pharmacist. Mr. Lee and his wife were out of town, but their seventeen-year-old son, Marcus, opened the door. He had been in a car accident two years earlier and had suffered a brain injury. Davis remembered pulling him from the car, his face bloody and smashed and unrecognizable, as the boy muttered some incoherent melody.

The accident had certainly changed Marcus Lee. For one thing, his eyes didn't seem quite right. When he spoke, even if looking right at you, it seemed like he was looking beyond you, as if he could see into your mind. He had also kept his head shaved after the accident so that the surgical scar, which split his skull down the middle, was clearly visible and unnerving.

Inside the Lees' home, Davis asked Marcus the same questions he had asked every other person he'd spoken to: *Do you know Vikki? When was the last time you saw her? Did you see anybody you didn't know in the neighborhood yesterday?*

Marcus answered the questions just like so many of his neighbors, but there was something about the way he stared at Davis that bothered the sheriff. It was even creepier than the boy's usual vacant stare. It was as if he were trying very hard not to smile but couldn't quite control it. Every couple of minutes a quick smile would appear across his face for a second and then disappear. Davis didn't know if it had to do with his brain damage or not, so he did something he had read about in a police journal, which was to surprise the interviewee and ask a question he isn't expecting. Davis said, "Marcus, did you kill her?" and Marcus smiled and said that he did. It took him a few seconds to realize what he had confessed to. He told the sheriff that she was wrapped in a blue blanket behind a stack of firewood inside his parents' shed in the backyard.

As they walked out the back door to the shed, with Marcus head-down leading the way and the pine trees forming a formidable wall in front of them, Davis looked back across the street, and could see the back of the Dobson house and three pairs of Vikki's jeans hanging on the clothes line. He couldn't see Anna at that moment, but he imagined her walking around the living room, smoking a cigarette. He thought of what he would have to tell her and his heart felt full and empty at the same time, like some neutral organ.

Vikki Dobson was where Marcus said she would be, lying behind a stack of firewood with a blue afghan covering her naked body except for her feet, which rested against the front of a bright green Lawn-Boy mower. In the heat of the shed, without prompting, Marcus had told the sheriff that while he was "making love to her," those were his words, she slapped him, so he hit her until she stopped moving. After handcuffing Marcus, Davis asked him what he planned to do with the girl and Marcus said he didn't know, that he was going to ask his father when he got back. He was found guilty by reason of insanity and sent off to the state mental hospital down in Miami where he would probably stay for the rest of his life. His parents sold the house and moved away, down south, Davis had heard, so that they could visit their son often.

Now, in the cruiser, Davis looked past the Dobson house and another backyard and across the street to the Lees' old house. From his angle, he could see that the shed was gone, replaced now with a sandbox and swing set. He thought again about Jimmy and the questions he had asked and it made him think again about Dot's murder, about the discrepancies with Truman, and if he had tried hard enough. And he didn't think it was so much a matter of not trying as it was not knowing what to look for or ask.

He also knew that so far he hadn't been trying as hard as he could on this Teresa Martin case. Sure, he was putting in the time, was at the crime scene, but wasn't really working it as hard as he could. Was it because he was getting old and was ready to retire? Or was it because he didn't want to find her? He was certain that if he found her she would be dead, so it seemed possible that if they didn't find her then she might be out there, alive somewhere, okay. But this made no kind of sense, even he knew that.

Davis looked at his watch and knew that he better get going if he was going to relieve Bird at the fair. He wished that he would have gone home and had dinner with his wife and stared into her sweet brown eyes instead of sitting out here, but he hadn't. He shifted into Drive and pulled out of the subdivision, back onto 144, as the sun began its long, slow descent.

Jimmy pulled into the driveway and parked behind the gray Corsica. He checked the address Carol had given him: 407 Sawgrass Road. Her house was single-story and block and painted an even blue. It was bigger than his two-bedroom brick house back home, and he wondered if her mother had left it to her when she died. On either side of her house, there were large fields, which were empty here by the road but in the distance were dotted with pockets of grazing cows. He doubted that the pastures were part of her property.

Before climbing out of the truck, Jimmy reached over and opened the glove box. He pulled out the money Truman had set there. The money didn't feel cold or warm in his hand. He counted it: $6,240. A new truck, a vacation, equipment for his business, re-build his back deck, the list of things he could do with the money seemed to go on and on in his mind. But it wasn't his. Would it be any different if somebody besides his father had put it there? Yeah, he figured, it would. The old man hadn't given him anything in the last twenty years and he wasn't about to start accepting gifts now. There was also the fact that this money was wrapped up with Truman's sick request to be killed. Jimmy dropped the money back in the glove box, shut it tight, checked his hair in the rearview mirror, then climbed on out of his truck.

On the porch, catty-cornered, were a pair of wooden chairs with pink alligator faces painted on their seats. Music came from inside the house, as if leaking under the door, some song vaguely familiar but unnameable due to volume and distance. When he looked in the front window, Carol was sitting on the couch thumbing through an oversized art book. As he knocked, Jimmy felt his heart rate increase, a twinge in his gut he could not help but identify.

The strong scent of spaghetti sauce came to him as she opened the door. Her smile was inviting and they exchanged hellos and he followed her into the house. Again, he liked the way she was dressed, oversized jeans and a white oxford shirt with the sleeves rolled up past her elbows, and she was barefoot with the ragged edge of her jeans sliding across the floor. She told him to sit down, that the sauce needed to be stirred and then she left the room.

On the pine floor, all around the purple couch, were various art books and sketch pads. One pad lay open to a drawing of an alligator with pierced eyelids and a small white Dachshund on its back. The dog's nose was pierced with a diamond pendant hanging from the septum. The gator's face held a sly smile; its eyes rolled back in its head to glance at the dog. Carol called from the kitchen, "Can I get you something to drink?"

Her voice startled Jimmy as it pulled him from the world the drawing had taken him to.

"Beer, if you got any."

Almost every square inch of the room's walls were covered with framed paintings of alligators: most of their bodies appeared to be relatively normal but the looks on their faces seemed to tell the stories. Some smiled where others wore tight, squinty frowns and in a few of the gators' eyes you could see tiny, mirror images of dilapidated farmhouses and pickup trucks and a store that looked like Dan's and a tiny body of water that could have been Miller's Pond.

Jimmy didn't know much about art, but he figured this was as good as any he'd seen. It caught his attention, made him look and look again. In one corner of the room there was a white chair with a stereo on the seat, flanked by a pair of tall speakers. He recognized the music now, James Taylor singing about the Carolinas.

Jimmy liked her house. Despite the fact that the paintings gave it the impression of being slightly cluttered, in their sheer volume if nothing else, there was something about the house that spoke to him of comfort and security, the kind of place he'd like to come home to. It made him think about the way he had been living. He worked six ten-hour days a week, either painting or giving estimates, got in around seven, drank a couple beers and ate a TV dinner or a hamburger he'd picked up on the way home, watched TV while doing paperwork, then was in bed by ten. On Saturday nights, he'd go to a bar and shoot pool or throw darts and on Sundays do yard work or go fishing. And it wasn't until that moment, sitting on her couch, that he realized just how structured and solitary his life had become. Not that he didn't like it. It wasn't a bad life. But maybe, he thought, there should be more to it.

Carol came back in the room and handed him a beer as she sat down, a foot away from him, on the couch. Jimmy said, "So, I see you got a thing for gators."

She laughed. "Yeah. I like 'em better than people. They don't ask for much, just something to eat."

Jimmy thought he heard sarcasm in her voice. He said, "Then when they get too big, they're slaughtered."

"Everything is slaughtered eventually."

"I guess you're right."

She picked up her sketchbook and showed him a drawing she had been working on. It was a gator with a paintbrush for a tongue and razorblades where eyelashes should be. She said, "Do you notice anything about the eyes?"

"Besides the razors?"

She nodded and he looked closer and caught the mirrored reflection of a swing, the kind you might find in a schoolyard. "I painted that after talking to you today, after you mentioned going by the school."

Jimmy said, "Don't blame me for that," and they both laughed. He liked how her laugh was easy and giving.

Carol stood and started to walk back toward the kitchen and said, "Come in here and talk to me while I finish the sauce."

In the hall, he passed an easel with a five-foot-tall painting of a gator with red claws and pink cheeks. He thought it was weird stuff, but at the same time found it interesting. Sitting down at the dining room table, which had two lit candles in the center, he watched her turn a long, wooden spoon in the silver pan, and took in the thick smell of the sauce: oregano, garlic and pepper.

Every few seconds, Carol turned back to Jimmy and smiled. She said, "Did you have a nice afternoon?"

He said, "It was interesting."

"How so?"

"Went fishing with the old man. He said he wanted to fix up the old house, so we ended up going downtown, buying some paint and flowers. "

She turned away from him, took a mouthful of beer and continued stirring the sauce. For a moment, he thought about the other stuff they had discussed at Miller's Pond. He didn't want to talk about that and was pleased when she started walking toward him with the sauce-filled spoon in her right hand, the left curled under it like a ladle. As she held the spoon out toward him, he leaned forward, opened his mouth, his tongue testing for temperature before tasting the hot sauce. Garlic and pepper.

"Um, good."

She smiled, ran her tongue along the edge of the spoon and walked back over to the stove. "Could use a little more pepper."

He said, "Tastes good to me."

She set the table and turned the stove down. "Come on, I want to show you something."

She parted the curtain and opened the sliding-glass door. Her fenced property was about the size of a football field and the cows he had seen earlier roamed freely on the other side. Straight back, there was a large cream-colored farmhouse, a row of red and green tractors lined up in front of it like over-sized toys. Between her yard and the farmhouse, just on the other side of her fence, was a square, unroofed concrete structure.

They walked through ankle-deep grass toward this structure, grass thickets and clover clinging to their jeans.

"What is it?"

She squeezed Jimmy's hand. "You'll see."

The pressure of her hand against his bruised knuckles reminded Jimmy of punching his father last night, and then earlier today wrapping his hand around that gun and firing at the tree and how close he had come to shooting him, and oddly enough how he was looking forward to working with Truman tomorrow. He still didn't know how to take what his father had said about Carol. To him, there was something about her that spoke of tenderness and not the lust Truman had described.

As they got closer to the structure, Jimmy could see that it was basically four waist-high concrete walls with no roof. The walls, which had looked solid from fifty yards, now appeared to be scarred and dotted with small holes. When they reached her fence, Jimmy heard splashing, like the sound a dog makes when it hits the water. He leaned forward, touching the walls of the structure, straining for a better look and saw the hundred small eyes of baby alligators poking out of a man-made pond. The noise he made caused half of the gators to go underwater. Others sat bobbing like anxious turtles, while some brave souls didn't budge from the mud-lined shore around the pond.

Jimmy said, "Wow."

"Pretty cool, huh?"

"What's the deal?"

"The guy who lives here hatches them and when they get big enough, he sells them to Gatorland or kills them for their back plates and tails. Tourist crap."

Jimmy had never seen anything like this before and thought it bizarre, yet strange and beautiful at the same time. The gators each seemed to fight for their own space on the surface of the water. A six-incher ran out of the pond, across the dirt toward Jimmy and Carol, made it half-way, then turned around as if realizing there was indeed a wall between him and them and ran back to the temporary safety of the water and his siblings.

"Some days, I come out here and just watch them for hours. Get ideas for my paintings."

Nodding to the farmhouse, Jimmy said, "Does he know you know?"

"He doesn't care. It's legal."

For a few minutes, Jimmy stared, mesmerized by what he had discovered, what she had led him to. Carol slid over so that their sides were touching. A bigger gator pushed three or four smaller ones down as it moved across the top of the water.

Carol said, "Bad gator, bad."

And Jimmy laughed.

Bobby's worst fears seemed to be coming true. It had been a mistake not to tell his father about running out of the principal's office. They had just passed Mrs. Floyd by the spinning tea-cups and to his right he could see that Wendy lady bent over, talking to a boy a few years younger than him. It might be somebody from school but he couldn't say for sure. It might even be her son. Bobby held his father's hand and walked as fast as he could, practically pulling him along. Darren said, "Slow down, boy."

There was a sweet smell coming off his father. Bobby had first noticed it earlier, as they ate dinner in the McDonald's parking lot, but now walking side-by-side the slight breeze seemed to be flushing the scent to the surface. When his mother still lived with them, his father would wear cologne when they went out for Saturday night dinner, but Bobby couldn't remember the last time he had worn it. In this way, the wearing of it tonight seemed to give it extra importance though Bobby couldn't say what it was.

"Bobby." He looked up and it was Nick walking toward him and wearing a red shirt with the word HICK printed in white across the front of it.

"Hello, Mr. Webster."

Darren said hi and turned away from the boy whom he had never shown any signs of liking. "Bobby tell you about his trip to the office today?"

Bobby felt his face flush red. His hands balled into tight fists. Throw the boy to the ground and pound him, pound him good, is what he wanted to do.

Darren said, "Nick, why don't you mind your own business?"

These words seemed to suck the life out of the boy's face, as the wide grin he'd been offering up moments before was now nothing but flat lips and wide eyes. Bobby said, "Yeah, Nick, why don't you mind your own business?"

"Make me."

Darren said, raising his voice, "Enough, you two. Nick, go bother somebody else."

Nick said, "Shit," and started to walk away. Then he stopped and turned back to them. "Mr. Webster, let me have a dollar."

"Where's your folks?"

"I don't know."

Darren looked around, as if he might be able to locate them

for the boy and thus save himself some money. But if that was his goal, he was not successful, so he pulled his wallet from the back pocket of his jeans and gave the boy a shiny new five and told him to go on.

The sight of his father handing somebody, especially Nick, money bothered Bobby. "How come you gave him money?"

"Because he doesn't have anything."

Bobby could think of nothing to say to that, so they started for the area of the fair that was mostly games and prizes. Mrs. Floyd and that Wendy lady were nowhere in sight. The first game they came to involved tossing a softball into an oversized milk jug. Bobby said, "I want to play."

Darren said, "You're not gonna win."

"How do you know?"

"Because they're rigged."

Bobby figured it was just another excuse so his father wouldn't have to give him any money. Darren said, "All right, but this is it." He handed the boy four one-dollar bills.

The man behind the counter took Bobby's dollar and set three balls on the counter in front of him. He explained that if you sank two out of three softballs into the oversized milk jug you won a prize. The prize Bobby had his eye on was a light blue dolphin with a white belly. He could see it on the wall, over his bed, swimming through his room.

He threw the first one and it hit the outer lip and rolled off, back behind the jug. The worker let out a fake moan. Bobby threw the next ball and it seemed to hit the same spot. His third toss was short by a good six inches. Bobby wasn't sure he wanted to play again, but he wanted that dolphin. As if taunting Bobby and the few spectators who had gathered to watch, the worker lifted two balls and dropped them straight down into the jug's top hole, as if to prove that he, and his game, were on the up-and-up.

In no time, the four dollars were gone. Darren, who had been standing quietly behind the boy with his hands folded across his chest, shook his head no when Bobby turned to ask for more money. Bobby said, "Win it for me."

Darren stepped up to the counter and handed the man his dollar and took three softballs. After watching his father lose ten dollars in less than five minutes, Bobby decided that yes, this game must be rigged, and that the dolphin would not be swimming through his room as he had hoped.

When they turned to walk away, Mrs. Floyd was standing behind them, smiling. "Evening, Mr. Webster."

With those three words, the air around Bobby became unbreathable. Something big and impenetrable lodged in the back of his throat. He wasn't sure if she was talking to him or to his father. He didn't think it was his father because, as far as Bobby knew, the two of them had never met. But her looks were alternating between the two Websters in a way that reminded Bobby of her innate ability to scan a classroom for that one student who happened to be writing on a desk.

Darren didn't say anything, and Mrs. Floyd stuck her hand out to shake. "Marsha Floyd. I'm your son's social studies teacher."

Marsha? He looked around quickly, hoping that Nick could see this but he wasn't among the blur of people, which seemed to surround this small meeting.

Darren said, "Nice to meet you."

"Likewise."

"He giving you any trouble in class?"

Bobby was sure that was the question that would nail him to the wall.

"No, he should do fine." Then she turned to Bobby, smiled in that fake way of hers. "You having fun tonight?"

Bobby didn't want to answer, wanted actually just to yell out that he hadn't made it to see the principal, because he felt certain she knew and was trying to will him into a confession right here, right now, in front of his father. It was just like her to ruin his fun. Finally, he said, "Yes."

Just then, one of the other students in the class, a boy named Doug who sat a few seats back from him, walked up with his mother and said hi to Mrs. Floyd. Bobby grabbed his father's hand and started to walk away. Mrs. Floyd called out, "Nice to meet you, Mr. Webster. We'll see you in class Monday, Bobby."

When they'd gone about twenty yards, Bobby looked back to see Mrs. Marsha Floyd talking to that boy and his mother and not looking in his direction. He couldn't believe he had gotten away with it. It was the kind of gift that surprised Bobby to no end, the kind he knew better than to question.

They came to the bumper cars and Bobby asked if he could ride them and Darren said sure. A few minutes later, Bobby smiled over at his father who looked odd and twisted in the small blue car he was expected to operate. Bobby gripped the steering wheel and waited for the cars to start. When they did, he lowered his head and stared at his hands and pushed the pedal to the floor and felt like he was flying for a few seconds before he ran straight into another car and looked up to see his father laughing back at him.

Jimmy and Carol walked forward, tickets in hand, as the battling strands of music blurred together into the simplest thud of a drum. Men, women and children all moved toward different rides and in different directions as if a sea that had no even tide. A red-headed girl ran past them and stopped in the center of the aisle, about ten feet away, and started to cry. Her hands were at her sides, balled into fists and her face was pink and stretched like a comic book character.

Carol said, "Somebody's not happy."

Jimmy laughed. "I'd say."

A man in jeans and a T-shirt came up and grabbed the girl's hand and dragged her back into the crowd.

Jimmy spotted the concession stand up ahead, turned to Carol, and said, "Funnel cake?"

"I'm still full from dinner."

"Me too, but a fair isn't a fair without funnel cake."

"How can I argue with logic like that?"

As they walked along, both taking small bites of the funnel cake, Carol lifted a napkin to wipe away the white sugar from her lips then wiped the corners of Jimmy's mouth with the same napkin. He smiled before looking past her at a small folding table with a man sitting behind it. In the middle of the table was a poster of the missing girl. On each side of the poster were inch-high stacks of flyers, the same ones that had been posted on almost every pole in sight.

Carol turned to see what Jimmy was looking at. "Hopefully they'll find her."

"Yeah."

When they reached the table, the man said, "Take a flyer. There's a number on the bottom. If you know or hear anything give us a call." His somewhat happy expression seemed at odds with the situation, as if he had no real stake in this but was performing some type of community service and what he really wanted was for his shift to be over so he could go have some fun on the rides all around him.

Jimmy stared down at the poster, which was just a larger reproduction of the smaller flyers. Again the word MISSING was above the picture of the girl and below that REWARD $25,000 and at the bottom, in smaller print, was a phone number to call with any information. The flyer reminded him again of his mother and the ones they had put up after she disappeared. The harder he stared the more blurred the picture of Teresa Martin became, so that her hair changed from blond to black, her eyes from blue to green and he was not a man of thirty-four but a boy staring at a flyer on a telephone pole.

Carol said, "Let's go sit over there." She was pointing at an empty bench. Jimmy, welcoming the reprieve from his thoughts, followed her. After they sat down, the music stopped for a moment and they heard a loud pop to their right and both turned.

Two boys, one older than the other by a couple of years, were standing at a booth and shooting a BB gun at multicolored balloons. The older boy looked about twelve or thirteen and held the rifle tight to his right shoulder, squinted in the direction of the balloons and fired. The music around Jimmy and Carol swelled up again so loud that they no longer heard the pops, only saw the mangled purple material, which had once been a balloon, hanging from the tack. The boy's shoulder jerked back again and another balloon exploded. The boys high-fived each other and laughed as the worker gave them a stuffed purple dinosaur. Twenty yards from the booth, the older one tossed the dinosaur into the garbage can and the boys disappeared into the sea of people. Carol laughed. "Kids."

Jimmy didn't say anything. While watching the boys walk away he had spotted Davis in the crowd. The sheriff was walking fast, with purpose, and Jimmy wondered where he might be going and what the hurry was. Did it have something to do with Teresa Martin? Jimmy figured that if he wasn't with Carol tonight he would go over and talk to Davis, see how he was doing, ask about his wife, something he should have done in his office this afternoon.

Carol said, "You ever think about having any?"

Jimmy said, "What? Kids? No. How about you?"

She turned to him and smiled. "I'd like three."

"Why three?"

"I like odd numbers."

Jimmy couldn't help but smile at this. "You are an odd one. What are you doing here in this town?"

"It's home. It's not so bad. Has its good and bad like anywhere. So you really don't want any, not even one?"

"Nope."

"Why not?"

"Too much shit in the world."

"Come on, there's good too."

"Not enough."

"Maybe not a lot, but there is some."

"Well, it doesn't matter because I'm not having any." He was thinking about his childhood, about his mother being taken away and him being shipped halfway across the country and then back again. Jimmy felt the need to move, so he stood up. "Let's go ride the Ferris wheel."

At the ride, Jimmy handed the worker two tickets and the greasy man winked at him as they walked towards the cart and climbed on the ride. Jimmy forced a smile; it was too good a night to get upset about it. The worker pulled a copper pin and the silver bar fell across their legs, tight like a child's car seat. Their cart ascended ten feet and Jimmy felt a small, comforting rise in his stomach. Carol scooted close to him and put her head on his shoulder and he wondered if she felt the same thing he did.

As the lower carts were being filled, downtown Portisville lay out in front of them, a string of lights up one street, beyond which various house lights flickered to the east and west. Then the ride turned and lurched them forward as they started moving and there were people on the ground standing there and then their cart was above the tree line and then back down again. Neither one of them said anything for a few minutes as if the silence was a reassurance of everything said and done until this moment, no past lives or loves, but only the unknowable future and what it might promise.

Davis leaned against the police car, breathing hard, while the man in the back seat yelled and banged his head twice against the window. Although he was upright, the sheriff felt like somebody was sitting on his chest. He turned away from the assembled crowd and slid a nitro under his tongue. The man in back seat's name was John Alred and Davis had arrested him a half-dozen times in the last year alone with charges ranging from shoplifting to sexual assault. The sexual assault charge involved a woman he worked with at the Coke distribution center in Tallahassee. She had originally said that he raped her in his trailer, but a week later dropped the charges. Bird spoke to the small crowd that had gathered: "Okay folks, the show is over. Go on, now."

After the greater portion of those assembled walked away, the deputy banged his flashlight against the window and yelled, "Knock it off." This seemed to quiet the man for a few minutes.

Bird said, "You all right, sheriff?"

He straightened up and took a few deep breaths. "Fine, son of a bitch just knocked the wind out of me is all."

"Why don't you sit down."

"I'm fine, Bird. Just let me catch my breath." Davis sat on the back bumper of the squad car and could feel the pressure in his chest gradually sliding away. He spit at the ground.

Bird said, "What all do you want me to charge him with?"

"Drunk and disorderly and assaulting an officer." A few minutes earlier, Davis and Bird had walked around the corner and found Alred, who was obviously drunk, yelling at a fair worker, saying the man had stolen his money. When Bird told him to settle down, Alred threw a punch at the deputy and then charged the sheriff, who tackled him.

Davis straightened up now and opened his door to get the forms for filing a report. Davis looked back at Alred, who was uttering *motherfuckers* left and right at a steady, low volume. Even sitting down, he was a short and squat, sorry-looking man with greasy, long black hair. Davis wondered for a moment why it was that people like this get to live long full lives, while other people are taken away much too young. Then Alred said, "I killed that girl."

Davis felt a chill. Alred smiled at him with his eyes wide and happy for a moment.

"What girl is that, John?"

"That blond bitch on the posters."

"That's not something you want to joke about."

"Got her tied up at my place, on my bed after I had her like she wanted it."

Davis watched a young couple walk by the car and wished for a second what he had been wishing a lot in the last couple days: that he wasn't the sheriff, that he was just another man walking along laughing and riding brightly-lit rides, which took him high into the air. But the position was his. That was clear.

"She kept saying, 'Oh yeah, them college boys can't do it like that.' She smelled like strawberries, tasted like peaches, sweet and sticky Georgia peaches."

"All right, the joke is over. Knock it off or I'll add an obstruction of justice charge."

"Fuck you, sheriff. She's there. Probably bleeding nice and slow from them holes in her wrists."

"I thought you said she was already dead."

"Probably is by now."

Davis closed his eyes again and took a deep breath. He was trying not to let this bastard see how mad he was getting. The car stank like liquor and shit and piss and all the sorry excuses for people he'd been carting around for as long as he could remember. He said, "We'll do it your way then. But you picked the wrong damn night to do this."

Davis climbed out of the car, nodded Bird over. "What's up, Sheriff?"

Davis blew out a heavy breath. "Our little prisoner there just decided to tell me that he has Teresa Martin tied up in the back of his trailer."

Bird said, "What? He's full of it."

"That's what I said." Davis thought of Marcus Lee and his simple, quick confession, but told himself that this was different, much different. He said, "Still, we have to check his place."

"You want to ride together?"

"Let's go separate. Call in Willie to cover the fair."

"All right, I'll follow you out there."

Davis put his hand on his car's handle and hesitated a second before opening it, not quite sure he was ready for what he might find.

Truman saw the headlights and stepped from the darkness out of his driveway. The truck slowed and came to a stop and Darren Webster smiled out at him, a cigarette hanging nonchalantly from between his lips. "Evening, Truman."

"Evening."

Truman climbed in without further ceremony and Darren pointed the truck north and neither man said anything for a few minutes. Truman hoped that Angie didn't wake up and step out onto the porch looking for him. He had waited until she had been in bed an hour before he called Darren.

Now, in the trees around them, an occasional firefly lit, drifted up, and then disappeared as if it had never been there at all. Over the trees, every few seconds, Truman could see the fluorescent light from the fair rides. He wondered if Jimmy was having fun there. If that girl was with him and if he would fuck her tonight.

Truman said, "You take your boy to the fair?"

"Yeah."

"How was it?"

"Fine."

"Business okay?"

Darren said, "As good as it's ever been."

"Any problems?"

Darren shook his head. "So what did you need, Truman?"

"Need you to do me a favor." Truman hesitated, knowing it was the kind of thing you didn't ask for, make an offer of payment, and then back out of.

Darren kept looking at Truman, then at the road, then back at Truman, as if his patience was growing thin. "What kind of favor?"

"I need you to kill me."

Darren turned quick to Truman. "Bullshit."

"I'm serious."

A long moment of silence followed in which Darren lifted his foot off the gas and let the truck coast to a near stop and then steered it over to the side of the road. After applying the brake, Darren turned his headlights off but left the running lights on so that the only illumination came from the dashboard in front of them. Night noises enveloped the truck. Katydids sang. Toads belched. Cicadas screamed. "Are you out of your fucking mind?"

"No. Twenty thousand dollars. I'll leave a suicide note." He wished that he didn't have to do it this way, that he could keep it in the family, but it was clear now that wasn't going to happen. Truman pulled a thick roll of money out and set it on the seat between him and Darren. "Here's ten thousand. I'll give you the rest right before you do it."

"When?"

"My son will be gone in a couple days. Angie, my nurse, she usually runs in the morning, so it'll be early. Sunday or Monday. I'll call you."

Darren said, "Do I have a choice?"

"Not if you want to stay in business."

Darren started the truck and eased back onto the road. Again neither man said anything for a few minutes while above them stars flickered off and on. Then from the distance Truman saw the first flash of a blue light and then a red one. *Son of a bitch*, he thought, *what are they doing?* He slouched down in the seat as Darren said, "Shit, shit, shit." But as quickly as the two police cruisers had appeared, they passed Darren Webster's truck and were gone. Truman sat up and Darren shook his head, letting out a sigh.

They passed the old billboard and were in front of the driveway and Darren pulled over and Truman climbed out. Darren didn't say anything, his silence speaking volumes as he pulled away.

On the porch, Truman looked out at the blackness of the trees that surrounded him. He held the gun in his hand and pointed at the sliver of light out there. Without firing, he set the gun on the floor and closed his eyes and tried to think of nothing, tried only to listen to the night's sounds, something familiar yet scary, those alive and dying creatures.

Davis drove on through the dark night with Bird following. Occasionally a light would appear in the woods from one of the houses behind the trees, and for the first time in a long time Davis found these lights somewhat spooky, even though he had lived here his whole life. But maybe it was just this night, this drive.

Alred was in the back of the car, staring out the side window. There was a small cut on the right side of his forehead from when they had pushed him in the back of the car. Davis felt a slight pressure in his chest and he tried to relax, told himself to take a few deep breaths, to take it easy, it'll all be over soon enough one way or another.

Davis flicked on his turn signal when he saw the sign hanging from a metal post announcing the Portisville Park, a trailer park off 144, a mile south of The Pines. The pressure in his chest had subsided but had been replaced by a steady chill throughout his body. He took out another nitro and slid it under his tongue and tried to recall how many he had taken in the last twenty-four hours. Six, he thought, and knew he was at his limit. The doctors had told him that in time the nitro wouldn't be enough and eventually he'd have to have the bypass surgery. He wondered if he'd already reached that point, but the last couple of days had been unusually stressful. He'd see how he felt after this was all over. In his rearview mirror, Bird's lights seemed to be bearing down on him, despite the fact that the deputy was a good twenty yards back.

A dirt road circled the fifteen trailers, which were arranged around a small man-made pond. Alred's trailer was the fourth one in from the entrance. Davis pulled in and shut his car off. Across the water, three men sat in lawn chairs behind a trailer listening to the Allman Brothers on a little boom-box at their feet.

Davis turned back to his prisoner. "You done joking, John? This is your last chance."

Alred smiled. "Go on and see."

Davis and Bird met in front of the sheriff's car. "How do you want to do this, Sheriff?"

"I'll go in. You stay out here with him."

"All right."

Davis steadied himself and then started toward the trailer door. Bird called behind him. "You need to get the keys?"

Without looking back, Davis said, "I'd bet it's not locked."

Davis' hand shook as he touched the cool knob. He tasted metal. The trailer's window unit buzzed to his left. He had been correct; it wasn't locked. As he opened the door, Davis smelled something rank. Bad eggs maybe, something with sulfur. The trailer was a single-wide and to the right of the door was the living room area—a couch, TV, and rocking chair—and to the left was the kitchenette, the bathroom and then the bed in the back. There was a closed curtain blocking his view of the bed. The bed was where John Alred said he had Teresa Martin.

The odor was worse as Davis passed the stove, definitely old eggs and bacon. He hesitated before going any farther back. He considered turning the light on but didn't. Instead, he lifted his little black Mag light from his belt and shined it down the hall. A T-shirt, three beer cans, and a paper plate littered the dark carpet. Flashing the light on the refrigerator door, he saw a twenty-year-old photo of Alred as a teenager in a baseball uniform. Someone had drawn a black beard across his chin with a magic marker.

As he made his way to the back, Davis again told himself to take deep, easy breaths.

Only five or ten more feet. He opened the bathroom door, shined the light around, nothing there but a toilet bowl full of piss. Davis shook his head, thinking, *How hard is it to flush the goddamned toilet?*

Turning back to the bedroom, he smelled it then. Perfume. Closing his eyes, he lifted his head and took in another deep breath. It was definitely perfume, smelled like the ocean or the beach, something tropical. Davis leaned against the wall and said a silent *Please, God, please.* He shifted the Mag light over to his left hand while pulling his revolver out of the holster with his right. Reaching up, he put a finger on the curtain, took another breath, then pulled it back. The woman in the bed rolled over and sat up with a fright, crossed her legs and folded an arm over her chest. She was pale and naked and too old to be Teresa Martin. When she realized he wasn't Alred, she slid back against the headboard and screamed. There were cigarette burns above both of her breasts and the top of her hands.

Davis said, "It's okay, it's okay."

She pulled the sheets up to her neck. It took Davis a second to recognize her. Her name was Rhonda Newton and she lived with her husband and three kids in the gray trailer closest to the park entrance.

Bird ran in the door. "Sheriff, you all right?"

"Fine, we're okay."

"Is it her?"

Davis flicked the overhead light on now. "No, not even close."

Bird stood beside the sheriff, his gun pointing at the ground and looked at Rhonda Newton. She said, "You two mind? I'd like to get dressed."

Davis shut the curtain and he and Bird went over to the living room area. Parting the curtain, Davis looked out at the cruiser where Alred was sleeping with his head up against the window. "Why don't you go out and check on him."

Bird went outside and leaned against the cruiser's door and looked back at the trailer.

Rhonda came out wearing a pair of cut-off jeans shorts and a pink T-shirt without a bra. When she reached for the door handle, Davis said, "Have a seat."

"I got to go."

Davis said it again, "Have a seat."

She sat down, practically threw herself into the chair across from him. "It's not a crime to fuck an idiot, is it?"

"Mrs. Newton, watch your mouth." He had never arrested her but had arrested her husband a number of times. Assault, DUI, domestic violence, a real prize.

She seemed about to say something but reconsidered and instead stared back toward the bedroom.

"How long you been here?"

"A couple hours."

"You heard about the missing girl?"

"Yeah, why?"

"You seen her?"

She pulled a pack of flattened cigarettes from her back pocket. "No."

"Your boy out there says he had her in here, says he killed her."

"John? Christ, only thing he could kill is a twelve-pack of cheap beer."

"He didn't mention it to you?"

"No."

"How'd you get those burns all over you?"

She took a long smoke off her cigarette, lifted her head to blow the smoke high in the air. "I smoke naked. I drink naked. Things fall on me."

Davis shook his head. "Which one did it, your husband or John?"

"I did it."

"Why?"

"Because I like pain."

"I guess you're one of the few people lucky enough to get what they want."

"Yeah, lucky fucking me." She laughed but it was the most insincere one he had heard in weeks.

Davis turned away from her, back down the hall. He'd look

around one more time before he left. Maybe if nothing else, he'd find some drugs or something he could add to Alred's list of charges. When Rhonda stood up and reached for the door again, Davis said, "Don't you have a family at home, babies and a husband?"

"That's none of your goddamn business."

"Yes, ma'am, it is my goddamn business."

"Haven't seen my husband in a week." Then she looked at him a second, as if asking permission to leave, as if saying, *Are we done with this shit?* and Davis walked past her, back toward the rear of the trailer. After the door slammed, he heard clapping and cheers from the trio of men sitting across the water. He shook his head and wondered how long it would be before he arrested one of her kids for something. The oldest one was seven. He'd give the kid three years, tops.

He pushed the curtain back again and surveyed the bed. The sheets were in a ball and there was a used condom in the far corner. Thank God they had used that, he thought. A naked picture of some blond actress with very large breasts, who Davis recognized but whose name escaped him, was on the wall above the headboard.

As Davis came outside, Bird was talking to a kid with a shaved head. The kid was no more than thirteen or fourteen. He said, "You get that son of a bitch, sheriff?"

Davis didn't answer.

Davis and Bird met at the front of Davis' car. "Tell you what, Bird, I'm gonna drive him in, toss him in a cell for the night."

"I can drive him in."

"No, I got it. We'll meet in the morning, come back out here and look the place over in the daylight."

"All right, I'll see you then. Hey, Sheriff, I'm glad it wasn't her."

"Me too."

Davis climbed in the cruiser, turned the lights on and idled out of the trailer park. Behind him, Bird began to wrap the yellow police-scene tape around Alred's trailer. When Davis drove by Rhonda

Newton's trailer, she was on the front porch smoking a cigarette and her seven-year-old was sitting on her knees. The boy waved at the sheriff.

A mile down Highway 144, Davis turned onto a side road, which seemed even darker than the highway. The cruiser's lights cut a line through the woods. Alred, who hadn't said anything since they left the trailer park, sat up now in the backseat. After driving on this road for five minutes, Davis slowed the car and stopped. He climbed out and walked around to the trunk, which he opened, then lifted the black, plastic fake flooring, and pulled the rifle out. When Davis opened the back door, Alred said, "Where are we?"

"Don't worry about it. Get out."

Alred looked around as if trying to find some familiar landmark. "Fuck this." He leaned into the back seat, trying to scoot away from Davis. "This isn't funny." His voice had lost all its cockiness.

"Get out of the car, John, get out now."

Alred slowly slid across the seat and then climbed out with his hands handcuffed in front of him. Davis walked him around to the front of the car. The headlights lit up the dirt road and the line of tree on both sides. Alred stood in the middle of the road, ten yards away from the car, in the middle of the lights.

Davis said, "Where is she?" The rifle rested on his right shoulder like a hunter waiting his chance to shoot.

Alred forced a laugh. "Man, I was just kidding. Just wanted to scare that Newton bitch." He wouldn't look up at Davis and the sheriff wondered if this was because the lights were blinding him.

"I told you not to mess with me tonight, John. Where is she?"

"I don't fucking know. I never seen her. I was just kidding. I'm sorry."

Davis pointed the shotgun at his face, and the man lifted his handcuffed hands up and turned his head away. Davis said it again, "Where is she?"

"I don't fucking know." Then Alred began to cry.

And though Davis knew what he had done was wrong, at that moment, he didn't care. He needed to know if this man knew anything about the girl and threatening his life was the only way he knew to get the truth out of someone like Alred.

Satisfied that Alred knew nothing about the girl, Davis walked over and opened the door. *Oh, how I'd love to leave you here hand-cuffed to a tree,* he thought, as Alred climbed in. They headed back out onto Highway 144. Davis felt more tired than he had ever felt in his life. Though he knew it hadn't been very likely, back in that trailer for a few moments he felt certain she was there. But she wasn't. Thank God for that.

Jimmy was atop Carol, moving within her as her fingers and nails slid across his chest, pushed against the muscle there, pinched his nipples. He opened his eyes, her humsong moan sweet in his ears, focused for a second on a painting above the bed of an alligator with two heads, and then came inside of her. They kissed deeply, as he began to soften, her legs wrapped tight around his back in a grip he had no desire to escape from.

Soon their breathing returned to normal, and music from the living room spoke in hushes and whispers. A candle on each nightstand bookended the bed. On the ceiling, candlelight played a shiftless silhouetted scene. Jimmy wanted to tell her how good the sex had been for him but stopped himself, knowing no matter how sincere the statement it was the kind of thing that would cheapen the moment.

From the nightstand drawer, Carol pulled a half-smoked joint. As she lit it, Jimmy saw through the glow of the flame touching paper her nipples gleaming and purple-red from the attention he had given them. She smoked, then held the joint out and he took it, toked long and hard, and passed it back to Carol, who set it in a clear ashtray. Moving his right index finger slowly from her belly-button to her left breast, he performed delicate circles around the dark nipples, causing Carol to moan faintly, until the flesh hardened beneath his touch.

Jimmy propped himself up against the headboard as she rested her head on his chest. *What a night,* he thought, *what a day, what a couple of days.* His legs and back felt sore, his pubic hair matted and yet he felt as alive as he'd ever been. Felt like he could walk a hundred miles, run a marathon, bench-press five hundred pounds; you name it, he could do it. It was as if everything that had happened in his life and in the last few days all built to this moment. He wanted to stay in bed like this for a long time, forgetting about all the other problems in the world. But as quick as these pleasant thoughts came, he felt guilty for having them, as if there were a group of people, including Jimmy, who were never allowed this type of bliss, whether it had to do with his mother or the fact that he had taken another man's life, even if it was in self-defense. Jimmy stared up at the ceiling again, gazing at the odd shapes forming above him—distorted squares, half-circles, folding triangles—and tried to concentrate on them, hoping the feeling would pass.

Carol said, "What's it like where you live?"

"In North Carolina?"

"Yeah. I've never lived anywhere but Florida—here and Tallahassee."

"It's nice. Some of the towns are big but where I live isn't. It's not much different from here, sizewise, except that where you have all these pine trees we have mountains. My house actually backs up to a mountain. There's a creek a mile away, full of trout."

"Sounds nice. Maybe I'll get to see it someday."

"Maybe."

Jimmy could feel her wetness against his thigh and the warmth of her breath against his chest. He figured she was listening to his heart, the way it beat quick and excited and he liked what that might mean. There were a couple women back home—one married, one not—who would come by sometimes. But those women would never stay in bed with him like this, easing into sleep.

He closed his eyes and thought of the missing girl. He had never known anyone named Teresa. But he knew, like Davis and his father and most people in town, how these things always seemed to work out. They would probably find her dead in the woods. But then, maybe because he was wrapped up in the warm arms of a woman, he thought there was a chance that somebody hadn't killed her. What if she stopped to pee and got lost in the woods and was living on berries, calling out for a voice to hear her? Maybe a boyfriend followed her out here and left the car on the side of the road and the two of them took off together. He knew it was strange to think of this girl, especially now with Carol lying next to him, but he couldn't get the image of that poster out of his mind. Her name *Teresa Martin, Teresa, Teresa.* Three strong syllables playing in his head.

Carol said, "You want to take a bath?"

"That sounds good."

In the tub, Carol sat behind Jimmy and began to rub his back and he closed his eyes. Her hands felt good on his neck and shoulders. The warm water was lulling, and the light was nothing more than a thin sheet from the candles in the bedroom two rooms away. He tried to remember the last time he had taken a bath and realized he hadn't had one since he was a child, with his mother.

On Saturday nights, when Truman was away on one of his out of town trips with Dan and Davis, his mother would run a warm bath for the two of them. Although he couldn't remember exactly when the baths started, he thought he was probably six or seven and they had continued, though much less frequent, until he was ten or eleven.

She would fill the tub with bubbles and let the water rise until it was about to overflow. Jimmy would say, "Stop it, stop it," as the bubbles climbed higher and higher. And she'd laugh as the first bubble or two fell over the sides of the white claw-footed tub. Then she'd let the pink towel fall from her body to the floor as she slowly stepped in, sending a wave of water over the side, onto the linoleum.

Jimmy would take off his clothes as his mother watched him, smiling with her head resting on the back arc of the tub and then opening her legs as Jimmy climbed in, sitting with his back to her chest. Popping bubbles and the warmth of the water sent what felt like a thousand pin pricks across his body. It felt good and Jimmy could smell soap mixed with the ever-burning cigarette in the small tin ashtray on the closed toilet seat lid.

She whistled a song he didn't know the name of until years later when he'd walked into a bar in Charlotte and heard "Into The Mystic" playing on the jukebox.

After rubbing his back, she would take a wash cloth and scrub his body, reaching around to his chest and face and legs and as she ran it against his crotch he'd stiffen there in the water. When she felt him harden against her hand, she laughed her cute, girlish laugh and lay back whistling her song, telling Jimmy how he was going to break some little girl's heart with that thing.

On some nights, she asked Jimmy to scrub her back. He would stand up and sit behind her—her back to his chest then—and feel the tautness of her skin and the single brown mole at the base of her neck before moving on to the rest of her back. They would sit there until the water cooled. Then she'd tuck Jimmy into bed where, with the sheets pulled to his neck, his skin felt clean and pure, alive, and he'd sleep better on those nights as if every pore had been opened to a thing he didn't understand but lived for. She told Jimmy he should never mention their baths to Truman, that it was their special time together. She said his father was a good man, but not affectionate and that what they were doing was perfectly natural for a mother and son.

"Will you do my back?" It was Carol again. He said sure and stood and she slid between his legs, reaching up and playslapping his drooping member.

As he began to rub her back, the music in the other room ended and the slight slush of the bathwater and her moans were all he heard. He tried to figure out what the memory of his mother meant, but it tired him and he hoped that Carol would say something to ground him here in this world. There was much to do tomorrow with the painting and planting. He considered asking Carol if she wanted to come over and help but it could wait until the morning. They would be in bed soon. The sheets pulled high, and the two of them clean and comfortable together. Dreaming, sweet and lovely dreaming.

Bobby woke in the night. He'd had a dream of his father and him in the front yard, playing catch with a baseball. The baseball was new, with bright red thread in the seams and the ball made a popping sound and stung their hands as it landed in their gloves. His mother was sitting in a lawn chair, a few feet away, watching. Tony was there too, behind her, playing volleyball with the big lady Bobby had seen earlier out by the pool and that Wendy lady. Marsha Floyd was mowing the grass under the volleyball net in tiny figure-eights. Bobby shook the image and walked groggily from his bedroom to the bathroom. After flushing the toilet, he walked by his father's room. The door was open and the bed empty. Bobby walked over and lay down in his parents' bed, stretching out, feeling for a thing to hold.

SATURDAY

JIMMY WOKE and opened his eyes to darkness. For a moment, he felt disoriented. The ceiling above him offered no clues, showed nothing concrete, only a dark line that could have been a starless night sky. It could have been the ceiling to his bedroom in North Carolina seven hundred miles away. Then he heard Carol's breathing next to him, smelled her hair. He climbed quietly out of bed, and in the departing darkness slipped on his boxers and walked out of the bedroom.

At the sliding glass doors, he smoked a cigarette and took in the flat, rambling countryside where two Black Angus cows walked slowly toward the fence at the far northern edge of her property. The square structure was there too, and for a moment he considered walking out and taking another quick look at the gators. The sun hadn't been up long and the grass was spotted with dew and at the bottom of the door there was still a foot or two of receding condensation.

She had set the timer on the coffee maker, and the pot was full, so he poured himself a cup, then meandered around the house, walked through the living room again and stopped at a closed door and opened it. A paint-splattered tarp covered the floor and on three of the room's walls was a mural of a country landscape. At the top of the landscape were a half-dozen white cows. A red pick-up truck with a cowboy sitting on the hood was parked by the wooden fence that circled the entire scene. The fence posts were small vertical alligators who looked as if they'd been tied to a stake and sat upright, balancing on their tails, staring into the sky, their legs extended out from their bodies as if trying to grab something. The cross boards sat heavy-looking in their open mouths.

On the fourth wall, the one not included in the mural, was a large painting of an alligator. What separated this one from the others was that it looked relatively normal. Jimmy studied the features, starting at the eyes, along the long snout, the back plates and the legs. But he could find no unusual markings or additions, which would make this one unique. He wondered if Carol hadn't finished it. If all of her alligators started by being painted normal and then she added her special touch.

The bed springs engaged in the next room and Jimmy quickly stepped out and shut the door. In the kitchen, he poured Carol a cup of coffee. When he turned around, she was standing there in a red robe whose sleeves were covered with white stars falling in small downward arcs.

He said, "Sleep okay?"

He felt guilty for having invaded the room, as if by doing so he had violated her trust, something he couldn't say for sure he had even earned.

"Yes. Like a baby. You?"

"Pretty good."

"You're up early."

"Gotta go help the old man paint the house."

She took the coffee he offered and nodded as if she were only now remembering his mention of it the night before.

"You wanna come over, paint a huge gator or two on the side of the house? Maybe one with paint brushes for teeth."

She smiled and said, "I have to work."

"Till when?"

"This afternoon."

"Come later. We'll be at it all day."

"We'll see. I've been working on a new painting that I want to finish. You want some breakfast?"

"No, I better get going." Jimmy went back into the bedroom and got dressed, splashed some water on his face in the bathroom and came back out in the kitchen where Carol was sitting at the table, both hands cupping her mug of coffee. When she saw him, she stood up and they walked to the front door where Jimmy kissed her.

She said, "You'll come see me tonight?"

"Yeah, I'll call you."

Then he walked to his truck, started it and backed out of the drive. The cab smelled of perfume. He breathed in deeply. She stood at the door and waved with her right hand, her left folded tight across her belly.

Truman walked out of the dark hall in an old pair of jeans and a T-shirt. The kitchen smelled of eggs and bacon and pancakes, of breakfasts and mornings long ago. It seemed possible to him that he had gone back in time twenty-five years and Dot had made this. She had always made big breakfasts for him and Jimmy. She wasn't much good at cooking dinner, would burn things as simple as bologna and cheese, but she could cook the hell out of some eggs and bacon.

Now, on the table were a trio of plates, each filled with hot steaming food: one had pancakes, another bacon and the third had eggs, which were separated into sections of sunnyside up and scrambled. There was a note in the center of the table that said *Enjoy, I'll be back soon.*

As Truman poured himself a cup of coffee, he heard Jimmy's truck turn into the yard. When he came in the front door, Jimmy smiled at Truman and said, "Let me just get changed and then we'll start." He grabbed a piece of bacon before heading back to his room.

Truman walked out onto the porch, looked at the woods across the yard before turning to the house. He had gotten a good amount of paint off the sides, but there had been more than one layer, which now gave the house a spotty pattern of grays and whites. The dirt in front of the porch looked good and fertile, black, ready to be planted in.

When he heard Jimmy moving in the kitchen behind him,

Truman went back inside. Jimmy was wearing the same clothes he'd worn when he'd arrived: the paint-splattered jeans and T-shirt. He grabbed one of the empty plates and filled it with a half-dozen pancakes, some eggs and two slices of bacon.

"The house looks good. Did the sprayer give you any trouble?"

"Nah, not really."

"Should we wait for Angie?"

"No, she said to go ahead and eat."

Truman made a plate for himself and sat across from Jimmy who was already working on his scrambled eggs. Truman ran a knife through his pancakes, cutting them into small squares. A circle of brown honey-maple syrup lay in one corner of the plate. The food looked okay, even smelled good. Because of this, he was a bit apprehensive about eating it, as if he knew that the taste wouldn't hold up to the presentation. But he started by dipping a forkful of the pancakes into the syrup. After tasting them, he had to admit that they tasted pretty good.

They ate in silence for a few minutes. Truman wondered why it was that she could cook like this one day and then awful, uneatable shit the next. He considered looking in the garbage can for any signs that she had ordered out.

Jimmy said, "Reminds me of the meals Mom used to make."

"Yeah." Truman could see her there, standing over the stove with a spatula in one had, a cigarette in the other.

"She would always have our plates full of food when we came out in the morning. I always like how the plates were hot, too."

Truman said, "She'd put them in the stove for a couple minutes."

Jimmy nodded as if saying, *Yeah, I remember.* "Damn near burnt my tongue that time I tried to lick some honey off the edge of the plate."

Truman laughed and Jimmy did too. After eating in silence for a few minutes, Jimmy said, "But she never seemed to eat, just sat there smoking, watching us eat. I always wondered if she dropped me off at school and then came home and ate alone."

"Oh, she ate. She ate plenty."

Truman remembered how she would pick at his food. She never did it around the boy, but when the two of them were alone she would feed him bite after bite and then he would take the fork and do the same for her. He was remembering that and the way she opened her mouth and closed her eyes, trusting that he would not hurt her, when the door opened on this Saturday morning and Angie walked in.

Davis parked against the curb. He could see Bird sitting in the diner drinking a cup of coffee, studying the newspaper. The sheriff felt even more tired than yesterday. He hadn't made it home until two and wasn't able to fall sleep for a while after that.

Bird looked up from his newspaper when Davis sat down across from him at the booth. A blond waitress, named Sara Huber, came over and poured Davis some coffee and refilled the deputy's cup. Sara was young and pretty and smelled of strawberries and was married to a man Davis had arrested twice for beating her up. "What can I get you, Sheriff?"

Davis looked up at Bird. "You already order?" The deputy nodded that he had. Davis said, "I'll have whatever he's having."

After Sara walked away, Bird said, "I drove by the scene this morning on my way in. Looks weird, all those trees wrapped in yellow tape."

"Lot of things seem weird around here these days."

Bird said, "You're right about that. Alred give you any trouble after I left?"

"No, he didn't say a word."

"That's good.

An image of Alred standing there in the dark, shielding his face, came back to Davis. He was not proud of what he had done out there. He tried to convince himself that the man had pushed him to that, but still it wasn't right.

After a couple sips of coffee, Davis said, "Bird, you given much thought to what's gonna happen around here when I'm gone?"

"What do you mean?"

"I'm not going to be sheriff too much longer."

"I don't know about that."

"About time for me to retire."

"Come on now, that's not true."

"Do you want to be the sheriff?"

"I hadn't really thought much about it."

"Well, do."

Bird turned away and the newspaper below him seemed to take on divine significance as his eyes fixed on an article about the recent rise in gasoline prices.

Sara came back and set the food in front of them—scrambled eggs, sausage links and slices of wheat toast. This seemed to relieve Bird immensely as he started into his food, as if he hoped that the business of eating might make the sheriff forget what he had just brought up. Davis decided he would give him his reprieve for now and smiled up at Sara, not sure how anyone could hit a face so sweet and innocent-looking.

Outside, a truck drove through Main Street with two boys sitting in the back on the wheelwells. One of the boys was holding a big brown dog. The light turned yellow and the driver slammed on the brakes and both boys fell forward. They righted themselves and laughed as if they could ask for no more entertainment than that on a Saturday morning. The man driving scolded the boys through the rear window. In response, they slid down so that they were sitting in the bed.

As they drove away, Davis watched a dark blue Buick LeSabre park in front of the diner. Strane climbed out of the car, looked into the diner, and Davis waved him in.

Bird said, "Should we tell him about Alred last night?"

"No, let's keep it quiet." Davis thought that if he told Strane about it, then maybe they would go and investigate the place, question the man and he could be done with him. But if they did that, then Alred might mention the side trip Davis had taken him on.

Plus, he was convinced that Alred had nothing to do with Teresa Martin.

Strane hiked up his dark blue pants as he made his way over to the booth. "Gentlemen."

Davis said, "Have a seat," indicating that Bird's side of the table would be the preferred one. The deputy slid over and Strane sat down. Right on time, Sara brought another cup and filled it with coffee.

Davis said, "Any news?"

"As a matter of fact there is. We got the results back on the pants. They aren't the girl's. We checked fiber samples from the car and the pants, and those pants have never been in that car."

Davis set his cup of coffee down. "So we got nothing?"

"Looks like it."

"What are you guys going to do today?"

Strane sipped on his coffee, made a sour face that said in no uncertain terms this was not the best cup of coffee he'd ever had. "We're gonna search the woods again, go deeper, stretch the dogs out. Plus, we got that list you gave us. We'll do some Q&As, but I gotta say if something doesn't show up today or tomorrow there isn't a whole lot more we can do here."

Bird said, "What list?"

Strane said, "List of local felons."

Bird turned to Davis, who was glad to see Sara was making her way back over to the table. "What can I get you?"

Strane said, "I'm gonna pass."

"Suit yourself."

Strane said, "What about you guys?"

Davis said, "We'll question some more of the people on the list, too." Along with those interviews, Davis figured they'd have to go over to Alred's. He'd also like to go over and see Truman and Jimmy, see how they were getting along. Either way, he hoped it would be a shorter day than yesterday.

Strane stood and said, "We'll see you later." He left the diner and walked a short distance down the street, stopped and studied one of the flyers on the telephone pole and then disappeared into an office they had converted into a makeshift investigation headquarters. Davis had visited the place yesterday. It looked like something out of a movie to him—photos of the girl on the wall, a detailed map of the northern part of Florida and sharp-dressed men sitting around on the telephone, tracking leads that had, so far, gone nowhere.

When Davis turned back, he saw that Bird was staring at the back of Sara's skirt, as if it might hold the winning numbers to tonight's lottery. He had to admit that the young lady had a body worth admiring, but it wasn't like Bird to act this way. Davis could practically see butterflies floating above his deputy's head as his mind swam in lustful circles, and he wondered if his deputy had already slept with her or if they were still in the flirting stage.

Davis said, "What are you doing?"

"Nothing, what?"

For this next part, Davis leaned across the table and lowered his voice, "Something going on between you two?"

"No."

"Well, there don't need to be. I'm gonna give you a piece of advice. Don't go messing around with another man's wife."

"I'm not."

"Don't."

Sara walked back over to the table, smiled at the deputy and filled his mug first. She turned the pot toward Davis' cup, but he put his hand up, indicating he'd had enough.

Bobby and Darren drove out of their front yard. A packed suitcase sat on the seat between them. Darren said, "What do you want for breakfast?"

Bobby said, "McDonald's. Where we going?"

"I don't know. We'll see."

It sounded good to Bobby. Fifteen minutes earlier, he had been asleep in his parents' bed when he opened his eyes to his father standing over him. At first, Bobby thought his father might be mad at him for sleeping in his bed, but if so he hadn't mentioned it. When he looked closer now, he saw that his father hadn't shaved and his eyes were red-looking and he had on the same clothes he'd worn the night before. He wondered where he'd been all night and figured he'd probably been out working. He did that sometimes.

Bobby remembered the dog and said, "What about Suzi?"

"We can't bring a dog to a hotel."

"How is she going to eat?"

"It'll only be for a day or two, until I figure out what to do, and I left her a lot of food."

So what Bobby knew was that this trip was for a few days and that the dog couldn't come. It occurred to him, out of the blue, as those golden arches shone ahead up on the right, something that made him as excited as his dad seemed nervous, that where they were going was to pick up his mother and that they would again, soon, be a family.

Jimmy looked out the window and saw Angie by the front porch, a fixed determined expression across her face as she loosened the soil with her gloved hands. She picked up one of the impatiens and the roots and tendrils hung down like bits of stringy, white hair. Truman stood to the right of the porch with the spray gun in his hand, the white paint shield across his mouth and nose like an oxygen mask. Out above the tree line, two turkey vultures circled overhead, and Jimmy wondered what dead animal they had their sights on.

He felt full and a bit sluggish. The breakfast had been too much, but once he got working and moving he'd feel better. He liked big breakfasts, liked how it gave him something to work off and the way a couple hours later he would be hungry again, hungrier even, as if the large meal had stretched his stomach. Although anymore it seemed like the most he got for breakfast was a sausage biscuit at a drive-thru.

His mind turned to Carol and what she might be doing now.

He could still smell her on his hands and arms. He considered, for a second or two, sitting in the cab of the truck and letting her scent fill him. On the drive home from her house, he had been numb, alive, and tried to think of nothing as the trees slid by outside his window. But now he thought of the time they'd spent together. What had he gotten into? Jesus, those gators. He smiled and shook his head. It did feel good being with her even if it had only been one day, hell, really just a couple of hours, but he hadn't felt like this in a long time. He couldn't help but think briefly of Helen and the only other woman he'd ever really been in love with, Merrilee.

Merrilee had come into his life when he was twenty-two years old and living in Kernersville, a small town outside of Winston-Salem. At the time he was working as a landscaper, the job that introduced him to the world of manual labor, the world of working with what is in front of you, one line at a time, where the satisfaction comes with work done being visible at the end of the day.

After work, he'd return to his studio apartment, shower and walk the quarter mile to the local bar — The Corner Tavern — where he'd eat a burger with fries for dinner and drink beer until eight or nine at night, listening to music, and watching baseball or basketball games depending on the season. On Fridays and Saturdays, he stayed at the bar until closing, throwing darts and playing pool and drinking too much beer before eventually making it home in a blur.

It was in this bar that he met Merrilee on a Friday night. She had long red hair, eyes the softest shade of blue he'd ever seen, a small upturned nose, and a tight body covered with freckles. The first night she beat Jimmy, three games of pool in a row. He had told himself, years earlier, after Helen, in the contempt of youth and a crushed heart, that he would not want or need a woman throughout his life. At the time, the job and his life were enough to satisfy him. He looked at the work as his apprenticeship period where he saved money and learned his trade, which he hoped would foster his dream of working for himself, being self-sufficient, depending on no one.

The next morning, lying in bed, with Merrilee asleep beside him, Jimmy sat up on his left elbow and with his right index finger traced the outline of the naked, slight bones of her spine and knew that it was too late; she had him. There'd been other women after Helen, but none of them had lasted more than a month or two. As soon as he felt himself being drawn in, thinking of the particular woman at work or as he showered, he'd break the relationship off. It was only in reflection that he could see this; at the time he would blame it on being too busy or young for anything serious.

A month after meeting, Merrilee moved in with Jimmy and a few months later she started dental hygienist school. Jimmy was as happy as he had ever been. He stopped going to the bar every night, only the occasional weekend trip where the two of them played pool together. She'd make him dinner and then they'd lie side-by-side on the couch watching TV until they were both ready for bed. They had their share of small problems—occasionally they fought over money or spurts of jealousy on his part if he caught her talking to other men—but despite that he felt then as sure that he would spend his life with her as he had a few years earlier that a woman would play no part in his future. He had even spent a couple afternoons in jewelry shops, shopping for engagement rings.

Two months after graduating from hygienist school, Merrilee left Jimmy and moved to Charlotte to live with her sister who was dating an accountant. Merrilee said that Jimmy had no ambition and would never be able to do the kinds of things for her that her sister's boyfriend could. After the initial shock, he told himself that it was for the best, that a woman did nothing but complicate his life and in no time he slid back into the routine which had been his before Merrilee: the bar every night and waking with a hangover on Saturday and Sunday mornings.

Despite his refusal to admit the impact she had had on his life, he missed her and over the next six months was arrested twice for harassing her. Both incidents occurred after a night of drinking, the desire to hear her voice and see those blue eyes light up outweighing the knowledge that they were no longer, and had never really been, his. He'd go to her third-floor apartment, an hour and a half away, and knock on her door. Through the door, she'd tell him to leave, yell and beg him to go away, but he'd stay until the police arrived—unable to leave even though he knew the outcome like an alcoholic does before taking that first sip.

To get away from her, after his second arrest, Jimmy moved back to the mountains where he had spent his teenaged years and began working as a housepainter, again vowing to never allow a woman to become a large part of his life. The experience with Merrilee was yet more proof that women were bad for him, a thing that could only lead to trouble and heartbreak. But here it was, he thought, all these years later and now Carol, this woman who made him feel things he had almost forgotten.

"You gonna hide in here all day or help us?" It was Truman, coming in the house to get something to drink.

"No, just taking a piss."

Jimmy went outside and surveyed the work they had done. Angie was on her knees, patting the dirt around one of the purple-flowered impatiens. It was the final plant on this side of the porch while the other side still had to be planted. Truman had already painted the front of the house to the right of the porch as high as he could without assistance.

Jimmy retrieved the ladder, which had been resting against the downed tailgate of the truck, and carried it over to the house. Truman came back outside and started for the ladder with the spray gun in hand.

Jimmy said, "I'll get the top part."

"No, I'll do it."

"The ladder isn't that sturdy."

"Just hand me this when I get up there." He gave Jimmy the

spray gun and began to climb the ladder. Jimmy turned to Angie, who shrugged her shoulders in a gesture he understood to mean *You can't tell him anything*, so he held the ladder as Truman ascended toward the higher reaches of the house.

After taking the gun from Jimmy, Truman said, "Damn, this thing makes it easy."

"Sure does."

"Last time we painted this house we had to use a roller, took three days. You remember that?"

Jimmy tried to remember the day but couldn't. His mind was still full of Carol and the way she smiled at him. How he would like to crawl up inside of that smile and forget about everything else, but he couldn't forget about his mother or Helen or Merrilee and how he seemed to be drawn to what he couldn't have.

He said, "Yeah."

"Your damn mother kept repainting everything I did."

Truman stopped painting for a second, coughed into the mask, and then faced the house again, spraying the fresh white paint across the old, faded boards. After a couple minutes, he looked down at Jimmy, who still held onto the ladder at the level of Truman's feet. "You gonna stand there holding your dick all day?"

Jimmy said, "No, I guess I better get my ass working, eh?"

Davis and Bird buckled their seat belts and pulled away from the tilting brown trailer. They had spent thirty minutes inside Alred's place and found nothing but a couple of joints in his top dresser drawer and a rather substantial collection of pornography under his bed. Davis shook his head, fully aware that they hadn't accomplished anything in the last couple of hours.

Before going to Alred's, they had stopped by the investigation headquarters and agreed to handle the first ten people on the list of Portisville residents with felony convictions if the men from the state could handle the other twenty-one. The first man on the list was Jim Bordin. Jim had done time down in Starke for trying to kill his girlfriend with a fork. She hadn't died but now had a dozen holes on the right side of her neck and chest. Jim Bordin hadn't been home, nor had the next man they had gone to question. After two misses, Davis had decided to stop putting it off and go on over and check Alred's place.

Now, Davis passed Rhonda Newton's trailer at the edge of the park. Her porch steps were empty and he wondered if she was in some other trailer with a man that wasn't her husband.

Bird said, "Why isn't Truman's name on here?"

The deputy had the list in his hand, studying it. He had already picked it up from Davis' dashboard, read it and put it back down twice. The reason Davis had not shown him the list before giving it to Strane was to avoid this. He was actually surprised it had taken Bird so long to bring it up.

"I didn't think it was necessary."

Davis could tell from the way his deputy avoided his eyes and looked out the window that he was trying damned hard not to get too worked up about this. "But they asked you for a list of all locals with records, not those who you think might be suspects."

"Yes, they did." Davis hoped that by leaving it like that the deputy would end the discussion, that this acknowledgement of something, although not exactly error, would be enough to quell Bird's pursuit. And it seemed to work for a couple of minutes, until Bird said, "Sir, I know you two are friends but shouldn't they have a complete list?"

"Bird, he's an old man. He doesn't have much time left. I just don't think it's fair to burden him with this."

"With all due respect, he didn't look too sick yesterday when you brought him out into those woods."

Davis stared straight ahead at the blacktop slicing a trail through the line of trees on either side of him. "Son, I'm going to try and not get too upset about this. I know we are all under a lot of pressure here. We don't know shit about what is going on with this girl and we may never find out. That is why I'm gonna let you question me this one time, today, in this car, but if you ever do it again you'll be working with your daddy over at the junkyard."

Bird's face flushed and he turned away from the sheriff. Davis knew that it was about the lowest blow he could throw, but the deputy had kept pushing him. Bird had played minor league ball for a couple years before throwing his shoulder out, and Davis believed the main reason he became a police officer after moving back to Portisville was to avoid working with his father at the junkyard.

They drove for a few more minutes without speaking. When they passed the dirt road Davis had taken Alred to last night, the sheriff felt his stomach go heavy and a sour taste he couldn't identify worked its way up his throat. He turned up the CB hoping for some report on something they could pursue, a speeding car, a stick-up, anything. None came and Davis decided that he would drop Bird off, let him question the rest of the people on the list. He was going to go by the Wills' and see what they were up to, maybe ask Truman a question or two.

Jimmy squeezed the trigger of the spray gun from atop the ladder. The black, paint-splattered cord rested against his pant leg. To his right was the back of the house and beyond that another wall of pine trees. Though it looked solid and impenetrable, Jimmy knew it was actually only twenty or so yards deep before it opened up on the other side to Highway 144. As a child, he had never played back there, behind the house and in those woods, and he had never seen his parents enter the area, as if it were a wall that one admired from a distance but didn't dare try to pass through.

The sun felt good on his neck and arms. He could even feel it on his back, through his T-shirt. As he was thinking about the upcoming winter in North Carolina and how he wasn't looking forward to it, the sound of his father coughing reached him. It was a long cough, deep and guttural and breath-catching. When it subsided, Jimmy returned to spraying the gun, covering up the old wood. The front of the house had gone well. About half of this side was done now. If he had more time he would have spent a whole day on prep-work, power-cleaning the house more than once and working on the paint around the windows with a chisel and he would put more than one coat on it. Still, with this quick fix, it would look better, much better, than when he had arrived.

A small band of house sparrows landed on the roof—ten feet away—chittered a quick, harsh song and quickly dispersed. One bird hung back a second from the rest, circled the roof and then ascended up and away.

No clouds occupied the sky, only a solid wall of blue like some vast blanket with no end in sight. Jimmy liked blue skies and always found them comforting. He figured blue skies were a thing most people liked, but he wasn't the type of person who thought everything he did and said had to be unique.

He climbed down the ladder and walked around to the front of the house. Angie was watering the plants and dirt by the front porch. She turned and looked up at Jimmy. He smiled and said, "Looks good."

She backed up a few feet to survey the work she had done.

Jimmy said, "Is he okay?"

"Yeah, he went in to get some water."

Then they both stared up at the house for a second.

"What kind of time frame are we looking at with him?"

She said, "I would guess a couple months. Could be as long as three or four. I can't imagine more than that. He has a doctor's appointment on Monday. They'll do some tests, take some new X-rays, see how it's progressing, but he won't let them treat him. I'll be lucky if I can even get him to the appointment. He refused to go to the last one."

"It's his choice."

"I guess it is."

"It would be really nice if you could stay a couple more days and go with him to the appointment."

"I can't. I have to get back." Jimmy wondered if he really did have to get back. Sure, there was work waiting for him, but there would always be more work. It wasn't that, really. He had to leave; this wasn't his home anymore.

"I understand."

Truman stepped out the door, holding a large glass of water, from which he took a generous mouthful. Angie asked Jimmy if he wanted some water and disappeared inside the house.

Jimmy sat on the porch steps a few feet from Truman. He considered saying something but couldn't think of a thing he wanted to talk about. Truman seemed to be of the same mindset as he hadn't looked up at his son since coming back out of the house. They were here, a few feet away from each other, and it seemed, at the moment, as if they had exhausted everything they could talk about.

The silence itself didn't bother Jimmy. He was used to jobs where men sat side-by-side without saying a word for their thirty-minute lunch breaks, as if the physical nature of the work they did had stolen their ability to speak. Jimmy decided that he wouldn't start the conversation but would stay close in case Truman wanted to. In the woods, a flock of sparrows, maybe the same ones he had seen earlier, spoke in their sing-song voices and though he couldn't see them, their presence was comforting to Jimmy just the same.

And then, Jimmy remembered the day his father had mentioned earlier, the other time they had painted the house. Jimmy and his mother mixed and carried the paint to Truman, who seemed to work atop the ladder all day long. At some point in the day, she had walked up behind him and painted a straight white line down his jeans. Truman had jumped from the ladder and ran after her, chasing her to the far side of the yard where he painted an X on the front of her red T-shirt. Then the two of them had laughed as they hugged and kissed in the baking Florida sun while a Merle Haggard song streamed from the house.

Bobby and Darren passed a pair of deer standing in the grass at the edge of the interstate. Bobby turned around and watched them run off into the woods. After settling back in his seat, he said, "Are we going to meet Mom?"

Darren turned to the boy, quick, his lips fixed in a tight, odd gaze. "What are you talking about?"

"I thought that's where we were going. Maybe she called you and we were going to meet her." Bobby had known after breakfast, as they pulled out of the parking lot heading south and not north, moving farther away from where she lived, that they weren't going to her house, but it still seemed possible to him that they might be going to meet her somewhere.

Darren shook his head. "I don't know where you got that idea. It's not going to happen."

"It could."

"Bobby, let me explain something to you. Your mother is not coming back to live with us." Then Darren paused, as if he were trying to find the right words, words that would be definite and not too painful and would not lead to more questions. He stared at the back of the small, red sports car in front of them as if it might hold these sacred words. "She's not coming back."

"She might come back."

"She's not."

Bobby kicked the floorboard in front of him and folded his arms across his chest. He didn't know what else to do.

Darren said, "Knock it off."

"I want to go home then."

"Not yet."

"Why did we leave?"

"I need to think about something."

"I don't care. It's your fault anyway that she left."

Bobby felt the slap of his father's hand crashing into his left cheek. His head hit the top of the seat. His jaw stung. For a moment, he sat there, unmoving, in stunned silence. Then he crossed his arms tight across his chest and stared out the window where trees whipped by. His father was looking at him, waiting and wanting some response. Bobby held his glare at the trees and told himself not to cry, that he could do anything else, could open the door and jump out and roll along the highway into the grass, but he would not let his father see him cry.

Jimmy looked down at Truman, who was watching the paint swirl in the compressor's square body, then up at the house, where he capped off the top arch with a back and forth spray. After handing Truman the sprayer, he made his way down the ladder.

Together, they stepped away from the back of the house. Jimmy had painted the top part first, figuring he could let Truman do the lower half after lunch. It would give Jimmy time to check the last side they had to paint, making sure the windows were still papered off and that there was no grass or dirt against the bottom of the house to slow them down.

Truman said, "Not too shabby."

"What did you expect?"

Angie called from the front of the house that lunch was ready.

Jimmy brought the compressor to the front yard so that he could fill it with more paint. Again, he admired the impatiens and camellias and thought the place looked pretty damned good. It was hardly recognizable from the house he had pulled up to two short and long days ago. Although he had seen his work transform many a building, it could still amaze him. He especially liked how the white flowers of the camellias provided a nice contrast to the bright pink and purple impatiens they bordered.

Angie said, "Is he coming?"

"I don't know."

Walking back around the side of the house, Jimmy wondered why his father had to be such a pain in the ass about everything. Why couldn't he just come when he was called?

As he passed the side they had already painted, he thought it looked okay, though he did see a few spots he might go over again if they had enough time. When he reached the back of the house and turned the corner, he saw Truman vomiting into the grass. Jimmy took a step toward his father, put his hand on his shoulder. Truman swatted it away and looked up at Jimmy with spots of vomit lining his lower lip. "Leave me alone."

"Are you okay?"

Truman spat at the ground. "What do you think?"

"Maybe you should go inside and get some rest."

Truman didn't answer but walked by Jimmy. He stood there a moment, then looked down at where his father had vomited. The small pile was mostly brown and yellow, from breakfast, Jimmy figured, but there were also smears of mucusy blood over the whole mess. Jimmy kicked some dirt over it before heading back toward the front of the house.

When Jimmy made it to the front yard, Truman was sitting on the tailgate of his truck, holding a turkey sandwich in one hand and a beer in the other. Angie was across from him on the second step of the porch eating from a bag of potato chips.

Truman said, "We gonna have enough paint?"

Jimmy said, "Plenty by the looks of it." He got a sandwich from the plate on the porch, then took a seat on the steps next to Angie. He wondered why his father acted different around her, not exactly nice, but not as mean as when they were alone.

The three of them ate in silence until they heard the car pull off the highway and enter the driveway. There was a delay in which they couldn't see it, only heard the hum of a motor down-shifting and the crush of tire on loose gravel. Jimmy hoped it was Carol coming around the corner. Then the front bumper of Davis' car came into view. He parked over behind Angie's car and climbed out. "Am I at the right house?"

Jimmy said, "Looks like our relief has arrived."

Davis walked toward them, with his hands in his pockets, admiring the work they had done. "Damn, it looks good. Tell you what, when you all are done here there's a gray ranch house a couple miles down the road…"

Truman said, "My ass."

Angie said, "Want a sandwich?"

Davis brought a hand up to wipe the sweat from his forehead and said sure he would take a bite to eat, if it was no trouble. From behind her, Angie lifted the plate with the three remaining sandwiches and offered them to him. The sheriff took one and sat on the tailgate next to Truman.

After Angie walked in the house, Davis turned to the younger Wills. "Come all the way here and he makes you work?"

Jimmy smiled. "Yeah, that's all he wanted. Son of a bitch."

Truman said, "Fuck you, both." All three men laughed as Angie came out and poured water from a pitcher into a glass and handed it to Davis who took a quick swallow and winked at her.

Angie said to Davis, "Hear anything about that girl?"

Davis shook his head. "Nothing yet."

Jimmy turned to his father. He waited for some smart remark, like what he had said the other night at Angie's first mention of the missing girl, but Truman didn't say anything about her. Instead, he turned to his old friend. "You ever use one of these paint spray guns?"

Davis said, "No."

"Makes things easy."

"Technology is something."

Truman stood and picked up the gun and walked over to Jimmy's truck and sprayed a white line across the driver's side back panel. "Squeeze the trigger and it does the work."

Davis turned back to Jimmy, who shrugged his shoulders and said, "Sure, why not." There were so many different colored spots of paint on the back of the truck that a couple more lines wouldn't hurt it. Davis lifted and sprayed over the same area Truman had moments before.

Angie jumped up and said, "Let me try." She added another line to the back of the truck.

Truman said, "That's the real reason he came back, so he could get his truck painted."

They laughed, then Truman grabbed the compressor by the handle and started to walk to the back of the house with Davis following a few steps behind him.

Davis watched Truman work the sprayer back and forth against the old wood. His friend had always been a tireless worker, not afraid to sweat and get dirty. The two of them had built Davis' house thirty years ago and he remembered meeting Truman on a basketball court, a short and thick man with a wild-eyed smile. Truman wasn't a good ball-player, was anything but graceful, but he moved with an intensity nobody was stupid enough to get in the way of, and which Davis had admired.

Now, Truman said, "Sure you don't want to do some?"

"I better not. Bev will kill me if I get paint on these clothes."

Truman sprayed another series of lines over the wood. Jimmy and Angie were at the front of the house doing something but Davis couldn't hear them well enough to say what that might be. He said, "Those jeans turned out to be nothing."

"Figures."

Seeing his opening, Davis went for it. "Where were you two nights ago?"

Truman said, "I don't know, why?"

"That's when the girl's car showed up."

Truman stopped painting and looked back at Davis. His face hadn't given any true signs of emotion yet, but the fact that he had stopped working was sign enough to Davis that Truman understood what he was getting at.

"What exactly are you asking me here?"

"Truman, don't give me shit about this."

"Ask then." Truman's face fell into that sick smile mode. The one that said he knew he had you and that he wasn't going to let you go until you did what he wanted.

Davis said, "You think I like this? Just tell me where you were and we can be done with it."

"I'm too old for that shit. I've been rehabilitated; think that's the term they used."

Davis stood next to him now, trying to keep his voice down. "Just tell me where you were."

"Same damn place I am every night, sitting on that porch."

"Can anybody vouch for you?"

"Angie."

Davis didn't know why he was bothering with these questions about the missing girl. Maybe he was trying to warm up, but this was the wrong approach. What he wanted to do was ask about Dot and the morning Truman had come home and she was gone.

"Want me to call her over here?" Truman cupped his hands around his mouth, making a faux megaphone.

"No. Do you always have to be so difficult?"

"Yes." Truman turned away and started working on the house again.

Davis stood there for a minute, watching him work, watching the house transform in front of his eyes. He knew that if he was going to ask, he'd better do it now before he lost his courage. "You remember the morning Dot disappeared?"

Truman turned to Davis again. His finger came off the spray gun and then his hand and the gun fell to his side. His eyes searched back and forth across Davis' face. "Of course I remember it. Why?"

"The morning you got back, after seeing she wasn't in the house, you woke Jimmy up, looked around outside for her, and then called me, right?" To Davis, his voice sounded shaky.

Truman nodded that, yeah, that is how it happened. "Why you asking?"

It took every ounce of strength Davis had not to say *because Jimmy said you never woke him up before I got there.* But again it was still possible that Jimmy had been wrong, a tired confused kid, not sure what he was supposed to say. Davis knew if he told Truman what Jimmy had told him years ago it might cause friction between these two. He didn't want that. It had been so long and it was good to see them together like this and Davis wasn't sure what he believed about that morning anymore. He knew the way memory could change over time, become something it never had been, whole events erased and created within the confines of the mind.

Before Davis could respond, he heard the rustling of leaves and someone coming around the corner. Jimmy smiled at the two old friends and said, "How's it going?"

Truman looked at Davis but didn't say anything. Davis said, "Fine. Actually, I gotta get going."

Davis turned back to say something to Truman—he didn't know what, a goodbye, something—but Truman wouldn't look at him, was concentrating on the house in front of him. It was as if Truman had forgotten that he was even there. Jimmy followed him to the front of the house. Davis said, "He's not in the best of moods today."

"I think working in the sun all day has gotten to him."

Davis noticed there were a couple spots of white paint by Jimmy's right eye. "You're probably right. Let me ask you something, Jimmy."

"Sure."

"Do you remember the morning your mother disappeared?"

Jimmy nodded slowly. "Yeah, pretty much."

Davis hesitated a moment. How far should he go with this? Was he already past the point where he couldn't go back? Was it all a waste of time? Just bringing up old memories, old nasty ones, that wouldn't help anyone? Maybe he should just shut his mouth and get in his car and drive away. But it was Jimmy who had first asked about it yesterday. He would have to be easy, careful with how he presented this. He thought he'd done okay with Truman. As calmly as he could, he said, "Now, the first thing you remember about that morning is your father waking you up, right?"

Jimmy nodded yeah, squinting his eyes as if he were trying to understand the question, maybe playing the memory through his mind again. Davis was sure the memory of that morning must have come back to him—sleeping in the same bed, eating at the same table, the house—more than once in the last couple days.

"Yeah, him and you together."

Davis smiled. "Right, that's what I meant."

"Why?"

"After you asked me yesterday about your father I started thinking about the case, and I wanted to be sure that I had my time-line right. When your father got home and all. I'm just trying to keep it all straight in my head, the times."

"You going to re-open the case?"

Davis shook his head again. "No, unfortunately, it's like I said earlier, things point to that drifter. Sad as I am to say it, finding a person that was in town for one day that long ago is damned near impossible."

Jimmy nodded twice as if he understood what Davis was saying, then looked past Davis toward the back of the house where his father was working. Davis turned around but Truman was nowhere to be seen, only the hum and tick of the compressor gave any signs of life back behind the house.

Davis set his hands on Jimmy's shoulders, squeezed a bit. "I'm glad to see you turned out the way you did."

Jimmy smiled, almost blushed. "I'm not so sure about that."

"You leaving in the morning?"

"Pretty early."

Davis reached up and hugged him, whispered in his ear, "If you ever need anything don't hesitate to call." He wondered if Jimmy would come home for the funeral and doubted that he would. Backing out of the driveway, Davis figured that was probably the last time he would ever see little Jimmy Wills.

Bobby held his new fishing pole in one hand on the shore of the lake. With his free hand, he threw a small stone across the surface of the water. They had driven a couple hours and stopped at this lake

Bobby didn't think he'd ever been to before. It was much bigger than Miller's Pond and Bobby couldn't even see the other side. His father had bought him the pole at the bait shop where they had stopped to get worms. It had a reel on it called a Shakespeare. He liked the sound of that name and he also liked how easy the pole cast.

Darren was asleep in the bed of the truck, his legs hanging down from the tailgate, his feet an inch or two off the ground. The drive had tired Bobby out, too. He wondered what his father dreamed about, if perhaps he was having the same dream Bobby had the previous night of the two of them and a baseball and popping mitts. If, in his dream, it was a football and not a baseball they played catch with. If his father was younger. If his stomach wasn't so big, and if on the sidelines Bobby's mother stood cheering them on, her long, blond hair swaying back and forth as she jumped up and down. Bobby closed his eyes and held on to the fishing pole.

Twenty yards to his right, a green station wagon pulled up and parked by a picnic table. A couple, about his parents' age, climbed out of the car and draped a red-and-white checkered tablecloth across the table. A blond boy got out and walked over to the water's edge. At the back of the car, the father opened the hatchback and a small white dog jumped out and ran toward the water and the boy. When he reached the boy, the dog lunged at his shoes and tugged on his shoelaces. Then, as if bored or unhappy with the taste of the laces, the dog walked over to the edge of the bushes and lifted a leg to pee.

The boy threw a small yellow ball in Bobby's direction. The dog turned and in mid-piss, urine spraying the air like a spitting sprinkler head, charged the ball, retrieved it and ran back. Bobby leaned against the side of the truck, which was warm from baking in the sun, as they played their game of fetch. The boy threw the ball high in the air and it bounced in front of the car and then over it. The dog charged the ball again, jumping clear over the car, flipping twice in the air and catching the ball before it rolled into the water.

After setting paper plates on the table, the mother called the boy over and whispered something into his ear. He smiled and walked toward Bobby, turned back to his mother once, but she nudged him forward with a gentle nod of her head. A few feet away, now, Bobby saw that the boy's two front teeth were missing.

"You wanna eat with us?"

Past the boy's right shoulder, the mother smiled and turned away and Bobby took this as another invitation to walk over to the table.

Up close, the man and woman looked older than he'd originally thought. The mother smiled up at him from her peanut butter and jelly sandwich and winked at Bobby with kind, green eyes and asked him his name. The father's mustache was dark and after every few bites he would lean over and tickle the boy. While the other three drank fruit punch in white Styrofoam cups, the father drank beer from a can. The boy chewed on the edge of his cup, making the top raised border look like a mold of teeth at a dentist's office.

The mother said, "Where are you from, Bobby?"

"Portisville."

"Where's your mother and father?"

Bobby nodded toward the truck. "My father is sleeping."

"Are you happy with them?"

Bobby shrugged his shoulders.

"Would you like to come with us?"

"I can't."

"Yes, you can, Bobby. Come with us." As she said these words, the father began loading everything—the napkins, the plastic bags, the cups, the tablecloth and the bags of chips—into the large basket. Birds of some breed Bobby couldn't name called out around them.

Bobby said, "My father."

"Come on. We're leaving." The father, the boy and the dog sat in the car watching Bobby. Waiting. It was up to him. The woman kissed him on the forehead and turned to the car.

Then Bobby felt the hard pull of a fish on his line and opened his eyes. The pole jerked out of his hands and slid forward through the grass and dirt toward the lake. Bobby dove at the pole. He wrapped his hands around it tight and looked to his left where the green car had been, but there was no sign of any car or family.

Darren jumped up. "What? What is it?"

He grabbed the pole out of Bobby's hands. Bobby climbed up onto the tailgate and watched his father reel in the small catfish, remove it from the hook and then toss it back out into the lake. Darren sat next to Bobby. "What the hell was that all about?"

Bobby was crying now. He wasn't sure what had happened. A family with a dog had been there and then they were gone. Was he dreaming? He couldn't remember ever dreaming during the day before. All he could say for sure now, looking where the car and family had been, was that there was an empty dirt road and a row of big, old trees with Spanish moss hanging down from them like unruly, gray wigs.

"Did you get bit by something?"

"No."

"Was it because I hit you?"

"No." Bobby could tell that his father was starting to lose patience with him because of the way he would ask a question quick and then turn away before Bobby answered.

"I'm sorry I hit you. I got a lot going on right now. I need you to tell me what's wrong. Is it about your mother?"

"No."

"Bobby, I need you to toughen up for me. We're going to be doing a lot in the next few days. You can't be crying like a little girl."

"I'm not a little girl." He wiped at his eyes, turned away from his father.

"All that crying makes you look like one."

"I'm not."

"Good, I didn't think so. You sure you're okay? You weren't bitten by anything?"

"No, I told you."

Darren put his arm around Bobby, squeezed once, and then let go and lay back down in the bed of the truck. Looking up at the sky, his father asked him again what happened and Bobby said nothing, it was nothing. Soon, his father started snoring and was asleep again. Bobby lay down next to him, closed his eyes and tried to sleep, but none would come. The branches of the trees above him danced with the slight breeze. Bobby had never stared at the branch of a tree long enough to notice how smaller branches come from the larger one and how those too grew leaves. Above him, still, and for some time, the leaves waved back and forth like flimsy, green hands.

Davis heard the helicopter humming and thrumming through the air above him. It was riding the length of the woods, along 144, about a mile from where they had originally found Teresa Martin's car. He wasn't sure he'd ever seen a helicopter fly through the air above Portisville. Of course, it must've happened at some point, but he couldn't recall ever seeing one here.

Davis hoped that he hadn't upset Jimmy or pushed him into thinking anything more about his mother's murder or his father's possible involvement in it. He didn't think he had. Truman's response to the questions, on the other hand, had surprised Davis as he had expected him to react more, to be angrier. They hadn't talked about her murder since the trial and Truman seemed more surprised by the questions than anything. Either way, Davis was glad he was done with it.

The news van with its logo, WJAK, painted in bright red along the sides, passed Davis going the other way. There was a blond woman in the passenger seat and he tried to see if it was that reporter Tammy Sullins, but he couldn't tell. He pulled in behind a pair of police vans, a couple of patrol cars. There were a few men he recognized from yesterday, leaning over the hood of one of the cars, looking at a map. Then beyond them, he saw Strane leaning against his LeSabre, talking on his cell phone. As Davis got closer to Strane, he saw him swat twice at a deer fly, which seemed to be honing in on his broad forehead. Strane hung up and said, "Sheriff."

"How's it going?"

Strane swatted the air again, though Davis no longer saw any flies, and said, "Step into my office," as he opened his door and climbed in the car. The car smelled faintly of cologne, something sweeter than what Davis wore.

"Anything?"

Strane said, "No, I think this is a bust. Out here and the Q&As we did, nothing."

"Us, too."

"To be honest, I don't think there is anything here. We have her car but nothing else here."

"So what are you going to do?"

"Well, I'll leave a couple of my men here to keep checking the woods, but some of us are leaving tonight, some in the morning. We're going to go back over the woods around the university, around her apartment, places we've already been."

Strane's cell phone rang. He picked it up, check the number on the Caller ID and muted the ringing phone without answering it.

Davis said, "How do you think the car ended up here?"

Strane straightened up in his seat and let out an audible sigh. He looked out the window for what seemed to Davis a long time. Davis noticed again that the top part of his ear was missing and wondered if he lost it as a child, maybe a dog bite, or if he lost it later in the line of duty. Strane looked back at him and said, "She didn't stop the car because of any mechanical problems. There was a half tank of gas and the engine checked out okay. It's possible somebody followed her here. Maybe they flashed their lights and she pulled over. Maybe somebody was on the side of the road and flagged her down as she went by. Maybe it was a hitchhiker or somebody faking an injury. For some reason she stopped and

somebody grabbed her and took off. But I doubt that another vehicle was involved. We don't have any other tracks, oil, anything
like that. But if somebody did get her where did they take her? It's
like she just disappeared."

Davis said, "I know."

Strane stuck his hand out to shake. "You know, sometimes we
don't find them. I'm not giving up yet, but we've got boxes and
boxes of Missing Girl files."

Davis couldn't help but the think of the Wills case. He shook
Strane's hand and climbed out the car as Strane said, "Thanks for
all your help, Sheriff."

Back at his car, Davis turned to the woods and the yellow tape.
He wanted to ask the woods, those trees, what they knew, what
they had seen, if the girl had simply disappeared. It was a crazy,
silly thought and Davis thanked God that nobody was allowed
entry into his thoughts. The helicopters passed again overhead
and soon the sound of the whirling propellers was replaced by the
harsh, barking of the hound dogs on what Davis believed was
their last day in Portisville.

Jimmy painted the final stripe at the side of the house. He looked
down from atop the ladder, searching for someone to celebrate the
completion of the job with, but Truman and Angie weren't there. He
ran the sprayer back and forth a few more times as if giving them another chance to come around the corner and see what he had just
done. When nobody materialized and it was clear that nobody would
see this last stripe applied, he climbed down. It was the one thing
about working alone that he had never quite gotten used to. The sense
of wanting to share the completion of a job with someone was rare but
when it came the solitude was painful. He had the customers, but
with them it was different because of money and the threat that they
would not be satisfied, though he could only remember two customers in twelve years ever complaining about his work. Both of those
he had known would complain the minute he took the job.

At the front of the house, Angie and Truman were peeling paper away from the windows. Jimmy said, "Well, folks, I do believe we are done."

Angie said, "Great."

The three of them walked around the house, observing with palpable pride the work they had done. On the last side they had painted, where the sprayer and ladder still stood, Angie jumped back when she spotted a large garden snake slithering through the grass. Truman lunged at the snake, tried to step on it but the snake seemed to sense he was in danger and picked up speed, disappearing into the woods.

After securing the compressor and ladder in the back of the truck, Jimmy grabbed three beers from the cooler and handed one to Truman and one to Angie, opening hers before giving it to her. He wanted to say something to sum up this day, to say how he thought the trip back had been worth it. Truman and Angie looked happy and tired, and because of this Jimmy decided not to say anything.

In Jimmy's opinion, his father had seemed strong working out there today, despite the evidence he had seen of Truman vomiting. In many ways, he still seemed like the man Jimmy remembered: confident, in control, more powerful than his small frame suggested. In other ways he didn't. Twice Jimmy had caught him staring off into the woods with glazed eyes, something he assumed had to do with the cancer.

Angie walked over to get something out of her car and Jimmy sat next to his father on the porch steps. Truman said, "So you going to that girl's house tonight?"

"Yeah. I'll be by in the morning to get my stuff."

"Leaving early?"

"Not too early, probably nine or ten."

Truman nodded. "Well, I sure appreciate your help. Couldn't have done it without you."

As Jimmy drank his beer in silence, the questions Davis had

asked came back to him. He agreed with Davis that finding someone who had been here one day, years ago, didn't seem possible.
He figured Davis' job must be awful sometimes because of the
kinds of things he had to see and questions he had to ask. Jimmy
thought of the way a person's job seemed to define them. He was a
housepainter. What did that mean? Maybe that he covered things
up. That he took a dull surface and shined it, made it new again.
He liked the sound of that, though he wasn't sure he believed it.

Jimmy went inside to take a shower and get ready. Outside,
dusk moved slowly forward, as the shade tested and changed the
color of the cars, trees, and the newly-painted house. The muscles
in his shoulders and upper back were sore, but he liked the feeling
and knew it meant he had worked hard.

In an hour, he would be at Carol's. Though he knew he should
be looking forward to it, he wasn't. It seemed clear to him now
that the reason he had come was to paint the house and ask his father about his mother's murder and now that he'd done both of
those things he was ready to go home. But he had promised Carol
he would come by and see her. Maybe he wouldn't stay the night
with her. Maybe he would just go for dinner and then come back,
spend the night and take off earlier than he had planned.

Still, he felt guilty for having chosen to see her tonight instead
of spending more time with his father. He had felt guilty for most
of his life, for having let his mother be taken from him in the
middle of the night, from lives destroyed by his lust and his hands
and for things he had said and others he hadn't. For having fun,
while others suffered. And then for not suffering enough. He
tried to shake this feeling, knowing, as he did, that it could lead
to nothing good.

Jimmy curled his right hand up to his head, flexing the biceps,
and looked into the mirror, which showed the flesh curled into a
ball. His biceps and forearms were thick and full and lined with
veins from over a decade of painting, first using rollers and now
holding the spray gun. He stepped into a double-biceps pose—

both arms raised like a prisoner being frisked—and tried to laugh at this but couldn't.

Digging in his bag for some clean clothes, Jimmy found the pair of white socks with the blue circle around them. He pulled them out and separated them and his mother's ring fell and landed on the bed. He wasn't sure if he'd ever give the ring to a woman he'd call his wife, but that didn't matter, he wanted it for himself and all it held in its tiny circle of memories. He moved it around his paint-spotted hand like a geologist sifting sand through dirt-stained fingers, trying to discover a secret.

Davis steered the cruiser into the lot in front of Dan's store. The front door was propped open with a garbage can. Before entering, he turned back and looked at the woods across the street where the pine trees stood not moving. Davis knew that anywhere he looked, on both sides of almost any street in this town, he could find these towering trees. When he was a young man, he had felt it was constraining but as he grew older he found it comforting and reassuring, a constant in a changing world.

He walked in the front door, but Dan wasn't at his usual spot behind the counter. This sent a quick bolt of fright through Davis. His first thoughts were of criminal action, and the second thought, that his old friend's heart might have stopped, seemed no better. It took Davis a couple moments to locate him. When he did, Dan was setting up a pair of rickety old sawhorses over by the coffee machine, partially shielded by a ridiculously large peanut display. The two men seemed to see each other at the same time. Dan said, "Sheriff."

"How's it going?"

"Better than you."

"You're probably right."

After getting a Diet Pepsi from a cooler in the back of the store, Davis walked over and helped Dan straighten one of the sawhorse legs. There was a piece of plywood balanced over the sawhorses and a small bucket of white paint on the counter by the coffeemaker. Dan had already painted FRESH FLORIDA on the plywood and Davis figured he'd add ORANGES next.

Dan said, "Any news on the girl?"

Davis shook his head. "Sounds like those boys from the state are leaving in the morning."

"That ought to make you happy."

Davis knew what his friend was getting at. "Yeah, but if they leave that doesn't mean she is okay."

"No, it doesn't."

Davis poured some Diet Pepsi into his mug. Dan said, "Go on behind the counter and get it, if you want some."

Davis looked down at the fizzing cola. "No, I don't guess I need that right now."

Dan picked up a Baby Ruth and opened it, chewed the whole bar in three big bites before throwing the wrapper in the can by the door. "Let's sit outside."

Davis walked out first and sat on the bench in front of the store. On each side of the bench was a green urn-shaped planter overflowing with cigarette butts. As he waited for Dan to come out, Davis looked up into the sky. There were still no clouds and it looked like the weather might hold for the fair tonight. Even though he wasn't going, since Bird had volunteered to cover it, some nice weather would suit him just fine and would probably make the deputy's job tonight a bit more pleasant.

Dan walked outside with a cup in one hand and a brown bag filled with the bottle of whiskey in the other, and sat done on the bench. Dan said, "Give me that," indicating the Styrofoam cup.

Davis didn't argue and offered his half-full cup, like a supplicant to Dan, who poured him a healthy portion. When he took a mouthful of the strong drink, Davis swished it in his mouth a bit before swallowing.

Dan pulled a pack of Marlboros from the front pocket of his shirt and started to peel away the wrapper. Davis said, "I thought you quit that."

Dan said, "I did."

Davis hadn't smoked in fifteen years but right now a cigarette sure seemed like a good idea. As Dan lit his, Davis said, "Let me get one of those."

Dan handed him one and then lit it off his own. Davis took in a deep, solid hit. It flooded his mouth and throat with a quick flick of heat and fullness and then he exhaled. There was a small knot in his stomach and he felt what he thought was a momentary jolt in the center of his chest. He told himself that he was just being silly, that it wasn't possible the nicotine could affect him so quickly. Still, he snubbed it out after taking only two more puffs.

Dan said, "It's been a slow day here."

"You should have closed up and gone out to Truman's. You wouldn't recognize the place. They painted it, planted some flowers in front of the porch. Damn place looks presentable."

"Who would've thought?"

"Not me."

"Him and Jimmy getting along?"

"Seemed to be. I mean, I didn't see them hugging or reminiscing over old times or nothing like that."

"Thank God." Dan laughed. "That might be a sure sign of the Apocalypse."

"I had to question Truman."

"About what?"

"The girl. Bird kept pushing me." Bird? Was it really about Bird? He damn well knew it wasn't and wondered how many more lies he would tell today.

"How'd he take it?"

"How do you think he took it?"

Dan laughed. "Man, your job has to suck some times."

Davis said, "You don't know the half of it. Do you think Truman is capable of doing something like that, messing with a girl?"

"I think Truman is capable of a lot of things. But I think given the right set of circumstances we are all capable of lot of things, many of them unpleasant."

Davis turned to Dan, who looked away from him out to the right of the store where a crow stood in the grass.

"Think he was capable of killing Dot?" The words came before Davis could stop them. Even though he had known where the conversation was heading, he planned for it to be smoother.

Dan said, "What are you talking about?"

"You know what I'm talking about. Did Truman already have those scratches on him that night you guys drove up to Kentucky?"

Dan sipped on his drink nice and slow, shook his head. "The prosecutor asked me this at the trial."

"I know what he asked you. I'm asking you again."

"Why are you doing this? I know you said Jimmy asked you about it. But, it's been so long. Nothing you can do about it now, just bring up old feelings."

Davis took a mouthful of his afternoon toddy. It tasted sweet and necessary and made him want another, but he knew that if he drank any more he might be willing to believe anything anybody had to say. He might be willing to let his guard down. "Dan, think about it like this. I got these doubts, like little voices in my head. Maybe the voices are Dot's, maybe they're Jimmy's or even Truman's. What I want to do is shut these damn voices up. Is it possible that Truman killed Dot? Yes. Do I think he did it? No. I just want to get rid of the doubts. Maybe once we find this girl, if we do, then I'll stop thinking about Dot too, but for now I can't."

Dan shook his head. "I don't remember seeing any scars on Truman's neck, but I wasn't really looking. I slept half the drive in the back seat."

Davis finished off his drink with one last upturned cup. Dan said, "You want some more?"

"No, I better get going."

"It'll work out."

"One way or another." Davis stood and made his way to the car, noticing how the trees across the street hadn't moved a lick.

Truman walked out of the bathroom, his hair still wet, wearing an old blue bathrobe. Angie was sitting at the table, sipping on a beer. He said, "The shower is all yours."

"I'll take one in a few minutes."

"Take one now, we're going out to dinner."

Angie said, "What?"

"Thought I'd take you out to dinner, get us some thick steaks. We've worked hard all day. I haven't eaten out in months. You haven't since you've been here."

"That's okay."

"Let me treat you to something."

"I'm not really hungry."

"Suit yourself." Truman waved his right arm quickly up and down at her, thinking, *I'm not going to beg.* He said, "Call me a cab then. I'm going."

Getting dressed, he heard the shower start. That's more like it, he thought. In the kitchen, he picked up the phone and dialed Darren's cell phone number. *Pick it up, Webster,* he thought, *pick it up, you bastard.* On the twelfth ring, Bobby answered.

Truman said, "Let me talk to your father."

There was a TV playing in the background and he could hear Darren ask who it was. Then he was on the phone. "Yeah?"

"It's me."

"Truman?"

"Tomorrow morning, sometime between seven and eight. I'll call you. But you'll only have about fifteen minutes, so be close and ready."

Darren didn't respond. The water in the bathroom stopped running and Truman turned away from the hall so that he was leaning over the kitchen sink when he spoke. "Listen to me, Webster, don't fuck with me. You have half the money. I need this done."

"It's just . . ."

"Let me put it to you this way. That boy of yours that answered the phone."

Neither one said anything for a short time. The sound of Darren breathing hard on the other end, taking in this last part, came through the phone. The door opened and Angie was in the hall a second and then disappeared into her bedroom. "I don't have to say any more."

"Hey, wait a minute."

"Be close when I call." After hanging up, Truman poured himself a drink and sat down at the kitchen table. He felt something wet on his forehead and reached up and wiped the sweat away. He wondered why Davis was asking about Dot now and figured it probably had something to do with Jimmy being here, maybe the boy had said something to him about her. It didn't matter. This time tomorrow he'd be gone from this world.

Jimmy knocked on Carol's door, feeling more nervous than he had the previous evening. Music seeped out into the night and flies circled the porch light like bombardiers moving in for the kill. Carol opened the door and smiled at Jimmy, kissed him on the lips. She was wearing the same robe she had on when he left her this morning. For a second, as he turned to shut the door, he wondered if she had stayed in the robe all day, working on her painting, but her hair was wet now and it occurred to him that he might have gotten here earlier than she expected. When he turned back around, she was wearing a one-piece silk chemise with thin, red straps across her shoulders. Her nipples were visible beneath the silk. The robe lay crumpled at her feet, around her ankles, like the end of a bridal gown. She smiled at Jimmy and began kissing him.

Taking his hand, she led him to the bedroom. Jimmy felt dizzy and didn't think it was from the two beers he had earlier but from everything he should and shouldn't do, places he wasn't sure he belonged. He didn't want her now, not like this. He resisted at first, but she pulled him to her and his hands and mind were guided by flesh and the wanting of more. On the bed, Jimmy climbed on top of her and thrust deeper and deeper into her as hard as he could—

their pubic bones crashing against one another—until she cried underneath him, her eyes winced in pain, saying how good he was, how good it felt.

Jimmy opened his eyes and turned away from the painting of the gator on the wall above the bed and saw below him, in Carol's face, Merrilee with her red hair fanned out on the pillow. Afterwards, he rested on top of Carol and their bodies were slick with sweat and alive with pain. He stayed in that position as long as he could in an effort to avoid conversation. She ran her nails across his back, tracing lines and directions as if mapping out what was next for them.

As he rolled off of her, he closed his eyes and thought, *Jesus, that didn't help anything.* She scooted close to him, and her hair scratched at his chest and tickled his nose and lips. After a couple minutes, she kissed him on his right ear and walked to the bathroom. Jimmy listened as her feet tap, tap, tapped across the floor, melting with the music. He lay there as long as he could, not wanting to stay, not knowing how to leave.

Davis drove slowly down a quiet Main Street. Flyers for Teresa Martin lined the poles on each side of the street. The one in front of the barber shop had been ripped so that two long strips of paper sat side by side with a line of stapled pole between them.

The Portisville Diner and the ice cream shop next door had extended their hours in the hopes of drawing some extra business because the fair was in town, but so far their gamble hadn't paid off.

Davis parked in front of the station and then walked across the street to the Winn-Dixie to buy some sauce mix. He had been on his way home, was only a mile from the house, when Bev called and said she was making London broil and they needed sauce. It was worth it, he figured, since London broil with mashed potatoes and green beans was one of his favorite meals. He knew she was cooking it in an effort to cheer him up.

As he walked out of the Winn-Dixie, someone called his name and Davis turned. It was Phil Abry, the store manager. Davis had arrested the man once almost a dozen years ago, when he was twenty-five, for selling marijuana to high-school kids. He had done a year of community service, here and in Tallahassee. Even though it happened over a decade ago and Abry had since gotten married and had two kids, Davis was still surprised whenever he saw him in slacks and a tie, counting money in the booth above the registers. "Any luck with the girl?"

Davis shook his head and wondered if the men from the state had questioned him about Teresa Martin. His name had been on the list. Stepping out into the evening air, Davis slid the package of sauce mix into the front pocket of his pants and breathed in deep. The air felt nice, better than it had in quite a while. Not too hot, a slight breeze. The kind of breeze that meant fall and winter were coming. Not that they had much of either season down here but he would take a couple months of seventy-degree weather, take it and damned well love it. He was about to climb in his cruiser when he looked over at the park across the street. It was empty except for a family of ducks walking under a bench.

Though he wanted to go home and see Bev, he felt like being alone for a couple more minutes. As he walked toward the park, and the streetlights buzzed on, the ducks headed toward the small stream, which was hidden by a thin row of cattails, at the edge of the park. He sat at the bench and rested his hands on his knees. Every once in a while he would see the faint green line of some baby duck's feathers.

He thought about Dan's comments in regard to what people were capable of. Davis tended to agree with his old friend. Wearing the badge for the last twenty-five years had shown him just how much people were capable of. Most of the people he dealt with were criminals and screw-ups, people who seemed to act without fear of retributions for their actions. But what about other people, someone like Bev? What was Davis himself capable of? Could he kill someone? He hadn't so far, but his job dictated that he was expected to, if put in the right situation. He'd shot three people but none had died, so he knew that he was capable of extreme violence because of his job.

Yet most people, Davis believed, like to think they are decent and that they wouldn't take another person's life but, like Dan said, the greater majority would if given the right set of circumstances. Of course, the right set of circumstances varied from person to person, but a few of the first ones that came to Davis' mind included self-defense, for your own life or someone around you, revenge, blind rage, jealousy, the list of things went on. If this was his criteria then certainly Truman was capable of killing Dot, but it didn't mean he'd done it.

He considered the evidence against Truman again and the discrepancies involving time and whether or not he had woken Jimmy and why he would lie about that. Even now, it didn't add up to anything more than some very slim evidence, possible mistakes or lapses in memory. Not enough to pursue. He still didn't think that Truman was responsible for it, and he hoped what he told Dan was true: once this missing girl case was resolved he'd stop thinking about the Wills case. And though they hadn't found the girl, it didn't seem as though she was here in town and so, in Davis' opinion, the case was pretty much resolved in Portisville.

Truman had insisted on taking the Cadillac. He said that her car was too damned small, made his legs bunch up to his chest, but they both knew that this wasn't true since he was only an inch or two taller than she was. Angie drove through the darkening night on Highway 144, heading out of town. Truman still had the conversation with Darren on his mind and it made him a little nervous. He didn't think Webster would back out of it, but who could say? He could take the money Truman had already given him and leave town.

Up ahead on the right, he saw the lights to Dan's store and asked Angie to pull in there. He hadn't planned on stopping, hadn't even considered the fact that their path would take them by the store until he saw the lights and the gas pumps. A moment later, as she pulled into the empty lot in front of the store, he wasn't sure if stopping here was such a good idea. Dan stood behind the counter and peered out at them. Climbing out of the car, Truman said, "I'll just be a minute." He took a couple steps and then turned back to her. "You need anything?"

"Some gum."

He cleared his throat, coughed, and went into the store. Dan stood behind the register, almost at attention. "Evening, Truman."

Truman nodded. "Dan."

"She your chauffeur now, too?"

Truman smiled despite himself and walked to the back of the store. He hadn't been here in years, not since he went away to prison. It wasn't that much different, really. The coolers in the back were new and that counter up front was new, too. He didn't know why the hell he was walking to the back of the store. There wasn't anything he wanted or needed back there. Passing the racks of candy, he remembered Angie's request for gum. In front of him was what seemed like a hundred packs of the stuff and all kinds of candy bars, too.

He called to Dan, "What kind of gum is good?"

"Don't know. Can't chew the stuff with my dentures."

"What sells the most?"

"Trident."

Truman located the Trident and got a pack. Along with the gum, he grabbed a couple of the .25 bullets from the old JFG coffee can and made his way to the register. He heard cheering from the television and leaned across the counter and saw that Dan was watching *Wheel of Fortune*. He had seen the show a couple times in prison and had heard all the guys say what they would like to do to old Vanna White. The black guys especially—the fact that her last name was White seemed to raise the stakes—but he didn't think she was that great.

Dan said, "Heard you painted the house today."

"Davis tell you?"

"Yes."

"It looks good for a change."

"Was nice to see Jimmy."

"He's grown up."

Dan reached up and turned the TV off as if this conversation required all of his concentration. "How you been feeling?"

"Fine. You?"

"It's a bitch getting old."

"We don't have much choice."

Dan said, "Davis was asking me about Dot's murder."

Truman nodded. "Me too."

Dan looked at him for a second, as if he expected Truman to say more. The coolers in the back of the store buzzed loudly. Dan said, "I guess he's just trying to tie up loose ends."

"Maybe. But it doesn't concern me anymore. He can do whatever he wants." Truman set the gum and bullets on the counter between them. "So what do I owe you?"

"Nothing. Take it."

"I'd rather pay."

Dan took Truman's money and gave him the change back. "It's good to see you."

Truman said, "Take care."

"You too."

Heading back to his car, Truman could feel Dan's eyes on him. There were a lot of things he could have said and would have liked to say, but he had stopped by and the fact that they had talked at all seemed enough.

Jimmy walked out of the bedroom. The sliding glass doors leading to the backyard were open and he could see Carol standing on her deck in front of the grill. She was dressed in jeans and a white T-shirt without a bra. A breeze came from somewhere in the distance, bringing a wave of her perfume mixed with propane Jimmy's way. Approaching her, he heard the grinding sound of the metal-wire brush scraping as she cleaned the grill. On the right shelf of the grill, next to a bottle of beer, a plate sat with four uncooked mounds of ground beef and a spatula with a long wooden handle.

Carol turned around and smiled at Jimmy. "Feel better?"

Jimmy forced a smile at her but didn't answer.

"Get yourself a beer from the fridge."

Jimmy pulled a Budweiser from the top shelf of the refrigerator and a package of sliced Muenster from the door. He got a knife out of a drawer and went back outside. Carol looked down at the cheese in his hands. "Cheeseburgers?"

He said, "Jimmy burgers."

Jimmy picked one of the uncooked hamburgers up and with the knife sliced it in half, horizontally. Then he took a piece of the cheese, bent it in half, and stuffed it inside the meat, before molding it back into a hamburger with no cheese visible on either side.

"Family recipe. The old man used to make them this way." He looked past Carol out into the darkness of the back yard. In the distance, the lights of the farmhouse stood out among the darkness and he knew somewhere between here and there those alligators sloshed around in the water, not knowing they would be dead soon. Fireflies danced in the yard, tiny balls of light rose and then disappeared, only to rise again. Jimmy added the cheese to two more of the hamburgers before Carol said she wanted to try making one. He watched her fold the cheese and press the meat together and bits of the pink-red meat slid between her fingers.

They sat down on the white plastic chairs and each took pulls of their Budweisers as the burgers began to cook and a thin line of smoke leaked from under the lid. Jimmy's hands felt greasy from the uncooked meat. He figured hers probably did, too. Carol said, "How did the painting go?"

"Fine."

"Did you finish?"

"Pretty much. Did you get some of your painting done?"

"A little."

Jimmy stood, took the spatula in his hand, and flipped the burgers. The pink meat browned with each minute over the flames. Jimmy tried not to turn and look at her. It felt good to be here like this but something inside of him wouldn't let it continue. He could, or would, not give himself to it completely, and he felt what he had with all those other women since Helen and Merrilee, that the closeness made him do what he didn't want to do, slide farther away.

Bobby walked by the telephone in the hotel's lobby. He set the bucket of ice down by his feet and called his mother collect. The operator asked his name and he told her but a few seconds later she came back on the line and said that nobody was answering. Bobby thought his mother might be taking a shower, so he decided to sit in one of the cushy brown chairs in the lobby for a few minutes and then try to call her again. The man who had checked Bobby and his father in a couple hours ago answered a ringing telephone and began talking. Bobby couldn't hear what was being said but the man behind the counter was laughing a lot.

After trying his mother three more times, with no answer, Bobby walked with the bucket of now-melting ice back to their room. His father was sitting up against the bed's headboard wearing only his jeans and watching a baseball game between the Braves and the Mets. There was a painting above the bed, over his father's head, of a pink wave crashing into white sand. Bobby placed the bucket of ice on the long dresser and sat at the foot of the bed, the only one in the room, a few feet from the TV. The Braves were up by three runs and at bat in the top of the eighth.

Darren said, "What took you so long?"

"I couldn't find the machine."

"We walked right by it earlier."

Bobby didn't answer but stared at the TV.

After a couple minutes, his father said, "What do you think about moving?"

"To here?"

Darren shook his head. "Somewhere away from Florida. Maybe out west."

"West?"

"Nevada or New Mexico, maybe Arizona. Somewhere it's still hot like in Florida."

"But school just started."

"I'm gonna make some money tomorrow and I've been thinking about opening up my own shop, working on cars again, somewhere besides Portisville. You could go to a new school, make some new friends."

"What about Mom?"

"You'll still get to see her."

Bobby said, "Not too much."

"You don't see her much now."

"I don't want to move away from her."

Darren closed his eyes and took a drink from the beer he had on the nightstand. Bobby heard laughing in the room next door. It sounded like it was far away and yet close at the same time. He turned away from his father, back toward the TV. Chipper Jones was up to bat and the pitcher looked mean and serious on the mound. Bobby wished he had a name like Chipper. Chipper Jones swung at a pitch and fouled it down the first base line.

Darren said, "You ready for bed?"

It hadn't been dark long and Bobby wasn't really tired but his dad looked like he might be. They had stopped and eaten barbecue sandwiches for dinner and his father had drunk three beers. Now his eyes were all red. Bobby turned the TV off. "If you are."

"I am."

Darren set the alarm clock and then turned off the light above their bed. Sleeping in a hotel room reminded Bobby again of that trip to Panama City with his parents when all three of them had to sleep in the same bed. It scared him that they might be moving away from his mother. Bobby tried to think of some reason to keep his father from moving, but none came, so he scooted over and rested his hand against the side of his father's head and said, "Good night."

"'Night, son."

Truman and Angie sat across from each other in the crowded restaurant. They had driven thirty minutes to Al Spritzer's Steakhouse—BEST STEAKS IN FLORIDA FOR 30 YEARS AND GETTING BETTER EVERYDAY, or so the sign out front said. The walls around them were deeply varnished pine and decorated with framed pictures of World War II soldiers. Dim light filled the room and Muzak fought the voices of the twenty-five or so other couples telling stories about the day they had just finished.

The plump college-aged waitress walked over and took their order. She had strawberry blond hair and a dimple on her right cheek. She looked as innocent as a newborn. On her chest, she wore a button with a picture of Teresa Martin in the center and the words "Find Teresa" wrapped in a half-circle over the missing girl's head.

After the waitress left, Angie said, "You been here before?"

Truman sipped a Jack and Coke and said, "Dot, my wife, used to love to eat here. She'd order prime rib, medium rare, and a big fat potato dripping with butter. She'd drink beer after beer and tell me stories about her and Jimmy. Tell me how he'd caught twenty catfish in an hour, or that they'd fed a duck a half a loaf of bread."

At the table next to them, a woman laughed at something the man she was with said. Truman asked Angie why she'd become a nurse. She told him that she didn't really know why she'd gone into nursing. Twenty-three and still living at home with no real plans, it seemed the thing to do. Her sister had been a nurse for a few years by then and one of her best friends was, too. All through nursing school she still couldn't say exactly why she was doing it, and she had wondered then if other people felt that way, like their lives were being led in a direction they had no control over. Still, all in all, she admitted, it wasn't such a bad job.

Angie said, "How did you meet your wife?"

"That was a long time ago."

"Oh, come on now."

Truman stared past her shoulder for a moment. Then he started, "She was still in high school and my dad, he worked as the night janitor there, where she went to school. I'd help him some nights. So this one night he takes me to work and I don't even think he knew there was something going on because when we pulled up he said, 'Fuck all, who do these cars belong to?' See, the parking lot was full and he didn't like people much. They got in the way of his drinking."

Truman sipped his drink again, shook the glass, rolling the ice around the bottom. Angie was staring at him, leaning forward, waiting for him to continue. "So he starts working in one of the bathrooms and I wandered over to the auditorium to see what was going on. It was a play. Dot was up on stage and she had this white dress on and was about the prettiest girl I had ever seen. I mean, she wasn't but sixteen or seventeen. I was twenty-one. I couldn't turn away. She said a bunch of words, but I didn't hear any of them. I was just standing there, leaning against the wall in the back. When the play was over and everybody started clapping, she came out and bowed. She was crying. I didn't know why. Happy, I guess.

"I went back to work with my old man. He gave me the broom while he went in one of the classrooms to get drunk. I was sweeping the hall when I hear this *click, click* and I look up and she is walking toward me in that damn white dress. Hell, I don't even think I said anything to her. Just stared at her like she was a movie star or something. She smiled and said hi and walked over to her locker, tried to open it but it was stuck. So she asked me if I knew how to open it. Well, I didn't know anything about lockers, hadn't even gone to high school. I hit it with the broom twice and it opened. She smiled, called me her hero, then got what she needed out of her locker, a book or something, and walked away. I stood there leaning against the broom, watching her. I couldn't move. It was like somebody had nailed my feet to the ground."

Truman finished off his drink, shook his head and smiled, then continued. "So I wasn't worth a shit for about a week. All I could think about was that white dress, about her hair and the skin between her neck and where the dress started. One day, I went to the school and waited outside. I don't even know if I would have said anything to her. It was like I just needed to see her. She recognized me right away, walked up and called me her hero again. I asked her out and she said yes."

Angie said, "Then what happened?"

Truman said, "Come on now. You've heard enough."

"No, come on, please."

Truman said, "We just started dating, seeing each other a couple nights a week. Of course, her daddy didn't care for me much. Her family really. Not that they were anything special. He was some type of number puncher for the school and here I was the son of the school janitor, the nighttime janitor at that, as if the sight of my old man during the day was too much for those kids. And me, I was nothing to them. I didn't graduate school. I had a hot-rod car and greasy hair. I suppose that's probably some of the reason she liked me, because she wasn't supposed to."

The food came and they began to eat. Truman cut off a wedge of his steak and dipped it in a bowl of horseradish and brought the meat to his lips and though it stung the tip of his tongue a bit, it tasted damn good.

Jimmy bent down and turned the silver nozzle on the propane tank off and felt the heat from the bottom of the grill close to his hand. They hadn't spoken much during dinner, had just listened to the music and the night sounds out in the dark.

He sat back down in the plastic chair. Carol came outside, holding two more bottles of beer, handed him one, and sat on his lap with her back to him. She said, "Damn, those were good," as she rubbed her stomach, laughed and then turned around and kissed him. She felt heavy on his lap and he moved his hips in an effort to try to redistribute the weight.

She said, "What are you going to do tomorrow?"

"It's a long drive. I've gotta leave early."

"Maybe I could call in to work. We could go somewhere in the morning before you leave."

Jimmy didn't answer but watched two of the lights in the farmhouse across the way go out. She climbed off his lap and sat in the chair across from him. "You plan on coming back?"

He said, "For the funeral?"

She nodded, then brought the bottle to her lips.

"No, I don't think so."

"That's too bad."

"There's nothing for me here."

"What about me?"

Jimmy looked at her a second and her eyes seemed to be waiting for some response. He lifted his beer and took a mouthful as he tried to think of a way to tell her about the reasons it couldn't work between them. But he had never felt he could tell anyone. He had tried to explain it to Merrilee one night, but all she said was that he needed to get over it, that everybody has problems and his were nothing special.

"I can't keep coming back and forth. I have a business to run."

"People don't need houses painted here?"

Jimmy said, "People around here don't want a Wills painting their house."

"I'd let you."

He tried to laugh but what came out sounded brief, tight against his lips. "Look, Carol, I have a life up there." He knew it had nothing to do with painting houses. It had to do with how his mother's murder would always be hanging over him if he lived here. And it had to with the fact that he wanted this, whatever the hell this was, to work between him and Carol, but being with her reminded him again of Merrilee and Helen and how good it felt to be with them and then how bad it felt afterwards, something he didn't think he was yet willing to risk again.

"Well, what about the house?"

"What about it?"

"Don't you think he'll give it to you?"

"I don't want it."

"You could sell it."

Jimmy wasn't sure what his father planned to do with the house. It hadn't occurred to him until she mentioned it that the house would probably be his and that was the reason his father had wanted to do some work on it. It made sense now, but he still didn't want the old house, and this connection to the town. "What good would that do?"

"You could at least get some money for it."

"I do fine without his help. Plus, I'd be stuck fixing the place up."

"I'm sorry. I just thought maybe you would have to come back and take care of that." She drank from her beer again. Across the yard, the final light from the farmhouse went out, so that the gator pit was no longer visible from this distance.

Carol got up to go to the bathroom. Jimmy shifted his weight in the seat again to try to get comfortable. He couldn't think of an easy way to leave. When he heard the toilet flushing, he considered standing up and walking out to avoid what he felt coming on.

She walked back outside, leaned down when she was next to him and tried to kiss him but he turned his head away. "What's wrong?"

"Nothing."

"I was just thinking it would be nice if you came back, that's all. I'd like to see you again."

Jimmy said, "We've had a couple of good days. Let's leave it at that."

Jimmy stood and she grabbed his right arm. Her hands, fingers, felt soft against his flesh. She was inches from him and her mouth was open. Her neck was white. He wanted to touch her neck, run his hand over it again, feel her smooth, white skin pressed against his.

Jimmy said, "I'm sorry. I'm just tired. Working all day. Got a lot of driving tomorrow. Maybe I should go before I ruin this."

"No, stay here with me tonight."

He said, "You sure you want me to?"

She hugged him and he hesitated for a moment before hugging back. And even as he hugged her and felt how good the contours of her body fit against his, he needed space, more than what this deck was providing. Pulling away from her, Jimmy said, "Whatever happened to your hair?"

"What do you mean?"

"In school, when you cut it all off. Why did you do that?" He knew what he was doing, trying to bring up old memories of hers to get her away from his past. He told himself to stop it; there was no reason to make her feel as bad as he did; she didn't deserve it.

She smiled and said, "Can't we forget about the past?"

"It doesn't go away." Jimmy's felt his tone slipping from friendly again.

She looked out into her yard, touched the end of her hair, and then turned back to Jimmy. "My father used to brush my hair every night and tell me how beautiful it was. After he died, we moved here from Tallahassee and when people at school would talk about my hair it reminded me of him, got to where I just couldn't take it anymore. I wanted to forget about my father because he was gone and wasn't coming back."

Jimmy listened to her tell the story, listened to the way her voice rose when she said *my father.* Her right eye began to water and her chin quivered. And as the first tear fell, he lifted his hand and gently wiped it away.

Davis climbed into bed, rested a couple of pillows behind his head, too tired to sleep. His wife lay next to him, reading the new issue of *Better Homes and Gardens.* Davis picked up a Tom Clancy novel he had been working on for five months, read a page and put it back down across his chest.

Over dinner Bev hadn't asked about the girl or pushed too

much. All she had asked was how his day had gone and he had said good and they left it at that. Now, lying side by side, Davis reached a hand under the sheets and rubbed her right thigh for a moment. She smiled at him. "You get enough to eat?"

"Yeah, it was good." Davis tried to read more from his book but the words blurred on the page before him. There were squares of print in paragraph form, lines and sentences and periods, but in his mind it added up to nothing. He put the book back down. "Went by Truman's today."

"Is he doing okay?"

"Yeah, him and Jimmy were painting the house, actually. They planted some flowers too."

"Seems odd they would do all that, especially if Jimmy is only in town a few days."

"Yeah, you're right." Davis had originally thought that it was Jimmy's idea. The place needed a paint job, and he had the paint, so why not do it? But now he wondered if it was Truman's idea. Did Truman know something the rest of them didn't? They say people who are dying feel it and know before the doctors or tests tell them. Maybe that was why Truman was doing all this stuff, tying up loose ends, because he did, in fact, know the end was soon.

Bev said, "Any luck with the girl?"

"No. They're going to leave tomorrow. They don't think she is here anywhere, not in the woods."

"Where then? Her car?"

"I don't know."

"They said that maybe someone got her out of the car on the side of the road here. If so, they took her somewhere away from here."

"What do you think?"

"I think it's possible."

When Bev didn't say anything to this, Davis said, "I think we should go on vacation."

"Where to?"

"How about the Bahamas?"

"That would be nice. Anywhere would be fine."

"How about California?"

She smiled. "Now, you're talking." She had asked him to take her to California a decade before and he had been putting it off for reasons he couldn't name. Now, he figured, it was time to go.

"When we get back. I'm going to see that doctor about surgery."

"Yeah, that's probably a good idea."

"Bev, I'm a little scared about it."

"They do it all the time."

Davis said, "Not on me they don't."

She smiled and said, "Good point. It'll be fine. They say in six weeks you're back on your feet, better than ever and it could add ten, twelve years to your life."

"We could use that time."

She kissed him on the forehead. "Of course we could. Get some rest, love. It's been a rough couple of days for you. I'll cook you a big breakfast in the morning."

Davis said, "Sounds good."

He lay back on the pillow and thought about how lucky he had been to have her for a wife. They hadn't been able to have a child, but if they had it would be about the same age as Jimmy. It occurred to Davis, not for the first time, how parents and children are connected throughout their life, whether they want to be or not. Even without children, he and Bev had a good run. He loved her. That he was certain of. He scooted over and kissed her shoulder, felt the scratch of her brittle hair against his lips. Then he closed his eyes and leaned again toward the sleep he hoped would come.

Truman opened the door for Angie. She nodded and walked into the house and sat down at the kitchen table. He pulled the bottle of bourbon from under the sink and poured himself a glass. "Want some?"

"Just a little." She lifted her hand and brought her thumb and forefinger to within a half-inch of touching, indicating what her version of "a little" was.

Sitting down at the table, Truman set the bit of liquor in front of her. She said, "Thanks again for dinner."

Truman drank from his glass and nodded a silent *You're welcome.* He was glad she'd agreed to come to dinner with him and figured this was as good a last night as he could ask for. He had to admit that he had grown used to her company even if they didn't talk much besides her damned medical questions: "How you feeling today? Any trouble urinating? Blood in your sputum?" Still it was a comfort having someone across the table from him. She had helped him, even if she was only doing her job, and he knew that life had been better in the last couple of months because she was with him. He wondered if she would miss him when he was gone and, without any hint of self-pity, doubted that she would. His only regret about this whole plan was that she would be the one to find him, but she was a professional and would know what to do.

Truman said, "You gonna run in the morning?"

She finished her drink. "Yeah. I actually should be getting to bed."

"About that time."

When she stood up, he said, "Would you consider putting me out of my misery?"

She smiled, "You didn't seem like you were in any misery tonight."

"No, I guess not."

She walked away and then disappeared into her bedroom. Finishing his drink, he wondered what Jimmy was doing and figured the boy was probably in bed with that Carol woman. He was relieved that his son wouldn't do what he had asked. If that had happened it would be a thing Jimmy carried with him the rest of his life, which is what Truman had originally wanted, but not now. The boy had turned out okay and Truman supposed he had Carly to thank for that, but he would never tell her.

Truman picked the phone up and dialed the first three numbers of Davis' phone number and then hung up. He'd sure like to talk to his old friend, tell him thanks for everything he had ever done for him. But it was late now, and the old bastard was probably asleep.

Truman shut his bedroom door and pulled the white linen suit from deep in the closet, and hung it on the copper hanger on the backside of the door. From his top drawer, he retrieved a piece of paper with the message, written in blue ink, *I'm in too much pain, I can't go on, Truman,* a two-inch thick wad of money, and a 5 x 7 photo of himself, Jimmy and Dot at the cabin when the boy was six or seven. He placed all three items in the inside pocket of the linen jacket.

He took his clothes off, folded them, and then placed them in the hamper by the closet and turned the light off. After settling into bed, as the darkness of night surrounded him, he remembered one other thing about that restaurant that he hadn't told Angie. It was the way Dot would wink at him and slip her hand under the table toward the end of the night, when the drinks had started to take their toll, and squeeze his knee. Though he knew she'd do it, every time it would surprise him, making his heart jump. He could see her in that white, fluffy shirt she wore. The cheap gold necklace he'd bought her early in courtship clung to her neck and she'd smile a smile so bright he could hardly believe she was with him.

Jimmy sat in the dark living room staring at what he could see of the paintings around him. Clarity was difficult to find in the darkness, but what he was able to locate seemed to be the featured parts of the gator paintings: a half tail, back plates shaped like the state of Florida, and eyes with more than one pupil glaring at him. It was a little after three and he had been sitting here for a half an hour, after climbing out of bed, unable to sleep.

He considered leaving Carol a note, telling her that it had been good seeing her and that he wished her the best of luck with everything, maybe even leaving his phone number or address in case she wanted to visit. He revised the message in his head a hundred times before putting pen to paper. What he finally settled on, *Take Care, Jimmy*, seemed to say what he wanted.

The streets were empty as he knew they would be and he drove on Highway 144, letting it take him south a few miles, past the cemetery, and then heading back north. It was comforting being alone here, driving, smoking a cigarette as the air came in the window. He thought again of what Truman had said about driving him around when he was just a baby, the hum of the car and road settling him to sleep and wondered if that was where he had picked up his love for driving alone through empty streets.

When he was a boy, his father would talk about how much he liked to drive around at night when there was nobody on the road, just him and the seemingly endless blacktop. How it made him feel like he was some last survivor in a world gone bad, like whatever it was that had captured or killed all those other people was somehow below him, or that everyone else was unaware of his existence and this being unknown offered the same amount of freedom.

After getting his license, Jimmy would go for long drives on those North Carolina mountain roads. It was distance, and miles, he wanted even if it was the same as it had been the night before and the night after and the way it would always be. He would think behind the wheel and not think. He wasn't Jimmy Wills but some nameless young man in a truck, moving and not stopping, staying between the lines, sure that the trees he passed on the side of the road didn't care about what he had seen or done or where he was going.

Now, he drove through an empty downtown Portisville, nice and slow, passing short and dark buildings—the diner, Winn-Dixie, City Hall and the barber shop—places he'd been in before and would never be in again. Not taking mental images to store somewhere in the back of his mind for when he was lonely or needed to reminisce but rather as if by driving past them in the dark, when the buildings were barely visible, he was attempting to erase them from his life.

When he passed Dan's store, all the lights were off and the gas pumps stood bare and witness to him as they probably had to his father so many times before. Up ahead, he saw the sign again that said MILLER'S POND.

It was after five and he decided to sit out there and wait for morning light. Spending the night at Miller's Pond was something he had fantasized about when he was a child fishing with his mother. He had imagined that at night fish slept on the surface of the water and raccoons feasted on the ones that drifted too close to shore.

He parked the truck by the picnic table, facing the pond, and turned the lights off and listened to the modulated cries of cicadas and the splash of popping bass rising deftly out of the water, mouths open, snatching night bugs who cruised mindlessly just above the surface. He tried not to think about Carol, but his mind moved to her nonetheless as he was sure it would again in the future. Any fantasies of a life together seemed silly to him now. It didn't make sense, but after thirty-four years he knew how his mind and the clicking chambers of his heart worked.

As for Truman, he figured he didn't hate the old man anymore, not that he was even sure he could call what he had felt for him hate. His father hadn't killed his mother; that much Jimmy had learned on the trip. He felt a certain peace because he had asked his father the question, which had burned in him for more than twenty years and he realized now that the not knowing paled in comparison to the not asking.

So Jimmy asked himself what so few people do, *What do I really want?* Sure, he wanted his mother back. He wanted to be able to call her and talk to her and wish her a happy birthday. He wanted to see her and Aunt Carly standing together on the shore of a mountain stream fishing. He wanted to be their bait boy, running from pole to pole, loading worms or chicken livers or tiny red salmon eggs on their hooks; whatever they wanted, he would provide. And he wanted someday to find a woman he could give himself to completely without walls or borders. But he wasn't a child, believing he could have whatever the hell he wanted. For now, the life he had in North Carolina, painting and fishing, what he'd been doled out by God or fate or some force he couldn't name, suddenly seemed more than enough.

SUNDAY

TRUMAN WOKE to the alarm clock at 6:30. He rolled over and heard the distant creaking of the hardwood floors and knew that Angie was moving about in the kitchen. He considered going out there and saying something to her, but he didn't see what the point in that would be. A minute later, the screen door rattled shut and he climbed out of bed and walked into the living room and looked out the window. Before she disappeared around the corner, he caught a last glimpse of her fine muscular legs and the bottom of her white running shoes. Truman drank from the bottle of Turkey on the counter and then went to take a quick shower, knowing he had about forty-five minutes before she got back.

As the water came down around him, he remembered the one time he and Dot had gone together to pick Jimmy up at school. They were heading up to North Carolina to visit Carly. After sitting in the car for fifteen minutes, Dot grew bored and ran to the playground and climbed onto the school's slide. At first, Truman felt out of place and half-expected someone to walk outside and ask him what the hell he thought he was doing in this schoolyard, but he soon forgot about that as he watched her play on the swings like a child. And he could see her now, as if she were in front of him: her hands in the air, her mouth open in a girlish scream, her jeans with the hole in the right knee, and the way she moved quickly down the slide into his waiting arms.

Truman climbed out of the shower and sat down on the edge

of his bed with a towel wrapped around his waist. His hand shook as he dialed the number to Darren's cell phone.

Darren picked up on the second ring. "Truman?"

"I'm ready." The phone went dead in his hand as he stood up and reached for the suit.

Davis sat on his front porch, sipping a cup of coffee, while Bev still slept in the back bedroom. He felt good, rested, and it looked like it was going to be a nice day. The sky, which was clear except for a couple of clouds that hadn't quite burned off yet, shook him with its blueness. His police car sat in the driveway between his Bronco and Bev's little Japanese car. And though he didn't plan on doing any work today, and for all intents and purposes he was done with the case, he thought again of Teresa Martin. He wondered if they would find any more evidence when they re-checked those areas around the school. He fashioned an image of the girl walking up to her apartment and asking what all the excitement was, her face tanned from a week in the tropics, and this made him smile.

On the other side of the driveway was his bass boat. The blue tarpaulin over it was weighed down from a month's worth of pine needles. Maybe he could get Truman to go out on the boat with him sometime next week. They had only gone fishing once since Truman was released from prison and that was a few days after he got home. Out in the middle of the lake, with nothing but water around them, he could ask Truman why he was doing all this work around the house, see if it really did have to do with Jimmy or if he knew or felt the end was near for him. It might work. Or maybe they could just sit out there on the water—no questions, no talking—two friends enjoying each other's company.

After filling his Thermos, Davis climbed into the police car, figuring he'd go on over and talk to Truman, ask him about fishing. Bev liked to sleep late on Sunday mornings, and if he stayed around here he'd probably just wake her up. He knew

Truman might give him a hard time, and that he'd probably have to apologize for yesterday, which was something he was willing to do. Backing out of the driveway, it occurred to him that he should probably leave Bev a note, tell her where he was going, but he would be back in a half-hour or so, probably before she even got up. Maybe he would even catch Jimmy before he left. That would be nice.

Truman was buttoning his shirt when he heard the sound of a vehicle crossing the driveway. It surprised him that Darren had gotten here so fast. Maybe he had been sitting on the other side of the trees, waiting for the call. That wouldn't be too smart, considering that Angie might see him, but Truman didn't care one way or another if they found out who did it; he just wanted this thing done.

When he looked out the window, he saw it was not Darren but Jimmy pulling in next to the Cadillac. Truman said, "What the fuck are you doing here?"

As he slid the jacket on, ways of getting rid of Jimmy flashed in Truman's mind: send him to the store for medicine or a newspaper or milk or eggs or bread or some damned thing. He even considered, if only for a moment, locking the door and pretending he wasn't home, but, of course, he knew that wouldn't work.

Jimmy walked in the front door and smiled at his father. If he was surprised to see Truman sitting at the table sipping on a bottle of Wild Turkey, in a linen suit, at this early hour, his face didn't show it.

Truman said, "Morning."

Jimmy nodded in the direction of the bottle. "Breakfast?"

Truman forced a smile. "New diet."

"Passed Angie on the road."

"Everybody passes her on the road."

"What are you all dressed up for?"

"She's gonna take me to church."

"Church?"

"Yeah, you know that place where people sit around and read from the Bible and the preacherman tells them how to be good." Truman's face felt hot and he was certain that he was starting to sweat, but Jimmy gave no indication that he noticed.

Jimmy laughed. "I'm quite familiar with the place, but I've never thought of you as the church-going type."

"I'm just full of surprises."

"I see that."

Truman said, "Thought you weren't coming back until later."

"I decided it would be best if I got an early start. I'm gonna take a shower and get going."

Then get in your goddamned truck and go, Truman thought. "It's probably best."

"Got to get back to work."

"Sure, I understand."

Jimmy walked back into the bedroom and then into the bathroom. The sound of the shower started and Truman thought, *Make it a long one, boy, get all those secret spots, the places nobody can see but you know are there.* After taking another generous mouthful from the bottle of Turkey, Truman headed out onto the front porch. *Come on, Webster, come on you motherfucker,* he thought. He heard a car on the road and his heart lifted, but then the sound and car were gone. He considered walking down to the driveway and stopping Darren before he turned the corner, convincing him that he needed it done out there.

His heart was beating so fast and hard that it seemed possible it might seize up on him before Darren got here. That wouldn't be so bad; he'd be dead, a lot less mess, but Webster would probably take the money anyway. Across the yard, in the woods, a couple of birds were squawking up a storm, darting in and out of the tress, chasing one another. Then the familiar sound of a vehicle coming up the drive erupted in Truman's ears like the first chords of a favorite song.

Darren parked next to Jimmy's truck, a few feet from the porch. He climbed out of his truck, left the motor running, a cigarette dangling in the right corner of his mouth, and walked up to the porch edge, looking around at the three cars. He hadn't shaved and looked like he'd aged a couple years since the last time Truman had seen him. "We alone?"

"Yeah, they're gone."

"You got the money?"

Truman reached into his pocket and pulled out the thick wad of cash. The sight of his own hands shaking surprised him and the more he tried to suppress the movement the greater its intensity. Darren took the money and studied it as if it were some foreign currency he had heard of but never before touched. He fanned the bills through his fingers, counting the prize.

Truman said, "I'm kind of in a hurry here."

Darren threw his cigarette at the front of the porch. It rolled between a pair of the freshly planted impatiens. "I'm counting this money."

Truman didn't know what Jimmy would do after hearing the gun shot, and he hoped he wasn't stupid enough to run out here and confront Darren and doubted that he would, knowing as he ought to, that this was a transaction he couldn't make himself.

When Darren finished counting the money, he put it in his front pocket. He looked past Truman, up toward the house, then over to the woods. "Where do you want to do this?"

"Out by that tree." Truman nodded toward his favorite bullet-torn tree. "Just put the gun in my hand."

"Where's the suicide note?"

Truman touched his jacket, around the level of his heart. "Right here, in this pocket."

Jimmy dropped the towel on the bed and pulled his jeans on. He could feel the roll of cash in his pocket. It was the money Truman had put in the glove compartment box. He pulled it out and set it in the top drawer of the dresser and then shut it. Despite the long drive ahead of him, he looked forward to it and wondered if the reason might be that tonight he'd be in his own house, eating a meal he made in his kitchen, filling his sink with dishes he had bought with money earned working with his own hands. The house he was supposed to start on tomorrow was a big split-level thing at the foot of a mountain, and if he got back by six, he could stop off and pick up some egg-yellow latex at Ferguson's on the way home.

He heard his father cough and this pulled him out of his plans, made him think again about the old man and how odd it was that he had been sitting there, dressed in a suit, drinking whiskey for breakfast. The drinking he might be able to excuse as an anesthetic of sorts, but it was the church thing that threw him; Jimmy still wasn't sure if he had been joking about that. Why would Angie be out running if Truman was waiting to go to church? Not to mention the fact that he was wearing that linen suit, which Jimmy had recognized as the same one Truman had on in the old wedding photo he found in the dresser.

Truman coughed again and Jimmy looked out the window into the front yard. His father was speaking to some man Jimmy didn't recognize. Although this seemed strange, especially considering everything else that was odd about this morning, he didn't understand the full magnitude of their conversation until he saw the gun. Then, he knew what this was. Truman had hired somebody to shoot him.

Jimmy ran to the front door. They were a few feet off the porch, walking away from the house. His first impulse was to call out and yell at his father to stop what was about to happen, but that didn't seem possible; words seemed a feeble defense against money and a gun. A gun he would have to get away from that man.

He opened and shut the door as quietly as he could. With their backs to Jimmy, heads bowed, Truman and Darren didn't speak as they walked forward and gave no indication that they heard him as he moved down the porch steps, his approach muffled by the truck's idling engine. Jimmy pulled a 2 x 4 from the bed of his truck. Truman reached the tree and turned around as Darren set his feet shoulder-width apart and began to raise the gun toward Truman.

Truman looked up, wide-eyed at Jimmy. As Darren began to turn, Jimmy swung the piece of wood. The 2 x 4 made a loud numbing thud as it connected with his forehead. Darren's knees buckled and he seemed to collapse in on himself as he fell to the ground, landing in a seated position and then falling onto his back. A gash opened just above his right eye. The blood pooled on his forehead, then started rolling down the side of his face, into his right ear.

As Jimmy dropped the piece of wood, he saw Gary Warsaw falling down the side of that bed years ago, heard Helen's pained cries.

Truman turned his gaze from Darren to him. "Goddamn you."

"You fuck." Jimmy started to walk away, his breath heaving within him. The porch in front of him fell out of focus. He felt the hand on his shoulder as it spun him around and then he was facing Truman again. Darren was on the ground behind Truman. Truman bent down and picked the gun up. He held it out to Jimmy. "Take it."

"No."

"Take the fucking gun, boy."

"Kill yourself."

"I miss her, Jimmy. I want to see her again."

"You're crazy."

"This is no way to live."

"Fuck you."

"Kill, not wound."

"What?"

"Take it." Truman held the gun out so that it cut the air between them. When Jimmy didn't take the gun, Truman said, "I'll kill him, boy." He pointed the gun at Darren's chest. His hand was shaking ferociously.

Jimmy said, "I don't care."

"I swear I'll kill him if you don't do this. I'm not fucking around here, boy."

Jimmy started walking again. He braced himself for the shot he was sure would come. Then he heard Truman's voice: "I killed her."

Bobby set three pair of underwear, two shirts, a pair of jeans and another pair of shorts on his bed. For shoes, he would go with the pair on his feet. He put all of the clothes into the orange suitcase his father had pulled down from the hall closet. He had left a few minutes ago with instructions to pack because when he got back they were leaving for good. His father had said he'd be about twenty minutes, so Bobby knew he didn't have much time.

After loading everything into the suitcase, he walked outside and set it next to his fishing pole on the porch. He was tired even though he had slept most of the ride home. He heard the car and looked up as it passed. It wasn't his father but Sheriff Davis in his squad car. The sheriff honked his horn and Bobby waved to him.

He didn't want to go with his father away from here. He wanted to see his mother, but it didn't seem like he would ever see her again. He had ridden over there and had tried to call, but nothing. It was like she had moved away. But no, she wouldn't do that without telling him. Bobby looked over at his bike and considered riding over to her house again, but he couldn't be sure she would even be there. Plus, he knew if he did that then his father would know where he'd gone and would just come and get him.

Bobby went back inside. His father had told him to get the dog and some dog food and one of her leashes and a water bowl. Bobby stopped at the sliding glass door leading to the backyard, and looked back at the blue telephone on the wall. He would try one more time. He picked the phone up and dialed her number. It rang eight, nine, ten times and then she answered. "Hello." Her voice sounded groggy as if he had woken her.

"Mom?"

She said, "Bobby?"

"Yes, it's me."

Jimmy stared at his father through a glaze of tears. Handle first, Truman held the gun out to Jimmy.

"Who?"

"Your mother. I drug her out into the woods, shot and buried her."

Jimmy's jaw stung. There was a buzzing in his right ear. "No, you didn't."

"I did. I killed her."

"But you said." Jimmy's head swam in darkness and confusion. He imagined gunshots from far off, imagined his mother being dragged by her hair through this same yard, a thunderstorm and more gun shots.

"Fuck what I said."

"It's all a lie. You're just saying that so I'll shoot you. You don't have to the balls to do it yourself."

Truman shook his head. "She was a fighter, cut me good."

The gun was between them and Jimmy felt his hand start to lift from his side, as if he had no control over it. He tried to pull away. Truman smiled wickedly and pushed it in his direction. Jimmy grabbed the gun and his hand fell to his side as if the weight of the weapon was more than he could support.

"She was a whore, boy, but I loved her."

"You call all women whores."

"She was fucking that fisherman. Dan told me about it. I drove back into town that night and shot her."

"Shut up." Jimmy felt his arm moving up. The gun getting lighter in his hand, as if Truman's voice held the power of levitation.

"No, I don't think so."

"I don't want to hear this."

"Too fucking bad. It's not about you want, but what you have to do."

Jimmy said, "Dan told you?" He couldn't imagine Dan having anything to do with his mother's murder. How could he live with himself all those years, knowing that he had pushed Truman in this direction?

Truman said, "Yes."

"He lied to you."

"No, he didn't. He wasn't the first man she fucked while I was away."

"Stop."

"Pull the trigger and it's over."

Jimmy squeezed the trigger. The bullet punctured the dented and distorted quarter behind Truman, singing out its hollow *ping*. The sound Jimmy had wanted to hear since watching his father fire into the quarter seemed so stupid and pointless now. He turned to the right and vomited, couldn't catch his breath.

Truman said, "She was fucking him that night."

"No, she wasn't."

"I watched her."

"She tucked me into bed." Jimmy remembered her leaning over him, her body full of perfume and the stink of cigarettes, dressed not in her usual night clothes but in jeans and a T-shirt and her lips freshly painted and her hair wet from a shower. *Yet still,* he told himself, *that didn't mean she was guilty of anything. It didn't mean what his father said was true.*

"Then she left you there alone in the house and drove across town and fucked him."

"No, she slept next to me."

"I watched them together and then she came home and climbed in the bed we shared."

"No, it's not true."

They both heard the car at the same time and turned as Davis pulled into the driveway and stopped where the gravel gave way to the dirt of the yard, fifteen or twenty yards away. He looked from Jimmy to Truman to Darren Webster, shaking his head as if trying to figure out what was going on here.

Truman said, "Come on, Jimmy. Do it now before it's too late."

Davis climbed out of the car, wearing jeans and a red T-shirt, and placed one hand on the roof and the other on the door, as if for balance. "What's going on here, Truman?"

"This is none of your business, Davis, just leave."

"I can't do that." Then he nodded at Darren, who had rolled a few feet away from Jimmy and Truman and was now on his side with both hands lifted to the wound on his forehead. "Does he need an ambulance?"

Neither Wills said anything. Jimmy turned from his father to Davis, back to his father. Davis said, "Don't, Jimmy. Don't. Put the gun down, son." His words were calm and soothing. Jimmy wanted to climb on those words and drift away from what had happened and what was going to happen. In the trees, past his father, a songbird spat a sad song. Jimmy searched the trees for the source, believing that if he found the bird he could right everything here in front of him. His blood thumped in his ears, heavy and persistent, and then disappeared as if it had stopped. It was still there, though, flowing through his body, and he could feel it in his hands and on the sides of his neck.

Davis walked slowly toward them, easing his way across the grass. He squatted next to Darren Webster as if to get a better look at his injury. Then he stood back up and said, "What's this all about?"

Jimmy said, "He killed her."

Davis said, "Who?"

"Mom."

Davis turned then to Truman, his eyes narrowing in on him, his head shaking left and right. His lips moved in a questioning motion, but if he said a word, Jimmy didn't hear it. Jimmy saw now that Davis had a .38 in his right hand, by his side. He tried to move away from his father but his feet felt stuck in the dry dirt, as if some invisible hand held his legs. Darren started to moan in a steady, low voice. Davis said, "Truman, is it true?"

"It's my time."

"Not like this, my friend."

"Has to be."

Davis said, "Did you do it?"

Truman didn't answer but turned to Jimmy who had lowered the gun back down to his side, and screamed, "Kill me." Jimmy took a step back, keeping the gun pointed at the ground.

Truman said, his voice calmer, "I can make it worth your while."

Davis was within five feet of them. He said, "Enough."

To Jimmy, the air around them seemed stagnant and suffocating as if it was filled with dust. He didn't want this, didn't want to be here at all, didn't want to believe what his father had said.

Truman lunged at Jimmy and the gun. The old man's strength surprised him as he grabbed at his hand and the gun. Jimmy fought for a second, tried to push him away with his free hand, but he lost his balance and fell back. When he looked up, Truman held the gun in his hand and was backing away from Jimmy and Davis with a sick smile across his face. He was breathing heavy. Davis pointed his gun at Truman and yelled, "Put it down, Truman."

Truman shook his head and lifted the gun to his mouth. Davis said, "Don't." The barrel disappeared in Truman's mouth, his hand shaking. Davis said it again, "Don't. Don't, do this, man."

All Jimmy could see of his father's face was the gun and his hand and the eyes above it all, scanning from Jimmy to Davis and back again. Truman took in a deep breath, then pulled the trigger. A muffled blast called out. Truman's head jerked and he fell onto his back with his hands out to the side. The gun was still clenched in his right hand.

Davis was on the ground beside Truman, feeling the side of his neck for any signs of life. Jimmy walked over and sat on the chrome bumper of the squad car as Davis began CPR. Truman didn't move or stir and Jimmy knew that it was useless, that he was gone. He cupped his face with his own hands and wiped away the tears. Davis continued the compressions for a couple minutes and then closed Truman's eyes and looked up at Jimmy. "Get the hell out of here."

Jimmy fought the urge to sit beside his father, next to Davis. He looked over at Darren, who was still lying on his side and moaning. "What about him?"

Davis said, "I'll take care of him. Just go, you don't need to be involved."

Jimmy walked to the house and went inside and splashed some water across his face, and grabbed his bag and came back outside. Truman was lying motionless in the pine needles under the tree with the quarter nailed to it. Davis was on his knees, leaning over Webster, talking to him. He nodded to Jimmy and Jimmy nodded back. Webster tried to sit up but Davis held him down until Jimmy pulled out of the yard.

Jimmy drove northbound on Highway 144, his hands tight on the wheel. He pulled a cigarette from the pack on his dash and lit it. Closing his eyes, he exhaled a little wall of smoke and felt something shake inside of him. He had come home and this is what he had gotten. He kept his foot on the gas, staying between 40 and 45, and passed Miller's Pond and the elementary school and Dan's store and the road leading to the cemetery where his mother was buried. The trees around him didn't stir as he passed the section of woods where Teresa Martin's car had been found. Strips of yellow police tape hung down from a row of tall, pine trees like flags guiding a traveler to his destination.

He tried to tell himself that what he had learned didn't matter, that his mother was dead, and had been for years, and what Truman said didn't change anything. What he hated most was that there were things he would have liked to know about his mother, things only his father knew, but they were gone now forever. Jimmy let his hand hang out the window, catching the air, which had already started to feel cooler even though he had only driven a few miles from his parents' house.

Eventually he traveled far enough on 144 so that all the yellow police tape was behind him and once again he was flanked by rows of naked, barren pine trees. Up ahead, on the right, he saw the cut off for Sawgrass Road, the road that led down to Carol's. Jimmy reached for his turn signal and thought of how he would like nothing more than to knock on her door and see her face and feel her comforting arms. But he didn't, couldn't, turn down her road, not on this day. Instead he kept on straight, his hands gripping the steering wheel and his eyes focused forward as the road leading out of Portisville unfolded in front in him.

ACKNOWLEDGMENTS

The author would like to thank Joyce and Chuck Snyder, Roger Hart, Susan Hubbard, and Jim Boylston for support and encouragement. Special thanks to Amy Rogers and Frye Gaillard for their help in making publication of this book possible.

ABOUT THE AUTHOR:

STEVE CUSHMAN, who grew up in Florida, received his M.A. from Hollins University and his M.F.A. in Creative Writing from UNC-Greensboro. His fiction has appeared in the *North American Review, 100% Pure Florida Fiction* and the *Raleigh News & Observer.* His first novel, *Portisville,* was named winner of the 2004 Novello Literary Award. He lives in Greensboro, North Carolina, with his wife and son.

NOVELLO FESTIVAL PRESS

Novello Festival Press, under the auspices of the Public Library of Charlotte and Mecklenburg County and through the publication of books of literary excellence, enhances the awareness of the literary arts, helps discover and nurture new literary talent, celebrates the rich diversity of the human experience, and expands the opportunities for writers and readers from within our community and its surrounding geographic region.

THE PUBLIC LIBRARY OF CHARLOTTE AND MECKLENBURG COUNTY

For more than a century, the Public Library of Charlotte and Mecklenburg County has provided essential community service and outreach to the citizens of the Charlotte area. Today, it is one of the premier libraries in the country—named "Library of the Year" and "Library of the Future" in the 1990s—with 23 branches, 1.6 million volumes, 20,000 videos and DVDs, 9,000 maps and 8,000 compact discs. The Library also sponsors a number of community-based programs, from the award-winning Novello Festival of Reading, a celebration that accentuates the fun of reading and learning, to branch programs for young people and adults.

This project received support from the North Carolina Arts Council, an agency funded by the State of North Carolina and the National Endowment for the Arts